# All
## the Comforts

🔲🔲🔲🔲🔲

# All
# the Comforts

*a novel by*
## Joseph Papaleo

Little, Brown and Company · Boston · Toronto

Published simultaneously in Canada
by Little, Brown & Company (Canada) Limited

PRINTED IN THE UNITED STATES OF AMERICA

*To Kurt Roesch*

It is only when the stereotype of the Good Good girl is challenged in *realistic* fiction, in novels which eschew the camouflage of gothicism and allegory, that the great audience is disturbed. The largest reading public, which is unaware of its vision of immaculate womanhood as a myth, does not rise to defend it as a myth; but cries out in horror when it is attacked on the level of fact — a simple truth about the wives, sisters, mothers, and daughters of America.

From *Love and Death in the American Novel*
by Leslie A. Fiedler

# All
## the Comforts

Vito watched her cheeks under the striped slacks while he carried the delivery in. On the elevator, he had cracked some new jokes, but she had said, *yeah,* only a limp *yeah,* cutting him off. He didn't mind the older ones doing that, but this one was his age, could date him tonight if she weren't married.

*The smelly pussy,* Charlie called her; one of the ones whose apartment smelled of perfume right into the kitchen: it came out of the rugs, the icebox, the closets, like a motor was pumping it in. They kept the windows shut, like the old wops, but they used the smell cans, French Mist, Country Pine, Old Lavender.

What did they want, like this, living with all this and yet not responding, not cracking a smile, a little laugh in the middle of the day, for him.

(The others, old and set, were locked in their boxes: you could understand: you just smelled the dry breaths, sometimes a little booze still in the air around them, their closed-in rooms heavy with floor wax or stuffy rug smell or the onions from last night. They got old fast; they dried up, but they fought it with dye and glued-on pants; up front it looked good, until you saw the chicken necks with hanging flesh, and when you looked close, hair dry as straw and bodies soft as dough falling down when you came in and caught them in robes, before getting on the girdles.)

But this was a young one. Just married, soft, but still tight enough to get your eyes, rugs on the floor without a spot, like fur coats, shiny, pale blue like water in a pool, and the kitchen in pink like flesh color in a comic.

He tried to carry the boxes into the living room. "Just leave it there," she said. "The girl will take it."

He straightened up next to her and looked down into her eyes. She never made him come up the delivery elevator and because of that he always expected to bring the stuff right in. She would not meet his eyes, but he thought, *she knows what the look is, she still remembers.*

She smiled a little, reaching into her pocketbook for half a buck. *Keep it, keep it.*

"That's not necessary, Mrs. Gordon." He waved it away and went out.

On the hallway carpet, Vito heard the elevator coming up, an easy, oiled noise, muffled as though by pillows, easing up to the floor that was silent and empty.

The door opened; he looked down towards her door and grasped his crotch to her, then stepped in.

Down in the truck, he sat in the driver's seat and lit a Camel and waited for Charlie to come back from the Tartan Towers.

Vito laughed as he saw Charlie coming, looking angry. Charlie walked into the back of the truck. He was the first Negro to work up here.

"Come on, come on." Vito began the game they played. "You had Bernstein. That's the real Macneil."

Charlie rearranged the boxes and looked at the white

4

slips for the next deliveries. He rummaged around in the back of the truck and did not speak, except to pronounce names and numbers of houses. Vito watched him.

"Is she giving it away yet?" Vito said.

Charlie looked up. "I'd eat it whole, man. In the front window on top of the Delicious apples."

Vito laughed, and Charlie came forward to the seat next to him. They drove down along the river and made the deliveries to the estates where you left the stuff with the maids, though sometimes you saw a woman in a dark dress in the garden or one standing about ten feet from a kid playing in the dirt with a shovel, her shoulders hunched forward as she watched the kid, waiting for him to be twenty-five right away.

On the way back, they stopped along the river road, near the tracks. By now they had perfected the amount of time for a stop, taught to them by Brophy, who graduated to counterman. Charlie brought his good transistor, and they listened to the music of the all-day rock and roll station.

Charlie turned up the music so loud that they could not talk. Each slumped in his seat, Charlie with his feet on the dashboard. The music, percussive enough to vibrate the speaker against its housing, set up a secondary sound, a hum like a force straining to burst out of the radio. Charlie hummed at the same frequency, blending his voice with the mechanical sound.

The disk jockey laughed, screamed, sang occasional phrases of music along with the records, made his daily jokes about the commercials: he would cut off songs unfinished, then switch in a recorded commercial, hooting after its sonorous and serious sentences on skin blemishes or unruly hair. The fragments were a private language the boys understood, and they listened and waited for the next song;

they never laughed, but sank back instead, going inside themselves to a place that was softened by the music and the accompanying words, shouts, chants.

Vito was uncomfortable with it these days; it was not real anymore. Since returning from college and getting around downtown, with Bobby Mitchell, he had begun to think about the person at the mike: phony-happy voices that sucked in the kids, but they were fat guys with wigs, with payoffs and free nooky from the young vocalists trying to come up.

Charlie was in it, a world of records, hits of the week, the latest group's song played over and over, the hit of six months ago (oldies) heard like ancient music, listened to with surprise at its thinness, with a smile for one's own innocence, for having thought it so complete, once the answer to the longing of a whole day.

Charlie carried his radio at the side of his face when he walked to the subway at night. It came in his ears so fast and so full that there was no time to remember. It went on for him every day and was the day's color and number and shape. Next to Charlie, Vito found it easy to sink down a while, like diving under the covers at night. It was loud but it was darkness.

Vito always quit first, starting the engine and letting it run until Charlie shut off the radio. They would talk for a few minutes, Vito filled with affection for Charlie, acting like an older brother. Charlie would listen to his advice and damn it with a few tired words, but Vito went on. He had discovered the colored guys, had seen them awake down South on the streets, and mad; it was as if the ones in his neighborhood had been hiding the years before and had come out when he came back home. Now he thought about them; he should be helping Charlie. He suggested the semipro league. "The scouts come out. You get *seen*." And he invited Charlie up for the Sunday games. To everything, Charlie said, "Sure, man, I'm gonna make it," by which it was clear he would never come.

But Charlie had his salary, his tips; he was making more than his father, he had said. He talked of his Saturday nights, his *jams*, his collection of records.

Vito could see it, looking down. He had a singing offer ready to start, had given up pro ball and plenty of things. He had the *Impala* and what he knew was himself — his looks, his body, his muscles. He turned away from Charlie; he had seen the women look at him as at a shadow, and the sense of this made Vito more friendly, like the brother pushing Charlie. "Sure, man, I'm gonna make it."

Charlie's voice was haunted by the voices Vito was ready to attack. Seeing that clear, Vito turned back to himself alone, to his own plans; there was no energy left to work for Charlie; Vito had to build his own army of ways, one thing said to the folks, another downtown in the singing business, some kind of plan to beat the draft, and a little bit of nooky for himself, for the nights, the nights.

## ▣▣▣ 2

Aᴛᴇʀ lunch, Mrs. Bernstein came in, in a white short leather jacket. Vito, standing in the back, hit Charlie's arm, and they both looked at her.

She was tall and thin, with a large round rear. "She's spreading nicely," Charlie said softly. "Yes, yes, ass me no questions."

"Tell me," Vito said. "You made that. You rolled in that."

"Oh man, tomorrow and tomorrow and tomorrow." Vito laughed at Charlie's dour face and walked to the back to comb his hair.

Conley the counterman had been watching him. "Got a date tonight, Vito?"

"That's right."

"Spend it all. I bet you spend it all on the chippies, your whole check."

"That's it," Vito said, looking at Conley's fat, smooth face, his fag smile.

Vito knew he should answer this way: Conley was a guy who always asked what they did on deliveries, mixing his dreams. He got his fat kicks watching. And he was the one all the women liked best; the *bastard,* he bowed to them and

8

rubbed the apples with a towel and put them in the women's hands to feel.

"Yeah, I just made Bernstein that went out. Didn't you see she was looking for me?" Vito watched it come up on Conley's face.

"She did? She did? You taking *her* out? Go wan."

"Sure. That's what I do. I take her out and my old man, he lets me spend all my check on her."

"Go wan, you prick." Conley lowered his voice in the store to say the word. "You don't take her out."

"I'll bring you pictures." Vito went to the door to get the afternoon deliveries ready; Charlie had brought the truck around.

"Go wan." Conley followed him. "Is it true? Listen, kid. If you want to keep this job —"

Vito went silently through the store. Now Conley followed him. "You don't get pictures, do you?"

"Get me a Polaroid and I'll bring you pictures tomorrow." Vito watched him.

"All right. I'll get one. I'll show you up to it. I'll *get* one."

Vito left Conley's breathing; the fat bastard was getting kicks out of this. "All right, get the camera," Vito said, and left.

He and Charlie packed the stuff and went off. In one of the new apartment houses, there was a new customer. Vito took it.

She came to the door herself, in tight slacks with diamonds of color, and a loose sweater. "You're new up here, Mrs. Steinman." Vito liked her eyes, sad eyes, light blue, with a suggestion that she may have been crying.

"Yes," she said, and smiled. "We've moved up from Manhattan." He followed her in. "I just couldn't take downtown anymore. The filth just got right in. You couldn't keep a thing clean. You couldn't take a walk without —" She looked at Vito. "Without getting robbed or something."

"I know. It's Puerto Ricans," Vito said. "They're even up in the Bronx where we live. Over in the East Bronx, around White Plains Avenue. You see them all over. You know, they just got off the plane. They read the creeps — that's comic books with the horror stories. And they give themselves these kookie names — Gorilla, China Lee, The Umbrella Man, Tarzan."

Vito saw she was listening.

"How old are you?" she said.

"I'm twenty. Graduated two years ago and I went on an athletic scholarship down South. But I couldn't make it."

"You *left* college?" She began to unload the groceries, placing the frozen foods first in the freezer.

"The Southern yuks, Mrs. Steinman. I couldn't take it down there. I said, well, who *needs* it? Down there it's yuks. Ever been down South?"

"Just resorts. Florida. Not what you mean."

"These people, they say they hate coloreds. And that's all. But they got something in the blood. They're still living it like kings and queens. So I came home. They're crazy."

She came to the table and took packages for her shelves. Vito watched her and waited for her response. "Well, I don't think everyone down there is like that. There must be good people."

"I met nuts." Vito stopped and waited for her to turn around. "I mean, look at it like this — I met people who kept the rebel flag in their room, and they talked about it like it was a country. A country *I* never heard of. What is that? It doesn't exist. Now what would you call that?"

She walked to the refrigerator: an impulse had come, to

offer him something to drink. A stranger, she turned to discover him again: it was a warm face; it had been here for a long time.

She smiled at the thought — silly and childish, an emotion worked by his face and the young hair, waved and shining and carefully brushed, not fitting the rough leather jacket.

"That's what I saw. I mean, that's the truth in my eyes, Mrs. Steinman. I mean it."

"I know, I know," she said. "I wasn't doubting you. I was just thinking. A person like you down there. How did you fit in?"

Vito stepped closer to the door. "Maybe I didn't fit in. And maybe it was me. I don't know." The doubt was annoying him. He wanted to curse them now, the dumb ones in the towns who worked behind counters, the girls who said *yankee* when they were in little huddles and laughed at you and then at each other, the guys who asked you if you lived next to *niggers* and laughed like the women: it was not a joke but some knowledge they had and kept to themselves, some pack of thoughts in their heads that was only suggested now and then by a few words and something in the expression of their mouths, the expression of a man with a girl stashed away uptown — it was that delight when they said *nigger*, which was supposed to be bad but which made them excited.

"Not hate," he said as he reached the door. "I don't think it was hate I found down there. Maybe it was how they made me feel shut out with that Southern *hospitality*. I was a foreigner. Maybe I am the foreigner. Everybody's a foreigner in some other place. Especially, maybe especially when you're talking to them who feel everybody's out to get them and *they*, they are the real minority. It took me a long time to get it — meeting people who acted like I came down to do something to them, like *I* was after them."

Helen let him continue leaving; her left hand held the refrigerator door. "I'd like to talk about that sometime. It makes sense."

"I'll see you tomorrow, then, most likely," Vito said, and left quickly.

Helen faced the door and smiled at the rush. "Nice," she said aloud, and went into the living room, holding the expectation of unfinished words from him.

When Vito came during the next few days, she was ready to talk. She watched him arrive, drop the heavy boxes gently and begin to remove the smaller bags of frozen-food cartons. Standing above him, it seemed she looked down like a person admiring a child or a statue from a balcony. He passed her face and she caught the odor of fresh cool air.

"Is it cold out?"

"Oh, there's spring in the air. But the wind still hits you good. It's good, except for your hair." Vito smiled at the confession of his vanity.

"I haven't been out," she said.

Vito looked around for the reason, but did not answer.

"Well, I suppose I'm getting used to a new place," she said, "and I don't know where to go yet —"

"There's some nice walks along the river." Vito thought of himself with Charlie, parked on the river road, listening to ABC on the transistor. He was sorry he had mentioned it, making it possible for them to be caught. But he could not withhold things from her. In this room, he already wanted to tell her all the thoughts that came up. It had happened in three days, in quiet, in the way she waited for him to talk, as if he were a messenger from some special place.

Helen took the bags from him and removed juice cans and boxes of vegetables for the freezer. As she looked into the refrigerator, the pleasant light on the bright foods, she thought of him standing near the table. "Do you have time for a beer?" she asked, and when he did not answer, shut the door quickly.

"Well, thank you, Mrs. Steinman. I'll say all right. Yes. If it isn't trouble."

"They're here waiting." She opened the door again, took a cold can and gave it to him. "I can't ever pop these new pull-tops."

"It's easy," he said. He held the can in his right hand and with his index finger, tore the strip back, holding the can still while the excess gas squirted up.

"You do that like a weightlifter," Helen said. She had stepped back, to disconnect herself from her invitation.

"I never did the weights seriously. That's for clods. Weights all day. The big mirror, you know; all that. With grease on the muscles. The olive-oil boys. But I was lucky I had baseball right away. I stuck to it."

She watched him take a sip. "Is that what you played down South?"

"That's what I could have done at seventeen. I had a farm contract ready after high school. Now that would have been only baseball. But they stopped that, my father and mother. They wouldn't let me go."

"They *stopped* you?" Helen knew why, though she asked her question: it was a form: politeness that said you didn't know the slavery to an old man and a tired woman.

"My people are old-fashioned in their ways. My mother, I think she would have let me in the end. But my father

13

wants me around, if you could explain that." Vito squeezed his hand around the can and looked down at it. "I don't help out in the shop — he's got a bakery." Vito was embarrassed to say it. "I don't like it. I just don't like the trade. Is that my crime?"

He drank again. "But you mean down in college. What was that. There, it was football fever. They'll give you a harem for a good halfback." Vito laughed at himself.

"Is it like that?" Helen sat down at the table; the coffee maker held a reflection of her face, looking hurt.

"No, not really. They're not like that with the women, no matter what you hear. I just got the usual salary and the sweat hours. Someday I'll tell you about it. I just came back. Maybe it *was* my father. I'm not sure. I came home for Christmas and I never went back. And he was happy."

Helen looked at the clock; it was uncomfortable for so much time to be passing. "You know how they are," she said. "How they like us around even after it's time we went." She shook her head. "I'd still be home —"

Vito interrupted: "He offered me everything. He'll pay my tuition. NYU downtown. Then I can be like all the other lucky guys. Be a CPA. Go into construction with the cousins and do their books. These are guys that when they have to go in the army are *happy*. They got out of the neighborhood; they can shoot somebody and get their kicks —" Vito saw his gloves and began to remove them. "Look at this; I'm drinking in gloves. Sorry. We go so fast I forget."

"Then the beer was a good idea. The pause that refreshes."

Vito raised the can to her and drank. "Usually, I don't drink. I don't like it very much." He was aware of the

14

silence in the apartment. "Mrs. Steinman, did you say your children were in school here?"

She laughed at his tone. "No children," she said. "Just me and my husband."

Vito drank again and finished; he stepped forward and placed the can on the white Formica table, looking down. "Listen, if you ever need anything, any shipment right away, a last minute for a party: just call me and ask for Vito. I'll bring it right up."

"Thank you, Vito," she said.

He turned and walked to the door. "Well, good-bye," he said, and left.

Charlie was waiting when he came down to the truck. "Man, you *are* making it," Charlie said. "Your face got the fish on it. They starting to give it away up there."

"Go home," Vito said.

"Oh man, oh man."

"Will you get out of here." Vito sat down in the driver's seat and started the engine. "I only had a simple beer from this *woman*. A nice woman."

"Ass me no questions," Charlie said.

Vito did not answer: he turned the truck abruptly, let out the clutch and drove away from the building. The speed and force threw Charlie off his seat, back into the cab. Charlie lay back among the boxes and laughed.

## 3

Hᴇʟᴇɴ went inside and turned on the TV. She sat for the last half hour of a daytime show, interviewing stars. Two comedians spoke about their religious beliefs and the war crisis in Asia. Helen listened carefully and felt serious and saddened, as though brushed by grief. She nodded to herself and thought of all the holidays abandoned, no one even suggesting a *seder* anymore. One of the comedians remembered his grandmother, who kept the tradition in Brooklyn, and told him stories she remembered, tales of beheadings and pogroms and village stories of monsters that came out of the mirror to bite you; these shook his dreams and never let his imagination alone and made him a comic, so he explained.

At three, the show ended and a rerun of the *Loretta Young Show* followed. Helen watched for a few minutes, not certain if she had seen it before. During the first commercial, the rest of the story came up out of memory, yet she could not turn it off once the actors began again; something about knowing made it better.

After that, she tried a soap opera, then *Queen for a Day*,

but they were both stupid today, and she shut the set in anger.

It was too early to start supper, and this was the time of year Cy was likely to be late because of buyers. She looked over at the telephone; she remembered three suits of Cy's not yet taken to the cleaners: they were in the bedroom closet, good enough in her eyes to be worn again, but Cy insisted on having his suits done every few days.

She walked to the bedroom and lay down and looked through *Life*, which had come that morning. The afternoon was darkening slowly, suggesting spring in its slowness.

When she had leafed through the whole magazine, feeling tired and blank from the pictures, which suggested the whole world but had no substance to make her feel or remember, the room had become dark.

The bedlamps gave it a soft glow, and she smiled: this apartment had come close to what she had wanted; downtown, they had arranged and rearranged but never had it right in those high-ceilinged old rooms with long dark halls and windows in the wrong places. Here she had gone into the empty rooms with the decorator, making Cy listen and approve their ideas.

She was looking at the pleasing creamy color of the lamp base — *potato,* the decorator had called it; it felt soft. It was all like a fine hotel; only the drapes had not caught on with the rest; they were fiber glass, which she had never liked, was liking less each day. But the decorator had made her do it, swearing it was the latest.

She shut her eyes and remembered the boy, Vito. Decent and white, a college kid: an example of this neighborhood.

She thought of going out and went to the living room window to look down at the streets. The evening taxis were arriving already, and the highway in the distance was filling up with traffic and slowing down in lines of red lights.

The apartment had a broad view of Riverdale and the park below, strings of lights wherever you looked, suggesting Fifth Avenue around the Plaza. Being on the fourteenth floor here had reminded Helen of the view from the upper Plaza windows, the apartment of J. S. P. Steiner, who owned the largest textile mills in the world. Going home she had asked Cy if they'd ever have a suite like that and he had said he'd have to steal, having already begged and borrowed.

Helen stretched her arms and felt stiffness in the back of her shoulders. She could see no people down there; it did not seem inviting for walking, a woman alone, and she did not know where to walk yet.

She went to the kitchen and prepared the corned beef; it was a fight keeping him away from his Yiddisher dandies, but they were all babies in the stomach. At least she had been able to keep his weight within reason, although she could not control their delicatessen-hunting while they were downtown alone. Men!

At seven Cy called; there were buyers in the office and dinner was included in the sale. Had to be. Cy heard the silence.

"I'd like to be home right now, baby." He had cupped his hands around the speaker; Helen could hear his voice muffled and knew the others were near him. "They're storming us with orders, Helen. I never saw it this way. I never saw a year like this. But I better not talk. I better not talk. Look, wait up for me."

He had rung off; his voice had contained exhaustion and joy, but his breathing was not good. His weight was just dragging him enough so that there was a panting behind his words. Unless it was a respiratory thing.

When he came in at ten, Helen had her food waiting and ate her supper from a tray in the living room while they talked. But Cy was impatient; he didn't want to talk, Helen thought. "What is it? What happened?" she asked.

"Oh my back," he said. "They have to feel every garment. You're never off your feet with some of them. I've got to take off these shoes."

He removed his shoes, looking anxiously at Helen, knowing she did not like this kind of thing.

His feet smelled awful, that acrid stink of subways; Helen looked at his black socks tight around his feet.

"At least you shouldn't wear a stretchie sock," she said. "They don't breathe. Get yourself a loose cotton. I should think you'd want to."

"And have the damn things fall around my ankles," Cy said, and looked down at his feet. "I know what you want, but I'm no college boy wearing those loose socks. I wear what everybody else wears." He looked at Helen, who shook her head.

"Look, honey, could we catch Carson? I just want to sit back and relax. I've *had* it this week."

"Sure, honey, can I get you something?"

Cy sat back. "No, no. I ate all that French crap. The further away they come from, the more they pick a French place." Helen was standing. "Just turn on Channel Four," Cy said.

Helen did, and took her tray inside. She returned with a bowl of fruit, which she put down in Cy's lap. He kissed her hands. "What'd you do today, baby?" he said.

"This morning I found a good beauty parlor. I had a rinse

and made an appointment for next week. Then I cleaned the place a little: still getting the dirt from downtown out. And I spoke to Esther and my friend Rachel. They may come over Sunday. And I ordered from the store. You *can* phone orders up here."

"Call my mother if you get the chance," Cy said, staring at the set.

"I want to ask her up, *formally*," Helen said.

"Yes, yes, that's nice. But give her a ring right away when you can."

Helen saw that he was watching the show while he spoke. She went back to her chair and watched.

When it was over, Cy watched the news and weather. While it was on, Helen went to the kitchen, rinsed out the few dishes and put them in the dishwasher. Then she started the motor and stood while the gears shifted; when she was sure it was operating, she returned to the living room, hearing the *Tonight Show* music.

"Shouldn't we check if there's something good on the late show?" she said, but Cy did not answer. She heard his snore and saw his head pitched down.

She sat down and watched some of the show, looking at Cy. Poor Cy. His breathing *was* too heavy; he'd have to get a complete checkup.

She looked at his bulging stomach going in and out; it seemed swollen because of his slumped position, pressing up against his shirt like a pained and diseased growth on his body; and he looked old. Old, Cy, old.

Suddenly, Helen was up; she switched off the set. "Cy, if you're going to sleep, then let's go to sleep."

"Just let me rest a minute here. I'm going to watch a little more. Turn it on." He had answered quickly, as though he were awake, yet his eyes had remained shut.

"You're not watching," she said. "And it's after midnight."

"Tomorrow's Saturday," Cy said, but stood up obediently and began walking to the bedroom. Helen followed him, after putting out the lights.

He was sitting on the bed rubbing his feet. "Helen?" His voice was in a reverie.

She began to undress on the other side of the room, near her dressing table. "Yes, what is it?"

"What do you want to do? Take a trip? How about that fur coat? I don't care. Sol Chapman went to Nassau and they liked it. Really Europe-looking, they said."

"You mean right away?" Helen was in her panties. "Cy," she said a little louder, but he did not turn to face her. "Is it the business? Really that successful?"

"Successful? Fantastic, I tell you. One of those years, the buyers think you planned every number special for them. I've never seen it this way in my life. And I been in the trade since I'm nineteen years old."

Helen walked to her bed. "I don't care where we go," she said. "Anything you say. What do you like?"

Cy was slowly removing his clothes, his head lowered as if concentrating on his feet. He sniffed at his T-shirt and shook his head, not turning to Helen, who did not like the habit. "I want this to be your wishes. But I'd like to see someplace. Maybe you can get some stuff from travel agents. And ask around."

Helen had put on her nightgown, then removed her panties. She lay down on her bed. "Cy?"

"Sweetheart." He answered as he walked to the bathroom for his pajamas.

"Don't forget to brush your teeth," she called, but Cy did not answer.

Helen smiled at the silence; perhaps he would sneak in on her; she did not turn her head, but waited.

When she heard his movements, she looked and saw that he was in his bed. "You didn't brush, did you?" she said, and sat up.

Cy pulled the sheets over his head.

"Cy. Cy. You won't have thirty-three percent fewer cavities." She waited for him to respond to the joke, but his head remained covered.

She called again and came to his bed and leaned over, her blond hair falling upon his sheets. One of her breasts slipped out of the loose gown, but she remained hovering over Cy's body.

He did not move; she pulled the sheets down, but he was asleep.

# 4

Helen had prepared English muffins, placed them in Cy's plate on either side of his boiled egg, and added little pats of jelly on top of each muffin — a new suggestion she had found on the side of the package. She watched Cy as he sat down to it and began to eat with his head lowered.

"Cy, do you like it like that?"

"What kind of jelly is this?"

"It's apple-raspberry. But I mean the way it's done; it's like a restaurant, isn't it?"

Cy nodded and ate too fast, his shoulders hunching over the food as if he were being kept from it, being starved, yet being forced to eat something bitter and bad.

"I can't figure out what you like for breakfast. I swear. Do you like this? Would you rather have it that other way, the egg poached and put on the muffin? Remember, I asked you?"

"Eggs Benedict," Cy said while he ate.

Helen sat down to her juice, sipping slowly; she never could eat until he was finished; something within her waited for his new wish even when he was satisfied. She watched his face patiently, slowly coming up out of the food, a little smile suggesting itself as he licked his lips.

Her father had sat in the dining room chair with arms; his fingers were large, swollen to her girl eyes. His hands had gone up and down; his face and head had barely, sleepily indicated commands. She had been eased by his sitting there and had followed her mother to get things for him, to watch him eat until his exhaustion was relieved for a moment.

Their hands were large; their stomachs grew year by year. Reaching over the dishes, their fingers were a blessing to all food and a curse to joy, for one awaited their gratification.

They were hunched; this was the place they sank into themselves, the way women did before their mirrors. Here they leaned into the duty of swallowing, of the stuffing that must take place, for men's strength and women's absolution.

"Another day, another million." Cy looked up and allowed his first full morning smile, one that was already half downtown. "Lennie said that last week. You know, a lot of them are moving out to Long Island. How about we get a house?" He pushed his plate to the center of the table and pulled his juice glass in before him.

"I don't know," Helen said. "This is nice, up here."

Cy drank his juice, throwing back his head. When he came down, he looked straight at Helen, noticing her in the sunlight. Her blue gown was translucent and shining.

"That's beautiful," he said. "Look at it on you."

Helen looked down at herself and smiled.

"That's an M. C. Shrank number, isn't it?" Cy said, and Helen nodded. "Ooh." It was a long sigh. "Now I have to go to work when I could pick you right up and take you right into bed."

Helen smiled. "Why don't you?"

Cy pushed his chair back and came to her; she hunched her shoulders in playful fear, but Cy only leaned down and kissed her cheeks. "I better go. I better go. They'd be calling me on the hour. Hey, Cy, what do we do about this? Hey, Cy, how do we label this?"

He was standing erect, with his hands on Helen's face. He let go and walked out of the kitchen and took his coat from the hall closet. Helen walked across the living room; he had stopped in the foyer and was arranging some papers. "See these," he said. "I haven't told you anything yet. If these things turn out, a little idea we got, we'll be as big as anybody in the trade."

Helen was near him; he zipped his case shut and reached his face to hers, kissed her, and went out.

She stood behind the closed door and heard the elevator. After its sound had stopped and started again, she walked back to the kitchen and drank her coffee. Looking at the crusts on Cy's plate helped her to skip a muffin.

She left quickly to avoid smoking and went to the bedroom to dress. But she removed her robe and sat down on the bed; she was sleepy enough to nap again; she shut her eyes and lay back and felt exposed. Lifting herself up, she pulled back the covers and climbed into the bed; she was in Cy's bed; the smells of Cy were around her: his Lenthéric men's cologne, the mustiness he brought home, an odor of dusty rooms and paper patterns and fabrics: she knew it as soon as she arrived at the business downtown, an odor that came to you as you stepped off the elevator.

Cy had been handsome; she had liked his wide, heavy shoulders — unlike the men she knew, fathers and neighbors who became hollow and hunched on the night subway after being on their feet in stores or leaning over machines.

Cy's shoulders had had time to develop: they were like the strength of money.

She would see him at the curtains while she was modeling on the showroom floors, knotted up half with shame and half with pleasure. Afterwards, she would dress fast and come down to meet him, welcome the broadness of his arms, his embrace and confidence. He was young and yet he was on a par with the men who hired her; he spoke with them and after a while they spoke differently to her, saving their kidding for the other models.

Cy took her arm, held her while they waited for the elevator. He removed the shame, stood politely next to her going down to the street. Then outside he always called a cab and went uptown, away from Seventh Avenue.

He seemed to know all the places on Madison; he was comfortable there, and they would have a drink before lunch and talk about the night and a movie or a play. He was full of places she had never seen, and his eyes were playful: she forgot the time, forgot she had to go back: all the places they sat in were his.

In theaters he loved to rest his body against her, leaning over, moving his arm until it was touching her; he did things quietly, as if he had the right and she were welcoming. She would look around, but no one ever noticed.

And on the way back, he would talk to her about his plans and his new ideas; she never asked whether or not they would happen because they were spoken like love words, something for her, a focus for Cy that became exciting now because of her.

When she touched his things now and remembered him through his odors, a good dream of what he was entered her thoughts. She remembered both of them, excited, running to things before the wedding, getting so much that it made the past disappear, as if she had been taken to another kingdom.

Now she wanted to confess her fear of this empty house, where no one spoke, where four years, first downtown then here, had made her alone, though their possessions had increased and she had no right to loneliness.

But Cy's real presence was different: he was busy; he was rushing away. He spoke like a demanding restaurant customer; she was an extension of the buyers who made him crack jokes when he wanted to be finished, and he yelled at her to get off his back when she confessed the pain of an empty house.

"I'm not complaining about *you*," she would say, and Cy would answer, "But what do you want me to do? Just tell me what I'm supposed to do."

He was in need of shirts or a rub for his stiff neck; he wanted a report on his mother or the list of phone calls and then mail.

The lists made her unthinking; she was rasping back at him like a tired waitress (she heard her mother's voice in the hot kitchen on Fridays). The words became the sound of hurt feelings, set off by Cy, leaving a wake of regret after he was asleep or when he had left her alone in the morning for work.

But then she was without him again; she could not make it up to him in words he could not hear, yet as long as he was gone, she could pace them out reasonably.

Sometimes they could slow it down at night and find what they had fallen into before it was forgotten so that it could rise only in shouts. They talked and found feelings; there was no need to argue; they were just tired as the world was tired, with bad feet or cramps. They went to bed and called the private names they had made for each other in their days of keeping company, bringing back the excitement and making love in the echoes.

Yet the hours without him were too long; he was changing shape more in his absence. The Cy who was becoming a man downtown, who came home to rest and ask questions, to have her join him over Chinese food, was hardly known. Remembering gave up the wrong surfaces of Cy: the rude slap of his shoes that came with his overweight body, a clumsy, flatfooted neglect.

*I want you to obey him; remember that.* Her mother or father had said that, long before her marriage. Her father had died by then, though. Yet he would have said it, too, because he became afraid of her after she had become a model. *Oh my poor Jacob!*

She fell asleep and was awakened by the doorbell, a fragment of a dream still in her head as she first became conscious: she had been showing the apartment to celebrities, to Elizabeth Taylor, Laurence Harvey, Governor Lehman, Jack Paar: it was an odd group, and it amused her as she thought of it.

When the bellsound persisted, she knew that something had happened to Cy and that she had been asleep, not prepared to help at the time. It was early morning, a time before callers. She went to the closet for her heavy wool bathrobe and walked into the living room; there she recognized the service bell, and hesitated, but the bell went on: she called out to the door.

"Mrs. Steinman? It's me. Vito."

She went through the kitchen to the door and opened it. "I'm in the neighborhood," he said, "so I thought I could take your order."

"No," she said gently; in her head, she was shouting, *Go*

*away. Leave me alone.* "Wait a minute, Vito. Come in and I'll write it down."

She left the door ajar and went into the bedroom. "I'll be a minute," she called to him. "Have a beer."

After a long pause, he called back. "It's nine-fifteen. You don't want me to start this early."

She heard his voice in the room with her and shut the door quickly, but without slamming it. *Don't insult them,* she thought.

She covered her hair with a pink kerchief and went to the kitchen.

"You wouldn't want women to see me staggering in." He was sitting in Cy's chair; the leather gloves covered his hands.

"Nice and warm out today," he said. "It's a good day to go out."

Helen did not answer; she smiled as she saw his discomfort. "I was just thinking here," he said. He looked at her but did not get up. "Sitting here; something brought back those days down South. The mornings, after breakfast. You were full so you didn't want to get up yet and go to class. The guys would sit there, this special dorm they have. There's other guys around you, but it's a time when you sit there with yourself. Not that you think about anything. You just sit there and you slow down and you start talking inside yourself. Maybe it's being five hundred miles from home; maybe it's something from the night before, the face of some guy who's on pot all the time. You see his face again and you have a vision of this guy dead. That one thing in his face you saw but you didn't realize it then. Now you see it —"

"Take off your gloves," Helen said softly. "I'll pour you a cup of coffee so you can think a little more."

She found the percolator still warm and poured a cup, then sat down. "Now let me write down what I need," she said. "Do you have a pencil?"

He had taken off his gloves; she saw his hand reach for the pen and had not expected the fingers to be so long and slender.

He placed the pen on the table near her hand. "Listen, you better come back, Vito." She had written a few items on the paper, then dropped the pen. "I'm not thinking yet. I'm getting a late start."

He was at the door before she finished. "Sure, Mrs. Steinman. I know a late morning. You don't have a head, do you?"

"A head? Oh, no. I'm just awfully sleepy."

"Then I'll come back later. All right?"

"All right," she said, and watched him leave.

When his body and face were gone and the closed door faced her eyes, she sat trying to understand what she had done: she had let him in and gone to get dressed as if someone were giving her orders. It was the presence of the boy, the presence of his wishes, perhaps, and something he had done.

The rest was unclear. She would have to go out and visit somebody. Go downtown. See the travel agencies. The feeling was in the apartment; doors would open any minute: it was in that.

She went quickly to the bedroom and called the limousine service for a place on the eleven-thirty car and then began to dress. She hurried through it, yet chose a very dressy suit, a gold necklace and bracelets for both wrists. There was no need for this much; she wasn't going to meet others, but very good clothes were always a protection: they kept questioners away.

Then she returned to the living room, hearing her heels loud on the floor when she passed the limits of the rug. She walked back and forth, as though trying herself out; it was a gesture from the days of modeling, before going out to the floor.

She remembered the list and sat down to call the store. Now she spoke briskly, almost in anger to the salesman's voice, which responded with patience and cheer through the whole conversation. His enthusiasm for all the foods made her increasingly suspicious; by the end the conversation was light combat, but the voice won with its consistent affection.

"I'm going out," she said. "So tell me when's the delivery? I might not be here."

"That's all right," the voice said. "We'll just leave it at the door; we do it all the time. Frozen food protected in a foil bag; all that. And credit your account. Don't you worry, Mrs. Steinman."

"But when's the delivery, anyway?" Her tone was angry again.

"Well, there's one before noon; let me see, no, they haven't left yet, and then you'll have to wait till three-thirty."

"Can you make mine in the early one?"

"All right," came the voice. "Don't worry, ma'am."

She hung up and sat before the phone, thinking that she was sweating under her makeup and that they were laughing at her in the store, saying she was afraid somebody'd steal her little order.

Her hand stroked the telephone, picked it up and placed it down twice, then dialed the number. "Hello, car service. This is Mrs. Steinman. I had a call in for eleven-thirty. I have to change that to later. The next car. Yes, that's right, the next one. I can't make the eleven-thirty."

When she hung up, she walked away, through all the rooms, back and forth. She turned on the TV, but its sound in the morning was loud and sickening, high-pitched and hysterical, a voice reporting on her to all the house. It was as if all sounds spoke of her whereabouts. What she had wished to do, what she had wished with the boy.

When Vito came, she was silent, watching him put the stuff down. She could not find her purse when he gave her the bill. "I'll give you a check," she said.

"We trust you," Vito said. "You're in a hurry."

She sat down and wrote the check, angry again.

"I'll pay it myself," Vito said. "Look, don't bother. Pay me back anytime. I'll pay it."

"No, you will not, Vito," she said. She handed the check to him, his gloved hand. And when she saw his smile, she was aware that *she* was smiling at him.

"You're laughing at the gloves," he said. "I forgot again, didn't I?"

"Yes, you forgot again, Vito."

"Well, I'll promise that you'll never see them again. I'll always take them off outside."

She smiled again, but it was harmless, light, only a reaction of face to face.

"You know about the car service, don't you?" Vito said. He was noticing her. "One buck, right into midtown."

"Yes, I know. I've called them," she said.

His eyes rested on her hair, like spun foil, fused together, nothing hanging loose; he saw her tight, shining stockings, thin, soft leather shoes, her hips against the skirt. "If you're ever stuck for a ride, just let me know. I have my own car here. And if you meet a driver named Arthur, just tell him you know *me*. Say Vito."

"Thank you," she said. "They know you all over, don't they?"

"They will," Vito said; he had not caught her tone. "If I use my breaks right. If I can just work it out."

"What's that? What is it now?"

"It's a lot of things. It's my future, Mrs. Steinman. Something I haven't told you about. Right now it's only dreams. You probably wouldn't believe me because here I am somebody pushing boxes." He walked to the kitchen door.

"Wait. Tell me what it is. Tell me the dreams. I don't mind dreams." Helen had found this hard to say, though the urge had rushed up to meet his confession of feelings.

"Someday I'll tell you. I will really tell you." He had not understood her tone. "If you ever want to hear about it. Because I think you're a person who would understand wishes like that. To go get it — what you *should* have." Vito held his hands in fists before him.

"I'd try to understand." She had to turn away to smile: the innocence was almost stupid, as if the world beyond his body, face, and hair did not exist.

"I'm serious. I'd like to tell you. I really would be grateful if you could listen." His hands were on the doorknob.

"Please go ahead. Tell me."

"It's too long. I couldn't right now. In two fast minutes. And it's not that straight yet in my head that I can spill it out, which way I go. To say it, I'd need time, the chance to get it all out." He left and quickly shut the door behind him.

Helen sat smiling. It was another man, with a man's crazy eyes staring at his plans: she had thought the excitement was herself. But she was mirror again, something that gives back the words louder.

There was another look he had: it was hunger, frightening if she were the only object of it. But it stared at the table with foods on it, at the high drapes, the washing machine, the dishwasher, as if they were messages to him, waiting for him, perhaps stolen from him. His face told it, and his face was a theft to come: it was handsome, strong in lines and planes, curling high dark hair, wavy but not tight, someone seen in a movie or on a stage.

There was nothing wrong. His was not the expression of the West Side streets, the Puerto Ricans with open mouths in their cells of not having, who forced you to walk away fast because they might tear something off you, take some fragment, then run away. Vito had plans and stood above himself in some way, unaffected by hate he had the right to have, ready to take up the things he wanted, like a man stroking a kitten come to him.

She stood up quickly and paced the apartment; then she went downstairs and walked about in front of the building, driving off feelings until her back hurt. The doorman came out to tell her that she was too early for the limousine. It startled her, but she caught herself quickly and said she was getting some fresh air first. She watched the big red face go back inside.

The car was early; once past the toll bridge, her thoughts were clear; the sight of the Washington Bridge brought the city to mind.

In town she had a sandwich at Schrafft's and then went to the two travel agencies near Rockefeller Center. At the second she called the car service for the ride back.

The car met her in front of St. Patrick's; she was the only

passenger. "This is gonna be a private ride," the driver said, "unless I get a call in the next two minutes."

He placed the intercom speaker on its hook, pushed his back against the seat. "Mrs. Steinman?" he said.

"Yes," she said.

"I saw your name on the board here. I'm Vito's friend, Arthur."

"He told me this morning," she said. "If I needed any help."

"That's right. For our friends, we'll bump somebody else off a car and take you. Any time."

"What is Vito's last name?" she said.

"Who? Vito? It's Filippo. We come from the same neighborhood, over near White Plains Avenue. But he's got a stage name. When I heard him. Vic Phillips."

She did not reply.

"He's a good-looking kid, isn't he?" Arthur turned his head. "Didn't he tell you they wanted him for a movie?"

"A movie? No, he didn't tell me that one yet." That was what he was going to tell her in the morning. "Is Vito going to be the new Tony Curtis?"

"No, he's a singer. Didn't he tell you that? I thought he told you all this already. Some guy heard him one night when a friend of ours gave him a chance to sing downtown. He did a few numbers at this club. Our best friend is Bobby Mitchell, the singer."

"Oh, that's your best friend. So Vito's going to take Bobby Mitchell's place. Right? I suppose you're going to be his manager. Right?"

"No, Mrs. Steinman, this is the real thing."

"Well, I wouldn't care. I'm not interested until he gets the Academy Award. Will you tell him that?" Helen turned her face acutely to the side, so that she could not see the driver at all.

"No, honest. I'm serious, Mrs. Steinman —"

"Then don't be so serious, thank you."

Arthur's voice changed; it was high; the youngness came into it, a little whine for disbelief, a little regret at being wise. "See, Bobby Mitchell is *really* a guy from our own neighborhood. His real name's Robert Agramonte; he changed it for the singing. I ought to know that much; I live three doors away from them." Arthur laughed at the silence. "It's all true, Mrs. Steinman. It is."

"All right, all right. So it's true."

"So Vito was going to be in this movie with a lot of young new singers in it," Arthur said. "But the deal fell through; the people didn't raise all the money. But they still offered him a contract. The way I understand it, he can take it anytime he wants."

"Then tell me why doesn't he?" Helen heard her voice cold and flat.

"*You* ask him, Mrs. Steinman. And ask him to show you the mug pictures they made of him. He's got pictures from when they tested him." Arthur paused. The car was approaching the tolls. "But why Vito doesn't take a contract? That's hard to figure out. Some guys say he's a born goof-ball, the kind of guy who always comes back, knocks around the neighborhood, with little jobs here and there, never anything steady. Look at the scholarship he had. He said his father made him come back. He was getting a *name*. The papers up here were picking him up. Nobody's going to call him home."

Arthur slowed the car, flung his dime into the automatic maw, and drove out fast. "I mean, his old man sweats for a buck. He's not going to pull Vito out of a deal, an opportunity. Well, let's just say Vito hates work. We all do. But he don't hate money. I'll tell you that. In that he's like the rest of us."

"That's right," Helen said. "Maybe he is *just* like all the rest of us, isn't he?"

"Well, yes and no," Arthur said. "Yes and no."

They were silent for the rest of the ride, but as the car stopped in front of the building, Arthur turned in his seat. "I'll tell you one thing about Vito that's different. He's a real pusher, a powerhouse. I've seen him do it. In basketball, in semipro football. Near the end, when guys are ready to drop. Then he'll push; he won't let up. He pushes like *he* wants to drop, like it's a pleasure to drop in your tracks. But that's the way to be, Mrs. Steinman. You push the other guy out first. It's money in the bank, if you ask me — that way to be."

Helen did not like this; she did not answer. She would not hear about these details.

Arthur opened the door for her without getting out. "Thanks, Mrs. Steinman. Thanks a lot." He held the money she had given him and smiled at her walking away.

She did not turn back to the face although she had put him in his place: he had told too much.

Upstairs, while she undressed, she thought she heard the service doorbell and went to the kitchen in bra and panties. "Who is it?" she called, but there was no answer.

Back in the bedroom, she became angry thinking about it. The phone rang. It was the beauty parlor calling about her appointment. She had forgotten, but would come right over.

She remembered Vito's offer of a ride and began to dial the store, then slammed the phone down and went to her clothes closet.

She dressed in slacks, a silk blouse, and a short coat and went out fast. Downstairs she began to walk and walked all the way, surprised that the distance was so short. The owner was waiting for her and not angry.

While he worked on her, she noticed his face in the mirror: long black hair and dark eyes, an Italian type, but he did not notice the women; he focused on hair, on curlers, the chemicals, the combs, the dryers that were available. Helen looked down the row of chairs and saw about ten pairs of legs, all different, all sexy, two in black mesh like whores in movies.

The beautician's body came round her, leading her gaze away; he did not talk, waiting for her to start. Down the row, the others, who knew their dressers, were talking to the mirror images and Helen knew how close they were, how intimate the details must be they spoke. It was like a magic, the way you talked to the face, the hands stroking but hardly touching you, as though the permission you gave with your hair was an offering: you gave your privacy to him and he reacted like an approving, admiring friend.

One Tuesday when she was living downtown, she had gone to Marcel, who had started years before with Charles of the Ritz, and in his own place that afternoon, she had broken down; it was a week after her mother's death.

As he brushed her hair slowly, she had begun to answer his questions about her eyes — was she tired? Had she been sick? She spread it all out about her mother, the last nights, sitting up holding her body while Mother moved out the last actions of her life, her breathing changing, her lips becoming blue, then coming back to life's color again, her fingers twitching on the bed, clutching without reason (it had made Helen shake with fear of dying), her voice going off until there were only abrupt sounds. Mother kissed her when she realized that her speech had gone, kissed her face over and over again whenever Helen did something to help, wiped her forehead or held her up to breathe. Mother was locked in those death movements for a week: the doctor had called them the "cheyne-stokes."

She had told Marcel in a way she could not tell Cy; it was too much when Cy was there to listen; Cy was there to comfort her and the feelings he brought out would make the story too horrible for her.

The tears had made a puddle in the plastic apron folded in her lap. Marcel had stepped back and sat down. He held the brush in his right hand and breathed out a long sigh.

"Oh, Mees Steinman, oh Mees Steinman." She did not hear his fairy voice that day. But what he did kept her silent for months to come, kept her mouth shut in beauty parlors.

He had been touched; he had brought her a glass of water and had sat down near her and even taken her right hand. And then he had told her about his own mother; underneath, Marcel had been a Puerto Rican kid who learned the business, had a quick talent, collected loyal customers fast. He had been so successful he had not had time to help his family. When he had gone back to Aguadilla, summoned by a telegram, carrying saved money, he had found his mother dying.

He had nursed her and taken care of his sisters and brothers. Even after she died, he still had four thousand dollars left, and left it with the family, rushing away with empty pockets and the haste of a stranger.

Helen had listened to the opening up of his background, dirt and pain. He had recoiled from his own description of the house down there: he could not stay to fix it up himself; he threw the money at them; he would send them more.

His whole story was not as sad as hers, but his slick hair

with curls and tint, his velour shirt, no longer hid him in the atmosphere of the salon.

(That was when she started to push Cy to leave Central Park West and go live uptown; everybody had a dirty apartment hidden behind them: the doctor's clean white nurse had dirty kids in a smelly flat. Countermen and waiters came down the steps of filth in East Harlem and put on black tight tuxedo pants and red vest-jackets with silver buttons over their greasy, stained underclothes.)

Her mother had disappeared that day; Helen had offered her in grief and received something worse in return. She would keep her deaths in her head, both Mother and Father, and being alone would be protected only by Cy, who took her with him, who gave her money in her own name.

From the very first dates he had tried to give her money — just hand it to her — *for whatever you need,* he would say.

She knew it was Bronx Park South he had seen driving up to get her from downtown, the change in his eyes when he saw her place.

Cy began to remove the stain of it when he stood at the entrance to her place and waited. He seemed proud and he had never stared like the other men, like crabs with claws ready to rip at her, with little come-on jokes, with that one thought: of getting a model on her back.

She loved the Tavern-on-the-Green and the walks they took after lunch. Cy would take her arm as they left and lead her into the park. They were always late returning, but laughed at it: Cy came in and joked with her bosses, told them the cab broke down, silly things.

They had been the best times, better than Miami or the Concord. He walked her away from the city streets around them: they looked up at the wall of Central Park houses, the stone lighting up in the sun, the windows catching sunlight, sky, all the light of the city.

They walked away from work, which Cy called *hustling*. You ran around and made a buck, but it was many bucks, and you even went down on Saturdays and sold wholesale to customers who came up the freight elevator, the dark part of your mind feeling the sweat of that coming bad season, of bankruptcy and the final fall into subcontracting, getting a little place in an empty store, borrowing to buy a few machines, hiring housewives who needed their buck and sewed the cheerleader skirts and school uniforms while you went out and begged for work.

Sam Shapiro had told her this on the first day Cy had taken her to see his operation, as he called it. Sam was the old foreman, who knew the older Steinmans from the beginning, who took Helen like a pupil, a girl, and kept explaining Cy, as if her beauty made it clear she would not understand. "You know why Cy does this," he would say. "You know why Cy looks like this," and would weave the tale of the bad season, the day of loss, the Manhattan money pogrom, when the *goyim* suddenly pull in all the money.

Cy had to beat it by growing. Everybody grew. "He'll make combinations," Sam said, and showed her the rooms of the place, the new expansion into slacks, into vinyl coats, into imported knitwear. "Everywhere they step, we got a garment waiting. That's the way to do it. Have an English line, an English name. An Italian line for shirts, tops, knit suits; even get a Paris designer name."

"What is your boyfriend showing you?" Cy would say when they came back from a tour, often with samples for her to wear.

"Don't joke," Sam would say. "This girl will at least

know what she marries. I'm teaching her the facts of life, you should thank me."

"I should thank you, you're giving her the merchandise," Cy would say, then embrace Helen and make her model the clothes they had given her.

Sam also told her about the wives, some who came in to pick up money, to feel the place around them like a velvet cape they don't get a chance to enjoy, others who refused to see the place, who never even left messages except to say *tell him his wife called.* Helen knew the eyes of the wives who came in to look the models over, to examine their suspicions and leave the threat of return.

One day she and Sam had come back to Cy's office to wait for Cy: Sam had been telling her about a TV show he liked, in which the man had a year to live and kept going to different parts of the world, one week in Italy racing cars, another in Mexico on speedboats. "I wouldn't miss a week. At that time, I don't answer the phone, I wouldn't go out to see my mother. If you should have an emergency you'd have to wait till eleven o'clock for my help."

Sam liked the actor. "He seems Jewish," Sam said, and laughed. "Even his face looks it, the expressions, the way he takes people's stories, the way he looks when somebody shafts him. But the name sounds Italian. Maybe his mother?"

Sam had then been called out and while she waited in the small room, she heard a scream. The sound was a woman's, and the anger forced Helen up to look.

She went toward the sounds, to the door of the cutting room and opened it to see the long dark room under rows of bare light bulbs, the high tables holding piles of cloth ready for cutting.

Between two tables, she saw the face of Arnold Kent, one

of the men who had gone in with Cy, bringing his little slacks firm under the Steinman name. Arnold was small, with thin, good-looking features, a beautiful nose and thin moustache that went with his changed name, as if the two made him close to what people wanted.

Facing him, with her back to Helen, was a tall woman with orange hair. Her hands were up, twisting about like someone about to go wild. She was shouting. "Fuck you, Las Vegas," the woman was saying over and over.

Helen stepped back. The words were like a beating: the hate was desperate, as if she would break down unless she screamed and drove her cursing violence into Arnold, who held his arms up.

"You don't go this time. Did you hear me? You don't go this time." The orange head moved toward Arnold, but the hands did not strike. They threatened; they tried to drive Arnold down with their swinging, down to his knees, make him smaller.

"But I got to go," he said. "They expect me."

"Shut up. You don't go this time."

"No, Linda. It's all planned. They expect me to be there."

"No, I said." Her right arm raised itself directly over Arnold's head and the hand quickly grasped at his hair, pulling back.

The neat toupee came off suddenly. Arnold was changed; he was older. His eyes were wide open, his face flat with shock, as if one of his arms had been ripped off. The woman let out a cry, a high moan, as if she had hurt herself, and threw his wig far into the back of the room.

It made a little whispering sound, like the stroke of a broom along the floor, and fell under a sewing machine among patches of blue cloth.

Arnold turned around and ran to his wig. The woman followed him, and as he bent down to get it, she stepped on his right hand. She was wearing an orange shoe: Arnold let the shoe press against his hand: he looked at it but did not cry out. When it released him, he sat down on the chair before the machine and covered his face with his hands.

The woman turned around and came down along the cutting tables. Helen did not move, but watched the face catching light as it passed under the bulbs. It was hurt; rather than old, it had only become like other faces, in color, in the swollen quality that comes from food, in the changes made by plucking eyebrows and dying hair to the color most recently advertised.

As she passed Helen, she said, "There he is," and went out.

Helen backed out of the room, finding Sam, who brought her to the small showroom and sat her in a green armchair. "You heard all of that," he said.

"Where's Cy?" Helen said.

"You think that's terrible," Sam said.

"I have to go back to work," she said.

"All right, so you'll go back." Sam sat on the teak serving table and looked down at her. "You'd better know a little bit. You just saw two decent people. I know them very well."

"Where is Cy? I want to see Cy."

"Helen. Listen. Don't say Cy. He can't change anything. You saw Arnold in there and that's his wife. You want to know what he did. Don't turn around. I'm going to tell you. Arnold's backing a big comedian and that's all. He goes along with this man's show; it's like an investment to Arnold. He puts up money and then he gets a cut from records, from a Broadway show the man is in. So what's wrong? Arnold will go with this man's party; they will have young chippies, too — some tasty *shicksehs* you shouldn't touch, because *shickseh* is *fleshe* and Arnold is dairy. You know how it is. But I'm telling you it's not bad. Arnold will just have a little flying around; his wings will go up and down."

Helen was listening; Sam lowered his voice. "So what now? So when he comes home, Linda looks not so good. She's working all the time to look good and now she don't look good anymore. Her hair is beautiful; her clothes you want to steal. But only one thing: she's older. She's older than the dreams you get in a nightclub. That's all there is to it."

"Did you see her face?" Helen said. "You'd see what happened to her, by him."

"I don't have to see her. What she did will go away. Arnold will wash it off, get a shave and a shine. It's all in a day."

"Let's go find Cy," she said.

"Come on, I'll take you. You haven't seen downstairs yet, anyway." Sam led her down to the sewing room, machines in long rows, women's heads over the black guitar shapes, shouting, singing.

At the end of the room, Cy was walking, examining skirts piled up on long tables.

Cy took her hand when she reached him and smiled at Sam. "Take her home," Sam said. "She needs a little fresh air."

"First come and meet Louise," Cy said, and introduced Helen to the chief operator. "She's my *paisan*," Cy said.

"How long have we been together?" Cy said.

"Don't ask," Louise said. "It's too long." She greeted Helen shyly; Cy was surprised but did not speak. Louise

45

became aware of her black smock, her cheap housedress underneath.

"We always fight about hems," Cy said. "And we'll always fight."

"Hems," Louise repeated. She looked at Helen.

"Yes, she calls me the perfection man," Cy said, trying to bring out Louise's sharpness, her wisecracks. But with Helen present it was impossible: Louise remembered women's things — hair and clothes, looking right. With the men she was permitted the loss of herself that ended in being a shouting voice, screaming jokes and taunts.

Helen looked into the dark eyes, sunken and staring. Louise showed the destruction of the sewing room: her eyes were stuck, detached from her expressions, locked by the dim lights and the concentration on the needle's work and the demand of Cy behind all her work.

While Cy led her back, Helen looked at the women's heads. Some looked up momentarily, but the skirts seemed to rush at the machines, like moths to light, and the women could not stop.

"She's a bigger Jew than all of us," Cy said at the end of the room, and looked down the rows. "When I offer one-fifty, she'll get one-seventy-five every time. She outsmarts me."

"Is the light always like this?" Helen said.

"We check the lights," Cy said. "The union would jump us if it was wrong. Don't worry about them."

Helen looked at the heads held down; they seemed to be sinking into the noise of the motors. The lights could not dispel the feeling of darkness around the women. Helen shook her head and went to the door.

"You can hit me if I ever complain again," Helen said when they were in the hall.

"Now don't start that," Cy said. "I don't run a sweatshop, a pirate shop. They make good money. More than you. And my dad was one of the first in the industry to clean up the rooms, to give time breaks and all that."

They went upstairs for Helen's coat and purse and started back to her office. "I wasn't complaining about you, Cy. It was just that place. Those were women."

"Well, yes," Cy said, but he did not understand. "That's true; many have families. But they really make enough to support a family. And women still make the best operators."

"I know, I know," Helen said. "And I'll never say another word to you about it."

"No, no, I want you to take an interest like this."

"I'll worry about the boss," Helen said; she was being pleasant, but she would need time to get the day out of her head.

"Anything wrong, Mrs. Steinman? Is it pulling?"

"No," Helen said, and forced a smile. He must have caught her face remembering.

Rachel took night courses at the Y: poetry and sculpture and the lectures of Erich Fromm and other psychologists. To open her up. But Rachel was always that way, reading and criticizing. If Helen were to do something, it would be something like dancing, something with her body.

She caught her face smiling. What was it? She was laughing at herself becoming a ballet dancer, thinking it seriously, though she had been serious in high school when Miss Adler in gym had said she had dancer's legs. She could hear them laughing now.

All the ends were fools' ends. You didn't do these things when you had an apartment and a husband. But what was that: shopping, beauty parlor, dry cleaner, dentist, a week in the mountains?

Rachel said children would change it, and Helen was ready to have them right now. But didn't kids come after you made your life a little, started doing the things you wanted, set up a place you were proud of? Babies were your second life. That was what she had said to Cy one night.

Her favorite aunt, Yetta, was proud of her May, who was in law school. Education. But May's eyes were darkened already, and her black-rimmed glasses were like chains of imprisonment for the woman inside. She would suffer, and men would make sure of it, and end up more alone.

The hands were touching her head, fingertips moving around it, like Marcel. This was Mr. Fred; he looked like he too had been downtown.

"Have you ever been downtown?" she said.

"Oh, yes; at Charles'; at Bonwit's — I've been around." He laughed at his own joke.

She was embarrassed by his private laughter. He removed the plastic apron and stepped back. "You have lovely hair, Mrs. Steinman. It really obeys."

She paid at the white desk and walked out along Johnson Avenue, to look at the shops. This neighborhood was still new to her; it had the pleasure of smallness, although the street was in the midst of apartment buildings. She stood in front of Bly's, trying to read the prices but noticing the looks she was getting instead. She turned to look at the street: these were faces she knew, but they did not have the pinched looks of downtown people. The women wore slacks and shorts; a few of the young girls went barefoot, though the sidewalk had pizza crusts and spit and even worse now that people were coming out for spring.

She went into Bly's for a bouclé-knit top with the new open neck; then she crossed over to the shoe shop. The window was full of sneakers: she had never thought of sneakers before this year and had even been out of the habit of wearing any flats. The man talked her into a pair with blue flannel tops and pointed toes. She laughed at her feet in the sneakers: it was like being a sweater girl again, the Lana Turner, Betty Grable years.

It was dark when she came out; night had fallen quickly and brought up the lights in the shops. She was happy for the day. The lights in the new delicatessen had a calling brightness, and she stopped at the window.

The hot dogs were a deep rose on a shining grill under hooded brass lamps hung from above in a row. Inside there were three wood and brass chandeliers and the walls were a padded pink. It turned a delicatessen into a nice thing, the lighting and the fabric walls, the stainless-steel counter and Formica tabletops. It was inviting, and it changed the past where every day she had seen Mrs. Pomerantz standing behind hot dogs on curling brown paper used to suck up the grease of the grill.

All the neighborhood school kids stopped there every day at four and five; the steam-clouded window gave off a short, shapeless, silent gray woman, with her dry orthodox wig, which gave Helen a horror image of being bald. It was a picture that killed being young, like the canned foods on the shelves, labels spotted with grease, leaning back in their dust.

But Helen went inside with all the others: it was a flavor that drew their loyalty yet kept them cheap. And the men never got over it; they always settled for what they knew before they had taste.

She walked back, past the teen-age kids who stood at the luncheonette, the girls in teased hair and birds' nests and French twists, the boys in blue and gray Bermudas or cut down, shredded jeans, somehow nice, though Cy had called it nuts one Sunday when they were walking.

A few of them sat in cars on the street; they all seemed ready to go out, to a dance or to a club. It was comforting, but she could not walk the streets anymore; she went quickly home; the phone was ringing as she came in.

"Helen, Helen. I'm trying to get you an hour." It was Cy. "Look, I know this is crazy. But I'm bringing two buyers *home.*" Helen did not respond to the joke. "No, don't faint. This is an old army buddy, Selwyn Siegal, from Alabama. They own Horton's Dry Goods down there. It's a department store. And the other is his chief buyer with him on the trip. I know it's late. You can just send out for Chinese. Siegal says he doesn't expect a supper; he'll *feel* bad if you rush and cook special. See — they don't expect much. They're only sick of hotels and they just want to sit for a night in a home. And they want to meet my wife."

"I'll make something, Cy. It's a little after six. I can get to the store."

"No, no." The puffing voice. "Just send out. Send out."

"You just tell me when you'll arrive."

"Helen, now I don't want you to go nuts making up a meal this late."

"What time?"

"Time? Well, that's the thing. Late. They want to finish ordering before we leave. Let's say between eight and nine."

"I'll have it," Helen said, and hung up and called the store, asking for Vito.

"Just give me the order," he said.

"I'm not sure of everything," she said. "A small supper, but with a main course, a dessert and all that."

"If it's a fast job, you could always grill a sirloin." Vito paused. "Wait. They have the barbecue chickens. Already done." She heard his voice, muffled, calling into the store; then it returned. "Look, I'll bring up the last three chickens; they're still hot. And some big olives. And maybe an ice cream roll, if you like them. He's even got some fresh strawberries, first ones in."

In a half hour, he arrived. Helen saw that he was dressed up. "You were going out," she said.

"Just home. But they don't care when I get in. I got time." He came in and unpacked the brown box.

Helen looked at his brown Shetland jacket, his blue button-down shirt and striped silk tie. It was no longer embarrassing for him to be here, but she turned away as he looked up.

"Do you have baking pans?" He unwrapped the chickens from their foil bags. "These can reheat anytime. Just like this. Look."

Helen turned and saw the chickens on the table; Vito was rushing about in his college clothes; she smiled, uncontrolled; she felt stupid and pleased; too many admiring things had surrounded her this afternoon. She could imagine Vito staying here; for a minute they were all of one place.

He came by her and put the ice-cream cake in the freezer. "This better go away," he said, and she stepped back.

Vito noticed it. "What is it, Mrs. Steinman?"

"Nothing," Helen said.

"I'm trying to run things. I get it. Pushing my way in here." Vito came back to the table. "I'm sorry. I get like that. I just did it for friendship."

"What's this? Did I order this?" Helen held a long box.

"No charge," Vito said. "Just put them on a cookie sheet in the oven. And you have appetizers. That's from me to you."

"No, Vito. Let me pay you. It isn't right, on your salary."

"Oh, come on, Mrs. Steinman." He held out his arms, to remind her of himself. "You don't think I come up here for *money.*"

She was silent and looked at him: his slacks were a soft smooth flannel; he was slender out of work pants. His gestures had been light — she stood still while he unpacked the rest and took the box to the door. "You changed your hairdo," he said.

"I had it cut a little," she said. "Nothing special."

"You have natural blond hair, don't you?" He leaned on the door. "Never get like these women around here — nobody knows what they are anymore."

"You're too young to worry about gray hair and things like that." She walked to the door. "You don't know how we worry nowadays."

"Not you. You'll never have to worry."

"They'll be here any minute," Helen said. "Thanks for saving my life." She began to extend her hand, but stopped. Close to him she was struck by his height: the leather work jacket had made him appear thick and squat.

Vito held the doorknob. "I met Arthur before. You know what he said?"

"What did he say?"

"That you're a knockout. It's true." Vito opened the door quickly and closed it on himself.

Helen was left with the flat of the door; she let her body rest on it, let herself smile a moment, then went back to the table. The tan box of strawberries lay ready for washing and paring. She looked down at them, then went inside to dress up first.

C Y AND HIS FRIENDS arrived at nine-thirty; Helen had had the oven going for an hour, and she came to the door hot and irritated. But they stood there, like boys, apologizing, holding out boxes for her.

Siegal had brought a white leather jacket and Cy an amber necklace he had bought from the other man, Rosensohn, a jewelry specialist. Both men spoke with Southern accents, funny on Jews.

They ate the supper after Helen served frozen daiquiris and the appetizers. Siegal praised the home-cooked meal a few times, and Cy was so pleased that his face seemed flattened with his smiling.

"The nicest kid who delivers helped me out," Helen said. "He set it all up; I didn't even order the appetizers; he thought of that himself." The men listened, quietly waiting. "It's such a nice neighborhood — the people are really human beings. Here is this sweet kid, thoughtful enough to bring all the food instead of going home. You should have seen him; all dressed up. He wants to be a vocalist. I think he came in his own car —"

"Yes, yes, that's nice." Cy looked at Siegal. "But could you let us see the jacket now?" Cy asked.

"Well, just let me get the coffee."

"No, no. Please. Come on, Helen." Cy was rushed. "Let Selwyn see the jacket. She was a model. The best they ever had. We couldn't hire her away so I had to marry her."

Siegal smiled politely at Cy, and Helen caught the criticism in his expression, but she put the jacket on to help Cy, and the beads, too.

The men stood up and walked around her. "Oh, that *is* fine," Siegal said. "You sure do make it look well, Mrs. Steinman."

"Helen. Just walk to the end of the living room and back." Cy turned to Siegal. "See the drape of it. They have that elegance, Selwyn."

"Yes, I see it."

"Our whole new line is like this. The conservative look, with a little youthful dash."

Helen walked back to them and stopped. Cy moved to open the jacket and feel the lining. "Just look at that," he said to Siegal.

"I know it, Cy. I know it. That's why I'm buying so much from you, boy." He was smiling but had noticed Helen's slight discomfort standing there.

"I just want you to see you got your money's worth," Cy said. "To me, you're a friend more than a customer."

"Yes, Cy, yes." Siegal touched his arm, then went to sit on the couch. Cy and Rosensohn followed. Helen waited, watching them. "It's very, very nice," Siegal said when he saw Cy waiting. "Very, very nice."

Helen walked to the closet and found a hanger for the jacket. "Are you taking this back?" she said. "Is it a sample?"

The two men turned, looking surprised. "Oh, please," Siegal said. "Mrs. Steinman, that's yours. We brought it especially —"

Cy broke in: "Hang it up, honey." He laughed with strain, still deferring to Siegal.

Helen thanked them again and went for the coffee and liqueurs. "Do you have a little straight whiskey," Siegal said when he saw the green and yellow bottles. Cy got the whiskey bottle for Siegal. "I always like a little glass of whiskey with my coffee," Siegal said. "I get the habit from my dad. It's an old Jewish tradition."

Helen saw Cy smiling as she served, pleased with her appearance. All three watched her as she poured; she had the feeling of having done what she wanted, a whole evening in her plans, step after step *by* her, the men reacting just as she would want and when she wanted it.

She sat down to listen. Siegal mentioned some movies he had seen, getting them off business. Cy mentioned Paar and it lead to the race question.

"We've hired colored," Siegal said. "And no trouble, especially when we put them in better dresses or jewelry — anything but budget stuff. Isn't that funny? I mean, what *works*. And if it was up to me, I'd hire them. They live there; they shop there. But you people up North. You take a man who gets on TV and hugs one and makes a little speech. *We've* got to deal with a population down there."

Rosensohn nodded at his boss. "Whatever we do, somebody is going to boycott and march around outside."

"How about that poor man in Mississippi?" Helen said.

"Oh, Lord, Mississippi." Siegal threw his hands up. "We once thought of expanding there. But it's hopeless. At least Alabama's got some Jews."

Cy was smiling. "Do you do business in Florida?"

"Dad bought Kennilworth about four years ago," Siegal said.

"Kennilworth's! Is that yours? I didn't know that. It must gross quite a bit."

"Yes, it's big," Siegal said.

Helen went out for a new bowl of ice; when she returned, Siegal was standing in the middle of the living room. He was brushing at his neat, pinched, tightly fitted suit, the type short men like to wear.

Rosensohn stood behind him. They thanked her before she could ask them to stay longer. Siegal said he had to sleep. "Tomorrow's the end of it," he said. "And I'm anxious to get home. I'm just a town boy at heart. I hate the cities, really."

Cy insisted upon taking a taxi with them. "Unnecessary," Siegal said. "No, no. I want to show you these little papers on the way down," Cy said. "It's something you got to see."

Helen cleared the dishes when they were gone, turned on the washer and went inside to prepare for bed. She read *Vogue* and waited for Cy, but finally fell asleep.

She awoke when she heard the doorlock and shut her eyes again when she recognized Cy's steps. She could not remember dreaming, but her nipples were hard.

She wanted to ask Cy to come to her bed but turned her face away waiting for him to come to her. He sat down on his bed, grunting as he undid his shoes. Slowly, his odor came to her; then he was in the bathroom and she fell asleep again.

In the morning, she had breakfast ready when he came in. Cy was cheerful. "I wanted to tell you last night," he said. "He liked everything. He liked my plans, too. And he said to tell you you're beautiful."

Helen walked out of the kitchen, leaving him there, but Cy followed. "Where are you going? What is it? Siegal says that. And Rosensohn, too. There's no harm in it. Helen, I've known that man's family twenty-two years."

Helen had gone to her bed and sat down, facing the wall. "And what did you say, Cy?"

"What did *I* say? Is *that* what it is? *Oy, gevalt.*" Cy slapped his cheek lightly.

He turned and went into the bathroom to brush his teeth. When he came out, Helen was still facing the wall. "I, Helen, *I*, who kiss the ground you walk on. What did *I* say? I look at you and I feel like a young kid again. Last night, when you put on that new number —"

"I'm sorry, Cy," she said, and stood up. She began to pace. "Cy. It's just a mood. It must be getting to that certain time of the month."

"I told you about these plans I had. Well, I can say this: thanks to you. It's all for you I do it. Everything I do. So what are you giving me, what did *I* say? You know what I say." Cy was getting into his emotion — of moral height — and unable to stop. "I may not say it every morning, but it's there. The feeling in my heart. And you know I've been faithful to that; I think, or at least I hope, you *know* me."

Helen had lowered her head; it was an involuntary gesture, something out of a past she did not remember now, a movement of contriteness in response to a male voice. But Cy could not continue; his anger was thin and could have been sustained only had she argued; defeated this way, there was nothing.

"I'll come home early tonight," he said. He was smiling. "Helen? Listen. It's about time we went out. Let's go for Chinese. And I'll tell you some more about my schemes." He came to her and kissed her head.

58

He left and went for his things in the hall; his briefcase was out already, from the night before. Helen came slowly after him, but he had gone. She walked across the living room and heard the gurgling noise of the elevator down the hall, stop, pause in silence, then start again, but she continued to the door, trying to remember more of Cy's words. Something about tonight.

$I$T WAS Cy's voice. She could not remember how the day had gone. The clock said four-thirty. "So we go out like I promised, only here in town. I was keeping my real secret until you got here. But listen to this. Your cousin Manny and I and Sol Chapman, including Arnold of course, we're going into a new partnership. And the reason maybe you'd guess by now. You know what it is? It's Siegal. He likes my idea for merging wholesale with retail — it's a deal with stores all over, a way to move inventory like you never had before. Retailers on every level. You can really move it around. It's like a dance with labels. Like Kennilworth's. Remember Siegal said they own that. Well, we can send that stuff all over, to other places. The Siegals bought into Lanzman in Detroit and they got a whole chain of specialty shops Jack Lichtenstein built up on the West Coast. It's a natural for my ideas. And Siegal said *yes*. They're taking us in."

Helen did not answer. "What it is is this," Cy said. "You got outlets, outlets all over. No matter how much you produce, it's got a place to go. You know, the retailer is a *schmuck* who sits. If you got to keep selling him this number and that number, you waste ten years selling him a season's stuff. So here we *got* the retailers in our hands. We can concentrate on producing. Then we ship it out and say, *here, sell this*. Don't open your eyes. Sit back and wait for the people to come in."

Helen was not holding the words, but she caught the excitement. "Oh, that's so nice, Cy. That's so nice."

"So get dressed. Take a taxi right down. We're eating at Leone's and then Sol, Manny and me go down to Alabama to meet the father. You know, with the lawyers, the papers, all that stuff."

Helen did not answer. Cy went on talking while she tried to find the hiding words.

"Helen? Helen? Listen, Helen. You're excited. I know. Now listen. I want you should get dressed up and take a taxi right away; we'll be at Leone's. Ask for Mr. Steinman's party. Hurry up, will you?" His voice stopped. "Oh, wait. Listen. Helen. Pack me a suitcase, will you? The air luggage, the tan bag. Pack a suit, a couple shirts, ties, socks. You know what. And the Remington cordless. All right?"

He rang off; Helen's hand rested gently on the phone as she placed it in its cradle. She stared at it, could see the grease of thumbprints on the cool black curve.

Finally, she moved away from it, into the bedroom. There was something here, forgotten: whatever it was, she was caught in it: it struck, like random blows inside her. It was hate. But there was no reason for hate.

Once she had dressed, she was all right. But she forgot her stockings and had to come back to the bedroom just before leaving the apartment. She could not hook the garterbelt fasteners round the stockings after trying and trying, leaning over until she felt blood in her head. It was like the disappearance of balance, though she was not dizzy. Finally, she sat down on the bed and rested her hands on the tops of her thighs and slid each stocking between the snap and fastener, then pressed them together.

It was like dressing in the room next to the showroom, pulling on nylons like this and having one of the men suddenly there staring, and when caught, watching him stiffen his face and order her out to the floor to model. And when he'd gone, his sneaky eyes left an odd, embarrassed feeling, like being caught fooling around with herself as a kid, lying in bed and seeing a big face above looking worried and angry.

Dressed, she went to the living room and walked, testing herself, her fit, the correctness, as though to reach the approval first of the eyes her mind imagined before the men actually walked up to her in Leone's. She pressed her hips, stroking her skirt smoother against the Playtex underneath.

She remembered going to ask her mother if she looked right on the nights Cy was due; and sometimes she would go back and change three times, until her teeth were clenched together, holding back screams. Her father was gone by then, but he had not been there earlier, never had had a word for things like that.

He went away from her and her mother, first into the private dream of some of the Poles and the Russians — going to the Worker's Guild even after the place was only a chess room for the old Socialists who wanted to play and talk Yiddish; and then, after politics died in lies, he went away to jobs, selling this or that — insurance, plastic cookware, stocks. He died of it all, breathing the cooked air of strangers' living rooms and parlors, saying what he didn't believe.

He had sat on her bed and played games earlier, years before — she did not remember their details, but the rest came up now out of time. He used to teach her bits of Yiddish and Russian; then it stopped; it stopped in one moment. He went away; he did not even suggest she go to Hebrew School; he abandoned the religion without abandoning: there were still *seders,* but they might have been birthday parties, and attendance at synagogue: a day came and they walked to the synagogue; there was no work. That was all.

When she was working as a model, after the fuss he made, he did not even speak to her anymore, except in questions about her welfare: was she eating enough? what money did she save? They were not the questions asked of a woman.

"He was waiting for a boy," her mother told her one night when they were alone. "Then why does he stay away so much!" It was the first time Helen had dared a private statement.

Her mother's answers were like words from the bottom of a long black tunnel. Respect your father; realize all the things he does to make you happy; remember that he works at night when other men sit and relax; remember his loyalty to the workers.

Helen had an answer from her own moment, from today: everyone with two TV's, with dishwashers, cars, summer places, winter weeks in the Caribbean, stocks going higher. What kind of meetings could you have for the workers now? Rachel's husband owned a candy store and took August off, a whole month in Florida. What benefits should we cry for? *Oh poor Jacob.*

She shut it off and dressed quickly now. Finished, she remembered Cy's clothes to be packed. His suitcase was in the closet, ready to go. She filled it with the stuff of the drawers, choosing what he would like to wear in front of new people. She put four pairs of his cufflinks in the small side pocket of the bag. Then she added the silver tiepin she had given him, with its small pearl in the center. She added more handkerchiefs than necessary because she knew him; he was never happy without a pile of at least twenty.

His shirts were all white: spread, high collars that were all the same, and his ties were all different, big patterns and flowers and designs she could not imagine matching all his suits. She went back to pick the right suit for his ties and finally took his gray, hand-finished worsted; it was a day-time color yet formal enough for any night wear. She began to latch the bag once it was folded in, but had forgotten socks. She opened the bag again, her hands shaking suddenly, and quickly took four pairs of his favorite Banlon stretch socks: the drawer was full of new socks, gifts, purchases he had made from the salesmen who come around with black suitcases and park in the office until you buy.

The limousine was waiting at the door, and the ride downtown refreshed her.

Leone's was immediately noisy and big, dispelling the traces of thoughts. Cy, Siegal and his friend, her cousin Manny, Sol Chapman, and the two company lawyers were sitting and eating.

Cy placed her next to him and called for the waiter. When he had ordered a drink for her, he turned to his food and the men. They passed plates to each other, leaned over and speared slices of salami, picked up wet olives with their fingers, forked up slices of red pepper and cold artichoke; and each broke bread: the idea seemed to be to push down all bites with bread.

"Let's eat like pigs," Cy said. "Before somebody says don't eat like a pig." "You already said that three times," Manny said; Helen caught Siegal's dour face.

Cy spoke softly to her. "Start on this. It's the big anti-pasto. Selwyn ordered another one just for you, but you can fill up on this one."

Helen ate some of the antipasto, picking carefully as the men slowly took her in, beginning to talk to her. "You look gorgeous, my little cousin," Manny said. "How does a fat slob like Cy deserve you, I'd like to know."

"Look at him," Sol Chapman said. "Eats like king of the world." He leaned to Manny and said something in a whisper. Manny burst into laughter. "Yeah," he said, "and he's king of the *goyim,* too."

"If he's a *goy,* I'm Barry Fitzgerald," Sol said.

"No, if I'm a Jew, you're Sammy Davis," Cy said.

While they joked, Helen had her drink and sat and watched Cy. She had seen how he went after food, especially in the last two years, but this was the worst. This was how they ate together in their lunch hours, at their delicatessens.

She placed a hand on Cy's back, to ease him, and he turned and smiled. "Don't you love this stuff?" he said.

Then he saw her face. "It's only a once a year kind of bust. You know, it *is* time to celebrate now."

He placed another slice of bread on her plate; the second antipasto had come, and he called for it down the table and placed it before her, holding it with both hands and bowing his head. Manny clapped hands and Sol joined him.

Helen noticed Siegal and Rosensohn a little back from this, closer to the lawyers, not comfortable with the fun. Something was wrong: Cy and Manny and Sol were too loud, showing too much: *that* story was in Siegal's tight little face. But she did not care; she would even shout with them now, if she could.

When the ravioli and the steaks came, there was a silence. Helen was able to look about and enjoy the people. One man looked like Merv Griffin, the TV personality; another was surely Henry Morgan, the comic, though she had not expected him to be gray and to have such flat ears. She wondered if he wore false ears on TV, then began to smile at herself for being serious.

"Having fun now?" Cy had taken a hand with his left, and squeezed. "This is our birthday, Baby. It really is."

He was happy, like a boxer who had won a fight; no, not a boxer: she was thinking of Manny's father, after the second Schmeling fight, when the Nazi had lost to Joe Louis, and Manny's father had won five thousand. He had frightened Helen, rushing in and kissing her mother, hugging her and dancing around, then picking up Helen, giving her a real kiss and hug, pressing his chest against her breasts and stomach, giving her the feel of a man's hardness and the sudden excitement of men, who exploded into moods unexpectedly.

She leaned over and kissed Cy on the cheek. He was surprised, and smiled, then touched her face with his hands. "That's a good girl," Manny said. "Kiss the boss and make him laugh." "Georgie-porgie," Sol said.

Cy smiled at them, pleased to be the butt; Helen saw a bit of the light his eyes once had — when they were engaged, when he had promises and never thought of the future because everything would one day be his.

Now there was blackness in the rims; his eyes were black against his pale skin, and their light would go down soon, as they turned away when he came home, hoping to close in sleep, sitting watching TV like a massage, staring at the floor while he undressed for bed.

She drank more of the red wine and lost her concern for

Cy; she gave herself to the food and went along with the talk, responding to Siegal's polite smiles and Manny's big jokes.

Cy at last pushed his chair back and leaned over the rungs of Helen's, his right hand resting gently on her shoulder as he spoke and added his remarks to the conversation, keeping his voice as strong as Manny's and Sol's, getting in a crack for every one of theirs.

His hand was familiar; he had done this at family get-togethers before they were married, whenever they had had to visit his relatives, begun first as protection for her fear, then becoming a habit and secret, a way of telling her that his words were first for her.

While she was in the midst of the pleasure of the sounds and shouts, the loudness she could not dare but which men had the right to create for her, they were suddenly standing, buttoning their jackets. They moved about like fighters, dancers in a game, slapping each other's shoulders, daring touch and squeezing one another's arms in the darkness of their restaurant. "Look at this belt; it won't fit," Manny said, and they laughed at his stomach and felt theirs. Even Siegal rubbed himself.

Helen looked up at Cy. "We've got to make that plane," he said, and leaned over to kiss her.

"Oh, Cy, can't you and I stay a bit?" She looked at the others. "Meet them out there."

Cy was happy with this. "Oh how I wish we could." He lifted her right hand and kissed it; he held it while the others smiled and walked around. Cy had found love again as he always did, at parties.

But the men began walking out, and Cy helped her up, stroking her shoulders as she looked along the table, still ready with food and drinks and coffee. "Did you like the meal?" Cy said.

"I wish we could stay," she said. "Please. Let's us stay."

Siegal had not gone out with the rest: he had held back and was at Helen's side. "We'll promise you a real party if all this turns out," he said to Helen.

As she turned to look at him, Cy spoke, louder. "It will, it will!" He placed an arm on Siegal's shoulders. "Next year, Selwyn, we *buy* this place."

"I think we may, at that." Siegal's tone changed for Cy, forbearing, swallowing other words. Helen felt that he did not respect Cy, but Siegal was like an old man, shriveled, whose voice breaks up parties: he was bigger than they were but he had no belief.

They walked out to wait for Helen's limousine service; the street was warm, and they looked at cabs and cars that came along. Manny came up to Helen and embraced her. "Here's our good luck!" Manny shouted.

The others liked the idea of a good luck charm and came to her, hugged her, offered a kiss.

She saw Siegal near the curb, talking to his man Rosensohn, who nodded and began to call for a taxi. When one stopped, Siegal came back to Helen, shook hands, then leaned forward and kissed her on the left cheek. "I think *I* deserve a little kiss by now," he said. Helen saw that he was standing on his toes.

Abruptly, he went into the cab, and the others followed him. Cy reached his arm out of the taxi. "Helen!" She came up close. "Maybe you could come out to the airport for a last drink. We could put you in a cab before we take off."

Helen looked into the crowded taxi. "You and I could go in another car." As Cy spoke, Siegal said something she could not hear, but Cy turned to get it. "No, no, it's too late." He called it out to Helen, though she was near him. "We'll just barely make the plane. Good-bye. Good-bye."

They rode away, shouting and waving, like kids going off. Helen stood alone, embarrassed, then proud, feeling like someone known, a celebrity suddenly out on the street. She knew that people who had stopped for the noise of the men were still watching her.

She let herself be seen — her mind flashed into nothingness, a dream of being seen on lighted streets like this. She remembered the old Steve Allen show and the man-on-the-street interviews: it was an off-Broadway street like this one, and the actors were really outside. She had been excited and thought of going down one week, at the time of the program, to be there and be caught by the camera.

She looked up at the lights in the night darkness, blue and black; it was a New York that had been a dream in the Bronx, as though the Bronx, with its weak, nightlighted streets, were the middle of Iowa, silent, dusty, asleep by ten, the dead streets around Bronx Park South, dead and somber — when it was cold, when the winter came; not in spring — in spring they were all out, like a Russian street, all talking in Yiddish, in little circles, under their wide gray hats and oversized suits.

The big car came as she was standing there, and she recognized the driver as Vito's friend.

"Hello, Mrs. Steinman. You got a private car again."

He came out and opened the door for her. "Thank you," she said, aware that the drivers did not do this.

"I'm right on time, right? Ten-thirty-five," he said. And when she was seated and they were riding: "Have a good meal at Leone's?"

"Yes," she said, and wanted to tell him to mind his own business.

"I went there once, a night Vito took a bunch of us out. He thought he was going to the Coast any day. To make that movie. You know. So we all went out, *on* him."

Helen was smiling now: it was the excitement in the boy's voice that pleased her, and she could turn to the sight of the passing streets without thinking. The windows were open, and the sound of passing cars was like a gentle splashing.

They were on Fifth Avenue, passing the glassfronts and lights of the fifties, then in the Plaza with the horse carriages and the park behind them.

The look of the Plaza brought up the edges of a memory as they passed, the feeling of it without the facts. She turned her head from side to side, languorously, in response to it — now her movements *were* the memory — as though someone were admiring her, saying things that made her show herself and yet not want to; she could not stop until Arthur's voice interrupted her, calling his office on the scratchy intercom.

She had lost count of the streets but she stared at the buildings, her focus at the edges of the sheen, the lights, the shining white stone of rich apartment buildings.

In passing, in rolling slowly by, stopping briefly for lights, then suddenly surging on a short distance (the rhythm set up and made by the black car), she was absorbing the neighborhood, feeling it to be herself.

She had forgotten Cy and the men but not what they suggested by their fun, in their cabs and planes, in laughter and tips, ten dollar bills held aloft in hands, being waved, to clear a path.

Helen shifted her position on the leather seat; the surface was smooth to the touch of her hands, but she was uncomfortable, sitting as though she might slide off. She held herself on; then she felt moisture between her legs: her panties felt tight and sticky: it was an irritation from nowhere, but it excited her. She hoped it was not that rash Rachel had spoken about — old Doctor Sidney had told her — that comes with boils: in Russia the women would say you had to get nine of them before you died.

"Look who's here. Look!" It was the driver's voice; she saw his face turn towards her. "Behind us, Mrs. Steinman. Look who's there. That's Vito. In the Impala."

Helen turned slowly and saw a white convertible just behind them; in it, Vito, waving one arm, and the car going slower, both cars in the same rhythm, then stopping.

Arthur had opened the door. She looked back, and Vito had opened his door. She looked at Arthur, who smiled. "Take a ride in a good car," he said.

"A good car," she said. "All right. I'll try it."

"Hello," Vito said when she came. "I thought that was you. I can drop you off. I'm going up."

She sat down and shut the door. As they pulled away, Arthur waved from the black limousine, still at the curb.

"Well, how much do I owe you?" she said, and Vito smiled but did not turn his head. "Where are we?" she said.

"Ninety-sixth. We're going west to the highway."

Helen did not answer but watched Vito, who drove slowly in traffic. He drove with his body resting against the door, turned towards Helen in the next seat; in this position only his left eye saw the road, it seemed. Helen was uncomfortable with it.

"It's a warm night," Vito said. "I put the top down and you'll get cool as soon as we get out of traffic."

She looked at him, with her back to the street, aware of the people her mind tried to put on the walks behind her. Finally, Vito turned up Riverside Drive, which was dark.

Her eyes had been on his thin blue polo shirt, his chest muscles broad, round mounds against the thin, shiny, clinging material (Banlon, she thought), bulging like small, taut, women's breasts, yet hard. His right arm, the muscles arching out of the sleeve, was too large; she could not conceive that his jacket had covered it; even on the night he had helped her in the kitchen, in his shirtsleeves, it had been hidden.

"Can you play any sport?" she asked.

"Any sport? What do you mean?"

"I mean all the sports. Basketball, whatever else. A track runner."

"Well, you know a college won't give you the scholarship unless you play three sports. I was all-city in basketball."

"Yes, I see." Helen was aware of her false tone, like an interviewer. "And how many years did you have?"

"Well, two years. I didn't go back after Christmas. Didn't I tell you all this?"

"Yes, you did. I was looking at you now. I forgot. You don't look athletic in that jacket of yours."

"You mean that leather jacket. It's pretty campy, isn't it? Maybe I wear it for disguise."

Her eyes were on his shoulders and his head; the shoulder hunch was almost frightening to her, though she could see it was caused by his muscles there and not posture, not the bull-like hunch of cruel men. "You need a haircut," she said.

"You're not kidding." Vito rubbed the curls on the back of his neck. "You know, you'd think, up here with this job, I could get a haircut every day. Down in school, and playing, too, I had one every two weeks. Now I have all the time in the world and I don't get to it. I'm getting like the guys on White Plains Avenue again. I keep a comb in my back pocket all the time. *Here I go again,* I've been thinking. I'm going to be one of the wopheads again."

"But doesn't long hair go with singing?" Helen was checking. "Isn't that usually true?"

"I guess so. Paul Anka. Dion. Those guys." Vito did not catch the allusion.

"Your friend the driver said you sing."

"Yes, that's right. I have a contract right now. I mean, anytime I want to start, I could go out to the Coast and start."

"Yes, that's what your friend was saying."

"But you don't believe it." Vito smiled. "Well, I'll show you right now. I'll come up to your house and sing for you."

"Right now? Without a band?"

"No, I'm bringing a whole band. Right into your apartment. You wouldn't mind that, would you?"

"I'm afraid I couldn't —"

"Don't worry. It's a demo record in the trunk. It's *me,* singing with a band. It's a few numbers I did at the second tryout. The first one was in a club on the East Side."

"I really don't think I could do it. I mean, I don't know when."

"Tonight," Vito said. "Right now. If that's all right with you. It isn't so loud on the phonograph." Vito turned to look at her. "You going home now?"

"Yes." Helen looked up at the sky over the Hudson, the rising hills of lights along the highways on both sides. "But I'd like to go riding tonight." The phrase had just entered her mind.

Vito did not answer but drove faster, switched on the radio; in fifteen minutes they had reached the toll bridge, driven through Riverdale and started up the Saw Mill River Parkway.

Helen had not seen roadside Westchester clubs in many years; going upstate, in the last five years, the taxi to the mountains had taken the Thruway in the morning hours, passing houses and trees. Now Vito was passing lighted clubs, low wooden buildings set back on the laps of their parking lots, with lights obscuring their size.

She had known them after high school, in a time of little bands and first discovering mixed drinks made with cream or fruit juices and Southern Comfort, which she still loved.

The boys in the crowd were mixed, and she had liked one named Tim Feeny and another who was Italian, who disappeared. And all of them — their emotions ran like sea tides then, not shored up by thoughts of who was right to marry, who would be a doctor, who would be something big in business.

She lost her reveries abruptly, startled by a double bump in the road; the rhythm had caused a remembered phrase: *thank you, Mom,* and she remembered Sunday rides with Uncle Jack, Manny's father.

"That's Slater's." Vito's head was looking towards the river alongside the road. "They have little paddle boats in the daytime. Ever been there?"

Helen looked back as they passed. "It's right after that famous bump in the road," she said.

"How about a drink? The bar is great."

She met his eyes, a brief glance without meaning or feeling. Vito turned the car off into the grass at the side of the road, then accelerated suddenly round to the other lane.

"That was *fast!*" she said, and Vito smiled.

They returned to Slater's, and Vito frightened her by

abruptly cutting the wheels into the loose, white stones of the parking lot. "Ooh, I thought you'd hit something," she said, and let herself out; she walked ahead, stopping at the water.

"This is so nice," she said when Vito came up. "How far are we from Riverdale?"

"Twenty minutes."

"You see," she said. "You have to have a car. And I was the one who said you didn't need it."

Vito took her right hand; he had been looking at her face leaning over the water and lines of it reflected in the water; she was light and yet painted, red and blond: the reflection, once he had seen it clearly, had made him reach out to take her.

Helen did not back away; the fiction of a ride home was gone, and she squeezed Vito's hand even in the midst of heat growing in her face, shame that did not cool itself.

"Let's go inside. It's very nice up there."

While they drank, Helen looked about the bar and the dining room beyond, imagining herself as a tourist, forming the conversation she would have if someone recognized her: she had been on her way home; she asked to see this new place for a future dinner; she stopped for a quick drink.

Vito was near her talking about the other clubs in Westchester, and she nodded and listened; then he began to suggest she buy a car, offering the name of a friend. Annoyed that she did not speak, he turned to face the bar and stopped talking.

"It's very comfortable here," she said after the silence was clear to her. "I've enjoyed it, but I have to go back. I should be back."

75

"Back?" Vito looked at the drinks, unfinished, and at Helen, but she stepped down, leaving her barstool spinning, and walked towards the door.

Vito followed her; he saw two men at the bar stop and look at her and then him, and nod. Her movement was exciting, but he was angry at her leaving him like this. He followed the shake of her body: it was jelly, dough, cunt — the words ran up his mind, then sank in feeling.

He came up close, then stopped, not sure how to address her. She pushed open the door herself, and he followed her out to the lot.

Helen reached the car first and opened the door herself. "Wait a minute." Vito's voice had changed. "We'll *get there!*"

He took her hand away and held the door for her; Helen turned and looked at his face, ready to speak, but afraid of his expression.

Vito released the handle of the open door and took both her hands, then dropped them and wound his arms around her slowly.

Helen found her body reacting too fast, striking his before he had set himself to press against her. In the back of her mind now, almost lost, was the anger that had pushed her; she had thought of hitting him, but with her hands held she struck at him with her body.

Vito slipped back against the door, but pushed himself back up, lifting her off the ground for a moment in the movement of regaining his balance.

She had never felt strength like that before; it was a magic — her body became light; her eyes were open as Vito kissed her and she saw the round curls along his neck shine in the light of the bulb that lit when the door opened.

She was lifted again, quickly, and sat down in the seat.

Vito kissed her standing above her; her head was held by him so that she had to look straight up, seeing the night sky behind his head. She felt his right hand on her dress, pressing with clumsiness against her breasts.

She tried to back her face away, but it was held there; her hands helped her, pushing at Vito's stomach: it felt like wood.

Vito lifted his head, releasing her, but she placed her face against his body; his hands stroked her hair briefly; then he moved away, gently pushing her back, and shut the door. She was silent while he went round, stepped into his seat, and drove off.

We must go home now, she said to herself. That was all. She would say it, simply. "Vito. Let's go home now."

Vito did not answer; the car drove off the highway and up a hilly road, with trees along its edges. A white sign came out of the darkness, reading TO SCARSDALE. The road passed a few houses set behind trees, with black cuts of driveways. Then abruptly it dropped down and at the bottom, the car turned into darkness, along a narrow, dirt road bordered with bushes that scratched the sides of the car; the sound made her shudder, like screaming blackboards.

"Do you know where this is?" The car had stopped, and Vito's voice was soft.

"No. Is it Scarsdale?" Helen could see only the waving lines of branches.

"No, that's way over on the other side."

The motor was running. "It's chilly, here," Vito said. "The top better be down." He let the roof come down; it struck, and there was an echo of it off through the woods; he clamped it in; turning from this, he took her hands again and pulled her towards him on the seat. She saw his head coming to her and lifted her chin. But he did not kiss her; she felt her dress buttons being undone.

"Vito!" She said his name in the silence, loud enough to have someone hear and come to get him. But she could not find words.

Her mouth filled with saliva and suddenly she wanted to spit. In a pause, his face came against hers. "Don't do it!" It was her voice, but not a voice of this night; it was a phrase that seemed recorded, the timbre of its sound flattened and nearly lost.

His head seemed to pause, listening; she sensed it in the dark air before her and wished to touch it, but the moment dropped: his hands had edged her dress along her back, his hands came round and unsnapped her bra, cutting at her skin, his hands had spread her legs on the seat, pushing her slip out from beneath her, bunching it high, under her chin: allowing this was like being held down by the material, the silken slip crumpled like her own power.

She was lifted by his arms again and sensed his strength in the lightness of her own body as it was lifted up. (It *was* this feeling that covered her thoughts and stopped words: she was up; she was a bird of his hands and could only follow.)

She did not think she was helping him, but her body moved according to his hands and knew the hands' directions. Helen felt the cold night air on her thighs; the cold frightened her — it was like the inside of Vito: coldness, blackness.

She saw parts of him in glimpses, when she dared open her eyes: his lips were sliding along her neck and shoulders, were then upon her breasts, sucking and pressing.

(Now this moment said she would be destroyed; cops would come; she would be exposed, taken to the station without her clothes; Vito would throw her out if they were caught. She tried to reach up for her dress, to pull it over her part way.)

But now Vito's hands and mouth were erasing thought. One focus remained: the feeling of his mouth on her left breast, her nipple rising, feeling tight and tender, and his mouth like pressure through her (rather than feeling), felt to her feet. She pressed her toes down against the rubber mat on the car floor.

Vito paused, taking his mouth away, and she heard her own breathing, the air of her exhalation scraping the roof of her mouth.

She felt him against her leg, his chin, his lips and the brushing of his tongue, and thought that she must scream; as his tongue curled inside her, her body twitched with its own control, not hers; but she was not outside the feeling: it changed her, making her thoughts believe that she was melting, dissolving; her head slipped slowly along the seat back, falling softly against the door.

His arms were pulling her down, placing her body: her head was back on the seat and her eyes opened: she was surprised that she did not call out. She lifted her legs, first her left along the leather seat, then her right spread out until it touched the floor mat. The obedience made her smile; her legs were small and light, his hands as large as half of her, working his power like big levers, high over her head, then down, down dipping and up again.

The thoughts ceased as she felt Vito within her; she heard her voice making sounds that resembled words, softly said, like a chant, without meaning.

Vito was silent until his body began to quiver and rock; he came down like the weight of stones, fading then striking, like a door that strikes shut. Near her ear his voice began speaking sounds, like words yet not words, exhaled rather than spoken, like the shout of a horseman to his horse, ending in groaning, the groaning of strength.

When his body had stopped moving, Vito jumped back and stood just outside the car door. She opened her eyes again and saw his body, a shadow of the whole door-way, grown in the night shadows.

She sat up slowly and dressed herself while he sat and watched. The night silence that had surrounded the car was gone; her ears were alert to occasional cars on the road behind them and even the far-off hum of the park-way.

Vito had lit a cigarette for her and placed it in her hand. "Hold it a minute," she said. "Let me comb my hair."

He waited in silence while she twisted the rear-view mirror to face her and combed her hair. She saw his still face carefully watching, and she stroked slowly for him. Her hair curled too well: she realized it was the damp-ness of the night. She had not been out in the night since —Helen stopped combing. Walks on Lincoln Road, with Cy, after a club, or the Concord. But it was not this, this cold spring weather, staying in it until its feeling covered all your skin; she had lived like all the apartment women, out only in the morning to shop and then back home.

She reached her hand for the cigarette, turning to look at him. "I got a jacket in the back," he said, and turned for it.

"Thank you," Helen said. "It feels much better." He had placed the jacket over her shoulders lightly, shyly. It was a grateful gesture but not done with delivery-boy politeness. He wrapped the bottom of the jacket carefully around her legs. "Why did we do it?" She said it when his face was leaning close to hers.

Vito straightened up to look at her, but he could not answer: in his mind was the word: *love*. He loved her. He loved her.

"Do you want the radio?" He leaned forward and switched on the car motor.

"You're not answering me," she said.

"You know," he said. "You know why." It was the first embarrassment he had felt.

The radio came on; it was late-night music, big bands from the hotels in Chicago.

She wanted to speak again and waited for the wind to die down, but the car rushed through it and the radio was too loud. She sat back for the rest of the ride, her face feeling red and flushed because she was wet and did not have a tissue.

At her entrance, she turned to him. "Good night." She let herself out of the car, her thought on the sweet tone in the two words: someone would pick that up. She walked through the lobby, looking down at the front of her dress as she came closer to the bright lights around the elevator door.

But the night man was half asleep and no one appeared. She turned away while she rode up; walking along the hall, she listened for her phone. Inside, the apartment seemed stuffy, the air stale and dusty: she had closed and locked the windows before going out; a habit of the old neighborhood, unnecessary but still done here where a night man was your protection and the cellars posted with gray signs of a detective service that threatened thousands of dollars in fines to outsiders, pilferers, burglars, salesmen — all people who could not get in, they were told.

When she undressed, she felt suddenly exhausted, unable to bathe. She lay back on her bed and touched her breasts, as though they might have been harmed. But she was too sleepy to go on thinking, and her eyes shut in sleep while she was still on her back, before she could go through her nightly shifting from side to side finding and molding a comfortable position.

# □□□ 7

THE PHONE was ringing: Helen had heard its sound in sleep and heard it now many times, higher, outside of herself. She reached for the phone. "Hello. Cy?"

It was the call she had expected last night; her delay in answering now would alert Cy. Even the lies she would tell would spell out her wishes in some way he would decipher: her dream moments were no longer idle or harmless: they were showing and moving.

"Hello? Cy? I'm here."

"Helen? Mrs. Steinman?" It was Vito.

"What is it? I'm sleeping."

"I'm coming to your building. Can I take your order?" The voice was too loud.

"Not *now*," she said, and let the phone fall into its cradle.

She turned on her back and looked at the ceiling. There was no need to be polite; she could say whatever she liked to him. He was growing at the exits and entrances of her mind, though; his weight was here, at the side of the bed. But she would damn him, somehow, when it was needed.

When the doorbell rang, she jumped up, this time fully awake. It seemed only a minute after she had slept; she could not understand his speed.

She put on her robe and went to the living room. It was the front door and she called from behind it.

The voice was new: a telegram from Cy. She walked to the kitchen reading it: MAKING BREAD, MAKING PIE, SIGNED YOUR LOVING HUSBAND CY.

She laughed at the words, the picture of Sol and Manny making it up with him.

She sat at breakfast and read it again; a suggestion of loneliness found her: she wanted to cry for herself left here.

The service bell rang and she sat still, waiting for the boy to go away. She was afraid of him now, of what he wanted to do to her. He was becoming an "it" — something that appears and reappears, demanding money, threatening, slapping and beating, ripping a housecoat down the front; her thoughts moved in and out: she knew they were falling into stories she had seen, movie stories that rested in layers in her head. Fragments came out, with her face in them; then the face of Lana Turner as she struck the bathroom wall.

She would have to pay him; the money from her purse; opening her purse she would take out the roll of bills, green bills hidden in a white envelope, hidden from Cy.

Yet she would not pay; he had no proof, but she had the proof of his face, his position; they would not believe she gave herself to a jaunty kid, just like that, like a diamond ring thrown out the window.

The phone rang at noon, at one-thirty, at two-fifteen, at four. She had spent the day waiting for its ring, ready to shut it in the bedroom if it went on. She did not answer and could not get out, go away from it. She ate a can of tuna and some Hollywood Diet bread at four-thirty and began to think that one of the calls must have been someone else. Cy's mother recurred; she would want to know where Helen was keeping herself with Cy away.

The phone rang at six, at eight, again as she was getting ready for bed, and she answered it. "I'm coming to see you." She cut off Vito's voice by slamming the phone down.

Ten minutes later the service doorbell rang, and she let it go on. When she heard fists on the door she shut the bedroom and the living-room doors and sat down before the phone; but there was no one she could call. The police. The police would know Vito and look and go away.

Then the noise disappeared; she went out to listen, coming slowly to the kitchen to check the lock again.

A note had been placed under the door, a white envelope and on the card in it: *Thinking of you. I am going away. Never forget.*

She opened the door and found a large bouquet of roses in soft, green paper.

He was not a criminal. She carried the roses to the bedroom and placed them in her square crystal vase. He was a young guy, full of life, full of a spirit she had had. She had. She wanted to call him back now.

But it was getting late; at least, it felt late for her after this day. She sat on the bed in her nylon gown and read *Reader's Digest* until her eyelids shut while she stared at the page. In this light sleep of moments, she dreamed a thought, that Vito was here in the room; just as it pictured itself, it dissolved; this picture recurred like a dim slide, five, six times, and then ceased as she slept.

# 8

I T WAS a phonebell; once awake, she was commanded by it, and her arm went up as a warm weight in her thoughts tried to bring her back into sleep; her mouth and body were empty, as if she had not fed enough on the contents of sleep.

The voice was a shock: Cy's mother. Helen had been preparing a tone for Vito's voice; now the old woman caught a feeling not meant for her. "No, nothing's the matter, Mother. I'm all right. It's only being asleep. Yes, I jumped a little when the phone went off —"

She was cut off; the old woman had heard but was interested in getting off her own feelings: why had Helen not called; what had she been doing; people want to hear about her; she shouldn't back away from others.

"Well, let me explain," Helen said. "Oh, I know we're all like that, digging into our own little holes."

The old woman cut in again, but Helen would not allow it. "I was actually waiting for *your* call." Helen spoke louder. "I said to myself, what do I do, as soon as Cy goes off, do I go and call up like a baby? You see what

I mean. Once I called *you,* instead of you calling me, then you'd *have* to invite me, and so forth."

"You're very thoughtful, Helen." The voice was suddenly warm; love had come up like a flash, but could go down again, Helen knew, in an instant of irritation.

"As a matter of fact, Helen, I did give you a ring on the phone that night." Helen's mind reached for the words. "What night?" she asked.

"The night they left, I called you up to ask if they got off all right. But you must have been downtown still."

"I didn't even know you *knew* anything yet." Helen found herself turning from her guilt. "Cy told me the whole thing just came up. That it was a big secret until the deal was signed and sealed."

"Which does not include me. Right? But Helen, that business is *my* business. What did you think I did, singlehanded, ten years? I ran it by myself. You may not realize Samuel passed on when Cy was five years old. Oh, just remember, we had our share of bad luck. But I'm *still here.* I am still here. And they must tell me."

"I would expect it, I would certainly expect it." The words were too intense for first awakening: Cy's mother moved from warm, motherly affection to suspicion of usurpers in one moment, and Helen knew that she had to ease the old tone. She had been used to this, from home, from her mother's winter evening moments of pogroms inside her head. Uncle Jack had said to her: you'll be lucky; you have the *shickseh* cover.

Mother Steinman was going on; Helen held the sides of the bed to hold down the dizziness that came. She allowed her face to move away from the telephone, and her eyes caught the red polish on her toenails: she tucked her feet under the covers.

"Helen? Are you there?"

"I was saying, yes, sure. But in this case, Cy himself had said —"

"*What, Cy himself had said.* Well, I know the whole thing. I'm in touch by phone all the time. You know, I still do the books. And I can still tell *them* a few things." Her voice paused for a laugh. "Oh, well. Look how excited I get. That place — it's attached to me."

"Yes, I imagine." Helen was getting lost in the purposes of Mrs. Steinman. "Why, you know how Cy talks about you; he talks about you all the time and mentions the things you say. He says to me, 'You know what the boss said' — he calls you the boss."

"The boss?"

Another shift in tone, and Helen's hand squeezed the mattress. "Well, it sounds cute, the way he says it. Don't you think? There's affection in it. Really. And respect." The silence frightened her. "Well, they'll be back in a few days. Why don't you come up and have supper here? We haven't had a real guest yet."

"A few days? Is that what he told you? Didn't he call? They just started for California. They have to look at the chain stores out there. They couldn't be back, the *earliest*, two weeks. Oh, that *shlepp*. He could give you a ring. But listen, what I was thinking was, why don't you come over *here* and stay a little bit?"

"Oh, that's nice." Helen's first reaction was sudden: the old woman did not usually do this; she kept her apartment as a special place, for people her own age who had retired, with businesses pouring it in while they collected paintings and charities. The other guests were invited for dinner at one of her restaurants on Madison Avenue.

Helen sat up. "It's Friday. I could come this afternoon."

"Now wait. I'm going away for a few days." Mrs. Steinman's laugh was another change: some guilt for extravagance, perhaps. "I made these plans long ago. But look. You come over next Wednesday for lunch. I'll call you Tuesday night. We can meet down here, and I'll take you to a new place. Italian. Northern cooking for a change, without tomatoes over everything. It's a brownstone they did up in genuine eighteenth century. That's coming back, you know. You're going to like it."

Helen wanted to go away, a weekend upstate, and get clear, and start anew.

But the old lady had hung up, like a businesswoman, with no extra words. Helen held the phone, then put it down, off the hook, and went to the bathroom.

Returning, she heard the busy signal and smiled at the phone and went to dress; but she began to worry when the phone's noise changed to a high whine: perhaps she had broken it. She placed the speaker lightly in its cradle and went out.

She was in the lobby when the noon siren went off: she had slept late, was enjoying it until the old woman's voice had set her off, like a starter in a race, her voice like a gunshot.

She walked to the Parkleigh Restaurant for a sandwich, then went to the store and gave her order. The walk home was hot; upstairs she changed into a light-blue shirtdress and came into the living room to straighten up before the maid's visit next day. The service bell rang, and she went to the door and found Vito.

"What a hot one." He carried the brown box to the

kitchen table and unpacked it and put the freezer foods away.

"What are you doing here?" she said. "I thought you went away." The shrill, the forgotten voice, a tone that went out to him, to the old lady, to Cy and the others who *told* her things but never asked her, who started actions and then left her in the moment of rising feeling.

Vito was standing and smiling. "I'm going to the Coast. I'm taking that contract."

She did not believe it. Vito had something in the box. "I wanted you to have my record," he said. He placed it in her hand and went to the door. "Tell me what you think about it."

When he had shut the door, she went quickly to the phonograph in the living room. She watched the record start, slowly, the automatic arm coming down, a hiss, then an orchestra, violins in the background, and Vito's voice, recognizable, the same person yet expanded; it was a voice beyond any neighborhood, its sound coming down from above, taking in great lengths: she could hear it at Jones Beach along the sands, coming from the comfort of a portable radio they all leaned to; or widening its breadth from speakers in the curtains of nightclub stages, all around, high in the air of darkness and smoky light. It was untouchable, insulated by its ability from the crowd around, far away and yet as uncreated as the creatures in TV.

When the record ended, she played it again, listening this time with more ease, getting to know the person of the voice and the smiling boy she knew and the person who had wrapped himself around her in the car. The hate she held like a filled, quivering pitcher in her hand was left to her to hold; always like this, she had been given the burden and then, as she was ready to hurl the heavy thing, was shown an offering, a blaze of light, a new gift in her hand, an exchange she must not refuse.

The third playing was for the music, and she went to the center of the room and began to dance, doing spins that whirled her skirt up. At the end, she sat down, out of breath and smiling. Oh if she had had the moment to dance, the chance to choose it: there would have been a time, to tell others, to show others: something she would know with movement.

She jumped up and moved quickly to the phone; while she dialed she heard her breathing come strong into her breast; her eyes looked down and saw her body heaving to the rhythm of herself, exhausted from the few minutes. It was as if she looked at excitement raised from a grave inside her; she looked at her body: she never ran; no one she knew ever thought of running or jumping or swimming enough to get out of breath. Everyone's body was moving towards the hope of sitting forever, waiting for an endless line of treats for their eyes and skin.

"Hello?" She heard her impatient voice and stopped. "Who is it?"

"This is Mrs. Steinman calling," she said. "Will you ask your boy to stop by this apartment. He left something off by mistake."

"Is there something else you'll need instead?"

"Oh no, the order's fine. It's just something he forgot. Something of *his,* by mistake." She was about to say *his gloves,* but saw them on his hands right now in the store next to the man who was speaking.

"Something? Well, what is it?"

"Just a personal belonging. Will you ask him to stop up, please?"

"Yes, yes. We'll send him up. How's about five? Will you be home?"

"Yes, I'll be here." She knew she had made a mistake as soon as she put the phone down to silence again. Now they will ask him *what* it is and he will tell them about the record: they would have stares ready for her when she came by.

She walked to the kitchen; she was hungry again, and ate cottage cheese from the waxen cup it came in (first scraping off a dry edge that had formed), and with it the last bagel in the bread box. Chewing the moist, salty dough, she stood over the range and boiled a pot of water for instant coffee.

With the cup, she went out to the TV. Her mood remembered the afternoon soap opera shows; they were not serious, but there was something in their happenings, like shadows of what really happens to people. And when she had seen a bit of the first show, she remembered some of it from months ago: it was the story of an older career woman, who loved a younger man, her niece's boyfriend. It proved her thought, and it was not the first time: these dumb shows guessed your life: somehow, uncanny: right after her mother's death she had found a parallel situation to her own.

She sat through the first show, then started to watch the next but lost her attention because it was about a woman locked in a garage and dying slowly of exhaust fumes from her car engine. The pictures were dull, and went from face to clock, back and forth, as if she would not know that time was going by.

She watched, but her mind was on Vito; after the slow, sweeping, erasing movements of the television (the countermen drifting off), the mood of the record came back. She left the living room restlessly and went to the bedroom: she was here to prepare herself for him, and she hated the thought and every movement she would perform. Some muffled, brittle order imposed itself; she was holding her box of equipment, the jelly, the rest. In her throat came the shuddering of sadness, like tears that cannot rise, a half-grief, for a person loved but not close.

Prepared, she sat at her dressing table. Lying back to get ready had been humiliating; in her mind today she was an animal: a grasshopper, she had thought, as she looked at her legs held overhead.

Now she rubbed cold cream on her hands and face, then sprayed Chanel on her hair. It was not enough; she went to the bathroom and washed her face and neck; then, for some reason, she poured a warm bath and sat down at the tub's edge and washed her feet, then wiped them slowly.

The doorbell rang, and she listened, rubbing and pressing her toes and her arch with the towel. She wore her silk robe and let Vito in, finally; he followed her to the living room.

"I liked your record very much." She turned to study his face. "Yes, I liked it. You have a really good voice. Slightly Tony Bennett style, which I like. But it's all you. Not a copy, I mean."

Vito smiled with the words and nodded. "Thanks for that. I mean it. Thanks. I need words like that; then I start to feel it. I think, now, I've got it. I've got the thing that's coming. What would you say? Should I go and do it? Should I sign that contract?"

"Oh yes, I'd take it. If it's still being offered."

"It's there, all right. But it means going out to the Coast. You start a whole new kind of life." He watched her face for the wild response, the words of yes that would get them going, the dream of racing to California in the Impala, the top down, blond hair and white luggage.

But Helen said: "In life we have to take a chance. You have to try it. I didn't do much, but I went and worked as a model, and a million old people told me it was a disgrace, I was wrong. But I did it. And I was scared; I was scared from the first day on."

"Listen!" Vito's voice was high, strained by the pleasure of her confession. "Let me talk to you. I'll come back here tonight. I've got to spread it all out and have you listen. OK?"

"OK, partner." She smiled, and reached out her hand in a joking Western handshake. Vito missed it, had already started for the door and the next thing to come in his day. She walked behind him and met him again as he paused at the door. He smiled at her, to produce words he could not yet create for the feelings he had. "I'll come back," he said as he left. Outside, in the hall he heard the echo of his words, others unsaid behind them; they were made of thoughts, feelings, of lines from a song he'd learned: *I'll come back to you, don't know where, don't know when; in the still of the night.* It went on until the elevator took him down to the street.

Helen walked back to the living room to look at the record, then turned abruptly and went to the kitchen. It was clean, the table holding one empty brown bag, open, standing lightly in the closed room. She opened the refrigerator door and picked out some celery and cheese spread. She ate it and was still hungry but could not cook any meat: the odor would be sickening.

The house must remain this way, still and unused, as long as Cy was gone. Then what she did would be temporary, outside of life, like the sudden summer adventures she had heard about; even Rachel had talked about these things happening. They could be out of time (like dreams acted in themselves) if the house were untouched, unused and lying asleep, with its life closed.

She napped when dusk came and awoke in darkness: the electric clock was dark, too. The lamp switched on brought the green dials up: it was eight-fifteen. She got up quickly, dressed herself in slacks and her new V-neck sweater, then went into the living room to put on some lights. The couch and chairs should be covered in times like these; she looked at them: the clear plastic covers. Rachel would remember where they were sold. She went to telephone and ask.

Rachel gave her the information. "Now tell me what's happened with Cy and the others."

"Oh, it's all business." Though Rachel was close, Helen would not say. "It looks like maybe very good news coming our way. If, if, if."

"Oh now, what is it, anyway? I spoke to Sarah Chapman and she's all excited. Did they corner the market or something?"

"Well, they have some kind of deal going. I don't know what it is, but I hope it comes through. Cy worked himself into the ground for it. Night and day."

"Well, I'm glad for you, Hel." Rachel's strong voice was serious; she was the only woman Helen believed.

"I wish I felt good about it," Helen said. "What is it,

all this? His mother likes it. They all like it. Everything's fine, but everybody's *shot*."

"That's what we do, here. We're expanding, now. It's all fine, but some days I don't even feel human."

"You're the one I thought was doing something. I mean, the courses you were taking."

"Don't worry about me, kid. What I don't like is you sitting up there all the time. Downtown was bad enough, but at least you were here. Riverdale, you might as well be a chicken. You know what I keep hearing: people are coming back from Scarsdale and places out there because they're half crazy living up there."

"Everything's wrong. Nothing's any good. You're getting me saying it now." Helen had changed her tone, to have some fun with the thought.

"Come on, Helen. Just look around. The men are all fat *drek*; the TV has all these skinny fags and stupid long hairs; the kids, you give them money and the best education and they pay you back with an arrest because they're smoking marijuana. I suppose you heard about Martha Bronstein's boy?"

"No, I didn't. But what have the kids got? Too much, or nothing?"

Rachel's voice did not reply; what was the silence? "Rachel, are you still on the line?"

"I'm still on the line. I'm trying to put something into words. Helen, if you could see the kids who come into the store; they talk there, you know. They say things I don't even think they say at home. I'd need a whole night to tell you."

"Then come up here and see me."

"I couldn't right now. We're at the store all the time.

But let me just say one thing about these kids. When you talk to them, you find out, number one, religion's gone. Ambition is gone, a certain kind of ambition. They hate the government; you should hear them talk about the president, everybody—"

"I don't think so much is wrong with them. I mean, the kids I see. They look better than we did." Helen saw the neighborhood.

"Something is wrong. I don't say they're made wrong. I mean, from the start. But they get so that the things they want is just for themselves. It's all alone. We weren't like that."

Helen saw the clock. "We have to get together. Why don't I come down to the store? I could help you out."

"Sure, I'll put you on the counter." Rachel's voice was happy again. "With your figure, you'll raise business two hundred percent."

"It's a date, then." Rachel said good-bye, and Helen sat at the silent phone. Rachel's voice was like a trip outside, her thoughts always lifted them away from the deadness of the apartment. She meant so much, though Helen had not seen her in almost a year; together, as friends, they had lost energy, lost the directions to each other. And friends were the best thing in life.

###### □□□ 9

AT TEN, she heard the elevator gushing up to the floor and knew it was Vito. She had been uncomfortable since darkness had come, had been walking the rooms since the phone call. A forgotten thing — an image or person — perhaps an uncle sitting in a chair — was growing; it was there, dissolving in each room when she came to look, reappearing in the places she left. They were creatures made to inform on the few who acted, to bring them down.

The doorbell brought her into the living room; she stopped on her way to the door and placed the record on the turntable; when Vito came in, it was playing his voice.

She walked in front of him, leaving him to shut the door and follow her. He stood beside her while she looked at the machine and listened.

At the end, Helen sat down in Cy's chair and looked up at him. "Well, I'm sure of it. It's really professional. There's no doubt about it, Vito. I know it."

"You really mean that?" Vito unbuttoned his jacket and sat down on the couch. "Because, to tell you the truth, some people have said the same thing. I believed it, too. But you know belief; there's always people who come around you and say you're great. Did you ever hear of a guy's friends telling him he stinks?" Vito clasped his hands. "But I've let it go. I'm not keeping up with the guitar enough. I had to call a guy to work with me."

"That's nothing. Little things like that. But if you're asking my advice on the rest —"

"Yes. I want your advice. You're somebody different. I mean this. You're outside all the voices I hear, the neighborhood. And my family." Vito spoke it fast, as if the words had just been remembered; his face became sad; the leap went out of it for a time. She watched it closely; it was losing its attractiveness.

"You don't know how it is in my house." He rubbed the sides of his face with his hands. "There's one way to be in my house; the other ways don't exist." He stood up. "No change. No changes, please."

Vito was plundering his feelings for words and moving back and forth, avoiding the coffee table and the side tables. "That's why I told you I was going away. I *was*. I wanted to get your reaction. A different one than theirs. I want to go out there and come back here, to *you*."

His face turned up to the ceiling; his eyes caught the glass and brass and walnut chandelier, which he saw as a badge of the rich, as a sign of her help.

"A person doesn't get a time to think straight over there. In my house. I appreciate —" His right hand came up in a sweeping gesture, to take in the entire room. "I mean all this, here. All the whole world, downtown. I have to tell them what it is; I have to explain this job to them, that it's going from place to place. I tell them it's *money*. *That*, anybody's going to understand. Fine! They like the idea of money. It keeps the wolves away from the door."

Vito shut his eyes and laughed; then he sat down again and leaned towards Helen to speak again.

"Vito, go anywhere and make money. Sing anywhere, but come home at night. Come back to the neighborhood. The neighborhood!" He struck his forehead with his right palm. "The neighborhood. You hear that?" He shook his head. "You'd think maybe they liked it themselves. They think it stinks in fifty different ways, they can't kid me. I can't talk to them, or even the guys I know my age. They get together and they think Heaven is a hundred bucks a week in some job where you can wear a white shirt. Behind some fancy cage, counting cash. The fu —"

He sat up straight, then pushed his back against the soft chair. "I'm not sure what to do. I really am not sure. I'm like a guy trying to concentrate on diving in the water. And people, they're on the shore, yelling, don't forget to come back for a sandwich first."

He saw Helen's smile and smiled back. "Then I think — going out alone. Like, to the Coast. Who's going to be there?"

"First, you make them hand over the contract." Helen heard her voice in a new tone, not passive, not the listener. "I look at you and I think, a lot of people make promises. They say contract, but they don't follow through. Our lawyer; my hus —"

She turned away from Vito to get a cigarette from the inlaid mahogany box; Vito reached quickly for matches on the coffee table and found gold-headed wooden sticks in a tiny ceramic barrel. He stopped, not sure if they were real or not, but Helen nodded his doubt away, and he struck one into flame for her.

By now she had swallowed Cy's name, though it had seemed quite natural to mention him. But having cut him off, she had to change the thought. "I could get you some legal help out there. I'm sure of it. Once you get a contract."

Vito sat down again. "Well, there's an office I am going to downtown. He's a friend of Bobby Mitchell. It's a big operation, but the guy I know's Italian. They have a record company and they own clubs all over the West."

His eyes watched her skin, like cream, gold in the light of a large lamp. And the V of her sweater showing up a little soft breast flesh, lighter than the rest, like the color of morning seen on the edge of the sky.

"Yes, I can get you that help. Some honest help. You'd need protection in a case like this. You must have heard stories about how they sew up entertainers, take sixty, even eighty percent."

Vito listened; he knew he had been right about her knowledge: this house would have it.

Helen had thought of making a drink for him, but had not yet gone to prepare anything. He had no pause: his times were a rush of actions, questions, plans racing, falling back to dreams, starting up again with a speed that held her suspended.

"I won't forget that." He was excited and stood up again. "I have the feel of it. I can do things, certain things I know are in me. Like singing. This is the thing I want. Even the football was not mine; you did it for somebody else, the coach's salary, to get a degree." He stopped to face Helen. "But this kind of work is the hardest. You don't get a trial; you don't know if you're a bum until they're laughing at you on the stage, laughing you right off the floor. You should *know* it."

"You can't *know*." Helen had responded without thinking. "You simply go out and try. If you like it, you try. You must." She was red; she had sounded like a mother or some high school teacher.

Vito had been holding the spent gold match and now placed it carefully down in a glass tray with brown bubbles captured inside the glass (another sign); he found his hands wet and pressed them against his jacket; he felt the small box in his pocket and remembered. "Oh, I forgot this," he said. "I got it to say my thanks. If you'll keep it."

He placed the box, wrapped in white paper, on the coffee table near her. "Open it."

Helen looked at the door leading to the kitchen. "Oh no, Vito. I couldn't take this. Really, I couldn't. It's very wrong, things like this. Look, you know I'm a married woman. I must stop."

"Stop? Stop? Did you ask why did you start? Don't you know why?" He shook his arms. "Just open it. Just look inside a minute." He tore the paper off and opened the box, taking a gold pin from the pad of cotton it rested on. "Look at it. It's a pin, a miniature. It's a record. Look at the label."

Helen took the pin and stared closely at the label: Vito's initials and the letters ILU were scratched there.

Vito was standing above her. "Put it on. Don't worry, it isn't a wedding ring. It's a friendship pin."

She looked up in anger; his tone was like a slap; the sarcasm opened a door into wishes.

Vito took the pin and attached it to her sweater, pulling the material away from her body to place the clasp through.

Helen sat still, held by the action. "Well, I haven't had this done since high school." She spoke to mock the procedure, but Vito did not catch it: he was inside the mood; he had some words, but they were too large; they swelled and were lost as things to say; they stuck behind his lips, falling back to become feelings inside him; they became melodies that played until he felt them in his throat and chest, becoming tears, drops that were not real but which fell from a face moving on a movie screen, something imagined but still himself, all in the echo of the word *love,* which is not said.

His eyes looked around in sad pleasure; he stepped back into the brightness of the room, shining like the interior of gold.

He stood up and came forward again and began to kiss Helen, leaning his face down slowly after he had secured the pin; his hands and his mouth together were like speech: with them he could show her what he felt and thought, and once he had touched her he would devise words.

Backing away, Helen felt stupid, already embarrassed by the words she thought of saying. "No. Now let's us stop this, once and for all." She heard her voice. "Now let's just stop it." The repetition stifled other phrases; she stopped. Then lines came up. "We just can't go on like this." They were more echoes; they were someone else's words; they would not carry her feelings.

Vito's arms had been left alone. "But I'm not leading you on." He tried to take her hands, but she drew away. He watched her: he could have grabbed her, twisted her down, but he tried facing her with the white little pebbles of words. "I'm no back-door caller. Don't you get that? I'm true. Don't you understand?" He had the word *love* ready again: the clowns, all the songs — it had been stolen: he would be laughed at.

Helen averted her face. Vito dropped to his knees, and the sound startled her. "Oh no, come on, stop it now. Get up, please get up." In her surprise, she moved an arm slowly towards him. "We're being stupid trying to go on. Are we children? You know what the truth is. I'm married. I have a husband."

Helen said the words to test them; they did not conjure Cy; Cy's presence was no greater than before and was inside herself, her own possession. It did not hurt him if she were here with Vito; it hurt none of them.

Vito had been talking, but she had not heard him. His black curls were beneath her eyes; her gaze caught them in the lamplight, which gave them color and made the hair seem solid.

"I'll do whatever you tell me." The words were coming up in Vito, each with a different feeling, contradicting one another, yet each true at the utterance. "I want you to come with me. Come away with me."

Helen stood up, to get away from him. "I don't *know* what to do," he said. "But I'm not here to *lay* you, to *get* you. I want to be with you."

"No. No. I think you'd just better go right home now." Helen moved away from the kneeling lover (a joke now), and the thief thoughts that already had planned leaving here. "That's the only right thing."

"No, that's not right. What's right is inside. You know what's right. You had the feeling. Tell me what you think about me. Tell me to go away. Then, I'll go."

Helen started to the front door. "Really, please now, Vito. Just look at it. Look at our ages. Look at what we *are*." Helen tried to undo the pin. "And please take this to some nice girlfriend."

Vito stood up quickly and brushed at his trousers; Helen

saw that his way had changed; he was not responding to her.

And immediately she was affected: it was as if his changed face created a pressure on her body.

Vito came to her silently, taking her shoulders and pulling her towards him. His kiss was painful; then the concentration of it against her teeth disappeared as she felt the rush of his hands under her sweater.

His hands, as they had been in the car, were heavy and too strong. But she could not shout against them without informing on herself.

While her mind tried to make some words, she found herself pulled down to the rug and again her body twitched as it responded to him and moved into wishes of her own secrets, wishes that had been preserved in her head: now the trails of the scenes in her head were floating into the air, coming out in each real touch, making the dreams an act.

Vito pulled at her clothes; the strength made her shrink; in her head, behind shut eyes, she was small. When he drew her slacks down, sliding along her legs, her body moved a few inches upon the rug.

The tufts of the rug rubbed her back, and she began to shift away from the pressure, but Vito's arms stopped her, held her in place; she lost the sensation of the rug and began to do only what his body did.

Again, his cold chest dropped upon her breasts and his hard stomach pressed her flesh until she felt herself shake in response.

Then the hair of his head, as smooth as wool, made her shudder, rubbing along her thighs, with the touch of lips and face, scratching her skin momentarily, then touching with a soft wet touch, a spot and another spot; her body was sinking without moving, becoming smaller, her legs responding by rising up slowly, moving back, spread wider than she could ever do in exercises, as though they had become lighter, as light as fingers.

Upon her, Vito was already familiar: his movement, his weight, even the pain he caused released her into some new knowing. She thought only of holding him, pressing him tighter to her, her arms against his back, touching and knowing the back with the face of her fingers.

Her voice wished to call out while they held together, but she heard sounds she could not control, deep in her throat, sounds of a pouring feeling, her only wish the giving of new sensations that went out of her, like the pouring of water, the riding and running of a waterfall.

Vito's body was still now, and her old thoughts came up: to love him was a disgrace; he was a nothing; there would be no reason for her to turn away from Cy. No one would believe this face of a boy without the sense to cut his hair or wear a proper hat.

But she had a feeling towards him that she had never had: she would protect him more than her mother or father; she hated these thoughts: they came because of doing this —

Her skin was cold. "Get off me, get off me." She pushed at his shoulders. His silent body rolled aside, and she rose quickly and went to her bedroom.

She put on her robe and went to the linen closet for a new box of tissues. Coming back to the bed with her hairbrush, she had forgotten Vito. She sat down and stroked her hair and was startled when he touched her.

"Oh! You scared me, you big dope. This is *my* room. You don't come in here."

Vito smiled and felt her hair, unaware that she was trying to order him out of the room. He stepped back and sat on Cy's bed. "All right," she said with her back to him. "Get to work. Go get me my hand mirror."

He held it for her; he was still smiling, enjoying her anger, permitting it by listening.

She looked at him while she brushed and saw the sweep of his shoulders and chest, his muscles tight and still, curving down to the hard, hairy squares of his stomach.

Vito smiled and blushed at her staring. "You're like stone," Helen said.

"I brought all my weights home." He spoke softly, as though confiding. "I work out a little every night." He found the subject he was attacking and raised his voice. "I'll never let myself turn to dough. Like those bastards at the store — even Brophy. They look like uncooked rubber — like —"

*Women*. Vito was about to say *women*, but stopped for Helen. She might not understand: she *could* be soft. Only soft men were something you liked to crush.

Helen's hands stroked his stomach gently; she noticed the lightness of the black hair, which she thought would feel tight and wiry.

She noticed that his body had become still and obedient to her gestures, and she set her brush down and pulled him closer, resting her face against his stomach.

She heard her heart beating in the ear that touched him, and she could not stop. She unbuttoned his trousers and let them fall to the floor. It was her own wish, the wish a reason.

Vito's body did not move, but she could feel a throbbing inside him and against her face his skin was like a substance shaken by breezes.

She tried to look at Vito's face as she caressed and kissed

his thighs; then she placed her lips around his penis and saw his brows furrow and his eyes shut.

Her experiment ended abruptly; his body pushed her back; his hands found their speed again, tearing at her robe. His body had not before reacted so violently, jumping in spasms. He seemed to have lost his control of her, and she was happy to have done this: her mouth held him and she increased the response of his body with her tongue.

The shuddering of his climax was frightening to her: he had grasped the sides of her head, holding her hair, and placed his legs against her shoulders.

He drove her to the floor; she was underneath him again, conquered even as she controlled his body. The weight, the hardness, the body of stone was the power. There was nothing beyond that, nothing that had reasons beside that. It was not even Vito, a strong young man. There was hardness and softness and the two striking, struck, and joined.

And hardness did not speak, did not telephone, did not travel for business, did not vacation: it existed, like a sleeping animal, in its own winter, unaroused until aroused. Aroused, it was a steady presence, pursuing what wished to be pursued, stable, gripping facts and moments of strength, and the two nothing but him, the beauty inside of Vito, that knew itself only by acting.

Helen had forgotten the night in her walking about; she was tired and the morning seemed too quick in arriving. Yet she could not stay in bed: her mind thought of things to do; she had gone down for the mail first. Coming back, she met Bea Bienen, her neighbor across the hall and leaned against the wall near her door, talking, enjoying the time. Bea was young and full of plans.

Back inside, she began to clear closets, remembering the

boxes that had been stored there since the move uptown, a labor she could not face until now. She found last year's summer clothes, like gifts from a stranger, and knew she could decide about them today.

She flattened them on the bed to recognize them — bathing suits, sunsuits, thin slack sets, day dresses — and began to separate them. She was drowsy but clear about most of it: she was preparing for the season ahead.

She modeled some of the clothes after looking at them, walking before the mirror to see if they had gone out of style. She picked up the new *Mademoiselle* and sat down on her bed. The flowered prints in the pages would make a few of her shirtdresses old. She saw Cy's face smiling, the way he studied her in clothes. His eyes came into the dream of Vito at the edge of her thoughts.

Neither could be canceled. But Cy could have locked doors, could have given her orders. Now his pale eyes only stared, and Vito's head stood up above her and all her other visions.

The two of them were stationary, like molded casts; they could not touch her anymore. She kept them in their places, Cy in his armchair, Vito at the outside door. They could exist only if she consented. What she had done with Vito had gone when the day had come: for the first time, she was owner as well as sinner, holding sway over the others, those who take orders.

The last few sundresses lay on the bed beside her, and she stood up and placed them on wooden hangers in the long closet. Then she came back and sat down. The bed was free of clothes, but there were new things to get. She dressed, called for the limousine service, deciding on the Westchester shopping center that Bea had mentioned in her conversation.

The car took her out to countrylike roads, houses on brown earth hills among thin trees, stretches of woods without a person.

First it was new, and the riding was like the ride with Vito, rushing away from the things behind them, faster than all the doubts and voices that home and her head created. Then slowly, because the daylight was different, it was like death. Her father and mother came into the dark seat: this was the ride she had taken on these country roads, to a cemetery.

She was covered by the thought; it hurt her in the sight of the unmoving trees and grass hills that suggested the people were buried. The trees were all newly planted and the earth was pale brown, brought in trucks to cover the scars made in building; and it was all like a cemetery, the whole suburb: all of it suggested that people were gone.

The silence enhanced it; even in the mountains, vacationing, the morning silence was without the relief the mountains usually gave. People confessed their insides in the silence. Cy walked through his early hours before swimming or golf and remembered his weight, his skin too pale and kept from the sun most of the year, his way being blocked by his mother. Human faults were no longer weaknesses you talked about but were like the breaking down of a machine, the sorrowing whine of something that was made to go but which came apart once you had the quiet to be aware of it.

The car left her at the glass doors of Gimbel's. The store aisles were unusually wide, and there were only a few shoppers here and there looking into glass cases.

Her walking took her past piles of new things ready to change her, clothes, jewelry and umbrellas, racks of leather handbags, striped ties and red sweaters, new shoes: the store was like summer; it brought up hotels and the beach, parties and restaurants. She thought she was near Connecticut, where the fishhouses stood in their bright lights along the Post Road. She had received a gift of salad dressing from Manero's and had a promise from Cy to go there for a steak one night.

She passed rows of shoes and saw two women, seated in regency chairs, neither aware of the other, but each holding a green shoe in hand and staring at it.

She wandered until she found a large sale sign at the blouse counter: there were no knits, but a blue, wash-and-wear tricot was being advertised. She felt it, and the imitation of silk was very good. It was something she could use: not too dressy, yet not so plain that it could not go out: it could be worn around the house, then dumped in the machine every night.

She left with the gray bag and went out to wait for the hourly taxi. There were men on the walks, dark men, walking along the mall of stores and stopping at windows. They were like the women leading them, their pace made neutral by the shopping: they stared like the women in the store trying to make the shoe decision — all their sight and thoughts over a shoe.

◧◧◧ 10

"Here I am, honey. Come over and sit."

Helen walked as gracefully as she could towards the voice, remembering her model's poise, then rushed to sit down as she saw Mother Steinman clearly, seated at a table, visible only from the waist, a white tablecloth and settings of silver and plates and glasses under her hands.

Helen had not been invited to the apartment after all, and the sight of Mrs. Steinman's face and heavy diamond earrings brought it up in feelings. The waiter led her through the room and handled the chair behind her; Helen kept her head down most of the way.

"Wait a minute. Stop." The waiter stepped back as Mrs. Steinman spoke. "You look positively gorgeous in that number." Helen sat down while the old woman spoke; her hands were being held. "Helen, you just look lovely. Tell me some good news."

"There's nothing to tell." She took her hands back, knowing that the question was about her possible pregnancy.

"Oh, then I know it well, I know it well. All day alone; you go to the beauty parlor; make up and dress, make up and dress. You get to look like a million dollars, but so what." She brushed at the tablecloth with her hands. "Why do you think I went downtown again?"

Helen removed her gloves and fought to get words, but the voice continued. "The first time I went downtown was in desperation. Even though I worked for years. Did I ever tell you that, Helen?"

"No, Mother." Helen watched the old, ringed fingers, curled, puffy, cramped from holding things, pencils perhaps, or the curving of age.

"Oh, yes, it was desperation. I don't know what you'd call it. There was only once I had a home life, you could call it — when I was carrying Cy." She took a water glass and drank slowly. "So, *do* I see you looking pretty because there's anything special?"

"I told you, nothing. Nothing that I know of." She could talk to Rachel about this thing, years of expectation, worrying what was done wrong, what spirit held it off; but not to Mother Steinman, whose questions stared into the bedroom.

"I thought you were shining for a special reason. I thought maybe it happened. For you, I was —"

"No, it hasn't happened." Helen picked up the slab of menu at her place, but did not look at it.

"Well, the best of luck to you." Mrs. Steinman was catching an invisible mood and was backing away. "I know you're hoping. You had a little bad luck; that's all." She gave the room a smile; it was dark, quiet, the table seemed miles away from the street just outside.

Helen followed her look about to the tables and the drapes and the faces: they were the retired old people of Manhattan, men of clean white hair, women's heads bobbed with the neatness of wigs. Some had young hairdos that seemed light and strange on wispy gray hair; a few had blue-tinted, waved sets.

Her face came back to her mother-in-law's smile: "You see what I mean? People are turning to look at you, Helen. You're a picture. That color lights you up. Stand up, stand up."

Helen obeyed for a moment. "Sure, you put on a little weight, up on top where you needed it. It's good, but I know Cy likes the skinny fishes in *Harper's Bazaar*. You can't live on birdseed all your life. You got to have a bust. Wait! I know what it is — it's the merger."

"Did Cy call you again?"

"I *called him*. I had to call, Helen. I'm only fifty-seven. Do you think I only sit and rock? I can't be put in the pasture, *already*. Especially with this — this is a *com*bine, with a chain-store setup, plus department stores — all over — all over. They can make garments; they don't have to think about limits. It's a dream. Say they have extra inventory in Florida; well, they can ship the garments to the specialty shops. The hicks come in and see the Florida label. It's a big thing. It's a dream, and it's so damn simple. You get three places to put inventory and even your *drek* has a new life. No more sweating inventory that's piling up dust until a Sam Klein comes in to give you a couple of pennies to take it off the hangers. My Sam used to say, somewhere there's a buyer for everything you make." In the triumph, Mrs. Steinman signaled the waiter, who came up to her side. She leaned to Helen, to complete the thought. "Now we don't beg anybody. No Sam Kleins; no nobody. They can all you know what. Now let's order."

The waiter took her menu, opened it and gave it back to her. "What do you like?" She spoke to Helen and looked along the list. "Too bad the Italian place was closed. This is Birdcage stuff — mayonnaise on meat and watercress with grapes. Oh, here's some scallopini. Let's take it."

The waiter wrote it down and went away.

"I was reading about this famous *research* man, who made the cholesterol studies: he's eating Italian and Chinese now. Scallopini — that's one of them. It was in *Time* magazine. It's unsaturated. Do you ever listen to Carleton Fredericks?" She noticed Helen's far-off face. "Helen, what is it?"

"My mind was wandering. I was just thinking, maybe Cy and I will be eating this in Rome. He's promised a trip, and I was just thinking, maybe, Italy."

"The Dennis Steins went to Denmark. Have you been hearing about Copenhagen?" The little face was blank. "Teak, the most beautiful things in wood. And L. L. Steiner, the younger brother, was in Hong Kong. The custom-made places are unbelievable: you fly in and they come to the hotel and take your measurements; they got tailors going around the clock: you have a suit in the morning." Helen was not responding. "He shouldn't leave you so much."

"What?" The statement had entered.

"Oh, I know what's wrong. But that's his life." The voice became low. "Look, you were a model, and you've had secretarial school. Go down. You could start by supervising the models and the openings. You'll add something to it with your good looks."

The waiter brought the food; it did not go down fast, as Helen had hoped. Mrs. Steinman sensed her own possible insults: she examined them and found nothing; she waited, and ate silently, too, but Helen did not offer anything.

"Helen, I'm just thinking." The tone was mild. "I can

remember the first mornings I started to go downtown with Sam. It was the Lexington Avenue subway, and I said, I'm married and I'm still here in this hole."

Helen smiled: the tone was offering peace and closeness. "I hated it," Helen said.

"But then we started going down in the company car. I don't remember when it started, but everybody had a company car one day; the tax law changed. And then I loved it." Mrs. Steinman ate slowly. "There's a spot when you're going from the Bronx to Manhattan: you come around this turn and you see the whole East Side. My mind would jump. I mean, every day it surprised me in the same way. Just as soon as I saw the buildings. I always felt — secure. *Now* we made it, too; something like that. As if the buildings were me. I don't know — ask an analyst. It got inside me: this is *me*. One of our customers, Johnny Adelsberg, already had a place there; I used to look for it —"

Mother Steinman took a large breath of relief; she was about to add her last thought, of the six or seven places that had refused Johnny on religion before he got a place. But it was almost boring; it was finished in her head; she was here now.

They sat back for dessert. "You could start that, Helen. Rent a Caddy. Today, everybody rents. You'd leave every day with Cy; you wouldn't be left with the milkman. I can see you supervising; you're quiet, but that can be an asset in business. Quiet and sure; you see more than you say. I bet you'd pick it up in a few weeks. What's the matter now?"

Helen had lowered her head. "Nothing. I'll talk to Cy. I'll ask him about it."

"Don't ask him. Think about it and then make up your mind and tell him. I'll even call him up as soon as he gets back. He could use you — now, more than ever." Helen's face was too wan; Mother Steinman reached for the young hands, touched them, but did not hold on. "If you're not having a family yet, then he can figure out something for you. They shouldn't let us rot, sweetheart. We do more than sweep up the dirt."

Helen raised her head. "I don't want to go downtown."

"Well, there's women who prefer the home. Me, I never —"

"No, let me try and say it. I like it. I like the apartment. It doesn't have a lot of work, but you have to be in it; you have to think about a place."

Mother Steinman smiled; it was a fine thought.

Helen continued: "You can't understand a house unless you're in it all the time. Otherwise, it's a reception room, like the dentist's." Helen put on her gloves. "Can you understand me?"

"Some women *prefer* it. That's what I said. They love to bake; they entertain. I was never that way. One day, Allan Cohen of Luft-Togs said to me, Sarah, you got a man in you. And he didn't mean the way I looked. It was the way I was made — not mannish; my figure was never mannish. That I know; men still look. I still get eyes, at my age. You know that, Helen. Looks and stares. And I'm vain about it; I don't care. I get all my bras made. Men still look on top; they can't see anything else. If you had to advise a kid to-day, tell her, above all, get a good —"

Helen had not been distracted. "I said I want the time to be in my place. And walk around. Maybe that's just me. If I'm home, I think of home things. Downtown, I'd get different. I'd fill up with what's there. If it was business, then it would be business filling me up."

"Oh, Helen, I could never stay in a house. I couldn't see myself marching around."

"That's where we differ, I suppose."

Mrs. Steinman went on. "Getting ready for one person all the time. It never seemed right on me. Maybe it's just that I can't see myself *waiting* on people. Like, look at this man waiting on us. Is this a man you spend a whole day of your life preparing for?"

"Well, somebody does if he comes home every night. Somebody's there. Home is the place that takes you in. This man has an agreement —"

"All right, all right. Don't worry. Please don't listen to my propaganda. Everybody should take me with a grain of salt." Mother Steinman was remembering something else, the bite of some lost way. "They said I was different. I was. So better Cy married a *you* and not another *me*. I'm lucky you're *my* daughter-in-law."

Helen could not take the suddenness of change, the desire to be beaten down. "You should never talk like that, Mother. It isn't right." Helen saw the defeated structure of the old face; she blushed at being a cause.

"It's all true, Helen; it's true. I made money. I kept the books, and the men looked up to me; they even made me boss when Sam passed away. I passed out plenty of *shekels* to cousins all over. But I didn't get *kissed*. If you know what I'm saying. I didn't get kissed. That's an end you wouldn't want. Because I'll tell you what it means: it means being forgotten, being forgotten in their hearts."

Helen had the fragments in her hands. "No, Mother. Please. Listen, you've got to come up and see me. We should spend a few days together someplace." It was rushing out of Helen, unmindful of consequences, only to scourge the dead emotions from Mother Steinman's face. "I want you to come up. Stay over. You know how much I like you. And *how many women* could do all you did?"

"Some are one way, some another." Mrs. Steinman was thankful. "Maybe you should have a boyfriend."

"What do you mean by that?" Her neck felt stiff.

"I'm crazy. Don't listen to me, Helen. My mind goes in muddy rivers. I was just thinking, one day — now that I'm getting old — some people go to work and some are too pretty for it. Is that possible? Some people are made for more pleasure than the rest. I go up to the hotels and I see the young women fooling around with a lifeguard type — what is he but a muscle between the legs? And that's all. All right, so let them do that a little." Her tone was excited; the idea was wrong, but the truth of it demanded voice. "Oh, they'd kill me if they heard me talking this way. And I don't mean it bad; you know me. If *my* boyfriend was the business — somebody said that once; if the other choice is being a cook and cleaner, or better, a schoolteacher — is that what *you* were made for? Look at you."

The old woman had said the thing that is not said, had leaped with her quick, strange mind into the future that was already annoying Helen. It was not that Mother Steinman could see the meaning of Helen's red face; Mother Steinman was luckily the whole world around herself, saying whatever she wanted because she created her own arrogant surroundings.

"You're ashamed of me, Helen." She looked and admired Helen's face and body. "I don't even care. What do you think being a woman my age is? Do you think that *I* have men? The thing with me now is I want to see somebody happy. I'm sorry for mistakes. With Cy. I'm sorry Cy is too much like Samuel. But that isn't you. You should have something that fits on you; it wouldn't hurt another. If I only knew you enough. I don't know you — to tell you —"

"I want to do things. This last week, I even had dreams of becoming a dancer. I'm ashamed to say it. And I want to do things for Cy. I want to do —"

"Stop it. You are; you *do*. You're doing things right. But you think you're a failure. Just like the rest of us — the women. What did you do for this one and what did you do for that one? It asks in your head every day; at the end of the day. I was ruined by it, so I know it. And that's why I'm crazy today. Because you can't go back; you have to change. For you, I wouldn't care what you did. I'd stand up and fight for you."

Mother Steinman was very tired. Was it any use telling this pretty bird, fearful and chained. She received a little energy from Helen's looks: her lovely, small nose, her hair, natural and softly blond, the blue eyes like a starlet's, hands that seemed carved white. "Keep this between us, will you? Just between *us*."

Helen gave her white-gloved hand and she squeezed back. "I love you, dear," Mrs. Steinman said. "And I'm sorry for you."

"Well, don't be sorry, Mother. I'm all right."

"Yes, you are. I know, I know. We all are. We're all all right. Young or old, anyway, we're not going to give in."

Helen smiled at the ambiguity. "What do you mean, *not give in?*"

"I don't know. I really don't know."

Vrro walked around his room, looking at the TV. He switched about, watching a mystery, some cowboys, a fight in a saloon, then an inning of a ball game. He turned it off abruptly. It was like a traitor these days, a lover promising delight but talking instead, shouting an occasional suggestiveness but quickly turning off and becoming cold, bland, like a girl who looks away. Even the ball game seemed to be played by uniformed ants: the screen destroyed the diamond, the grayness destroyed the green air of the stadium.

He picked up his guitar and played it awhile, singing some phrases softly. It would be best to let the guitar go, get a sideman, to concentrate on the voice. The last few days he had been thinking of Tony Merola, who had played the Hickory House and single dates in good places downtown.

He went out to call; it was only ten-thirty, but the house was quiet, the phone down in hall blackness, his parents in bed or his father down at the bakery while his mother slept. From his sister's room he heard soft radio sounds, Crosby or Como.

Tony's father answered. "This is Vito Filippo, Mr. Merola. I'm calling Tony about the guitar. I want to get him some work." Vito kept his tone jovial, for the suspicions all fathers have.

"The guitar? Very nice."

Tony came, and his voice was low, the musician's affectation. "Hey man, what's the gig?"

"I want to talk to you about accompanying me."

"*You?* What are *you* doing?"

"Well, you know Agramonte got me a tryout downtown. Don't you know?"

"Yeah. I think I heard. So what are you doing?"

It was hard to explain to the tone in his voice: Tony had the sideman's meanness; he was a born sideman, good at his work but made for the shadows, with a wisecrack out of the dark for anybody up front at the mike.

"Well, I got this contract coming up. They'll set me up some club dates. Long Island and Jersey first. And I can't concentrate on guitar and voice at the same time. So I thought you could play back of me. I like your stuff."

There was no answer. "Did you hear that, Tony?"

"Well, you get the date, Vito. And then you call me up." Tony might be about to fall asleep.

"All right. I'll call you. But will you do it? Are you free?"

"Vito, you get the dates and then call me."

"I'm using Vic Phillips. What do you think of that name?"

"Just call me, man. Get the gig, get the gig, first."

Vito went back to his room; it took a few minutes to rid himself of Tony's sour mouth. *Get the gig first.* Vito thought about going over right now, showing the little bastard the fist. The fist would make him remember some words.

He turned to his tape recorder and started the tape; it was some old guitar practice; he flipped the tape farther forward until he reached his voice, and listened while the voice sang "I Have But One Heart," "San Francisco" and "Just Say I Love Her." He stood up and tried out the few gestures Bobby's teacher had showed him and did them along with the songs played a second time. It satisfied him in the mirror, and he played them again and synchronized his movements exactly.

While he sang, he could imagine it. There was not much more to do to get it on a real stage, if he could only drop this room around him. He understood why Robert Agramonte had to change his name to Bobby Mitchell and why they all called him Agramonte, to bring him back, to pull him back down.

He picked up the weights and pressed awhile. When he felt sweat he stopped and went to the mirror. He saw the person who was large enough for her. He took off his T-shirt and watched his muscles, making fists, bending his arms. He shook his hair with his hands; he would get it cut because she liked the college style.

He walked round the room and sat on the bed; he saw the wood headstand, dark like the room. He punched the pillow. The bureau was curved and old: the legs, carved claws round a ball, made him blush. Helen would laugh at this, at the lace covers over everything.

It was like a snap in his mind. A snap and this whole place was gone. He was going and going on, with her, with another name, to LA, away. The walls were brown, imitation wood grain. The wood chair was hung with his delivery jacket; his gloves lay open on the seat. He got up and kicked them. The room was a wooden cage.

He put on his shirt, combed his hair, and went quickly downstairs and out. The Impala was in the street; he started it soft and drove two blocks before gunning it.

First he drove up White Plains Avenue, checking the open places with his eye: lights on in the candy stores, bars, the Laconia Theatre. As he drove under the El tracks, he looked left and right. On Two Twenty-fifth, he saw six guys he knew: they worked for the taxi service, and he watched them while he stopped for a red light, but drove off again when the light turned green. In the instant, he had wanted to stop and talk with them, but they would not know the plan now; they would be sour like Tony; hope to them was only the things you could show: gold ring, diamond links, black Caddy.

He drove to the city line and then turned east, out towards Mount Saint Michael School, where he stopped. His mother had wanted to get him in, but his father refused to pay.

"This one will *be* something." He had heard his mother say it to him one night.

"Then he will do it without the monks slapping his hands with a stick."

His father's voice scared him, but he liked it, even if it was impossible to get it to talk nicely back, to say he understood what Vito was going to do.

His father had gone on about the monks and finished the idea there. "Men who do not have women are not men. If he ever does anything, he must wear pants. Let the skirts remain on the women."

Vito looked at the dark school grounds, the football field. Their games had more writeups in the papers; their games had the girls.

He started the car. The East Bronx was dark, but he knew all the ways to the parkway. He thought of going out to La Guardia but turned north instead and drove into Westchester. Along the parkway there was one clubhouse, set back on a hill behind a golf course; seen from the road he could imagine the rooms inside, the clothes. He still had the white jacket he got from one of the football-crazy kids in the dorm; it was new, a kind of pay for winning games. Peanuts. But he thought it was great then, when the kid came in with it.

Once he had a date with a girl down at college who came from Mamaroneck; it was a prom. The town sign came up in his lights. She would still be down South. He rode off the highway, into the streets of the town: no walkers, just like Riverdale. The suburbs were like graves, except for the little blue lights in the houses: they were all sucking potato chips and watching the cowboys.

He would call Helen. He drove back to the highway, looking for a phone. He would go up to her once more. But first he would go downtown and get the contract in his hands, to show her.

The thought stopped him. Signed, he would be trapped. He would be on the road they chose; he could not back out, could not get away from anyone who wanted to say he was rotten: you were there onstage and any fat fink with money could say you were a nothing. A nothing.

He drove faster, checking the speedometer, pushing seventy, eighty, ninety-three — until he saw lights behind him and eased off.

The car went through the blackness to the Bronx. It was a fight inside him to turn into the smelly streets, towards his room.

He parked in front of his house, then walked to the avenue and peeked into the bakery. Lights. His father was in there, but he would start with his mouth: *what have you done today,* with some crack about not helping out. If the old man pushed, Vito would tell him about Helen, the marriage to come, the whole thing he would do.

The old sonofabitch would look down like a king he thinks he is: *very nice, go do it on the ten cents a week that you make.*

Even the weights, the football, had never stopped his mouth.

He would leave these crusts, these crusts of bread. They own the Bronx and let them have White Plains Avenue and the greasy provolone on their lips and sit back in the chair on Sunday afternoon with cousins laughing around them, until they bust a tube and croak.

He walked home fast and went upstairs. The room was the same. His bedsprings creaked, remembering him, making the same sounds they had made when he was sick with scarlet fever, and when he jerked off, and when he had come back from the South, all locked up, like a guy thrown out of Heaven. He let his head go back.

*Arms that touched me they were more than her words of no and gold soft fuzz shining on them and her hair shining when I looked up at the light the little strands catching light like golden wires Christmas tree icicles on the legs of her the way she opens I'll bring her flowers every day he'll never know it if he comes home the fat fuck whoever he is and why don't he come and take his own wife is he one of those bastards who take the showgirls of the clubs the pussy chasers all they want to do is throw the C notes around the table and stuff a couple between some tits that's what the bastard is let him come let him see us I'll stand up to him I didn't leave a good woman home to rot his time is up he's finished the fink I'll go to the Coast and work and she'll be waiting and I'll get her I was all-Conference halfback re-*

member that I have stories in the Post the Journal the Tribune they all wrote me and the record date I sat at the table with Agramonte and producers and pussy ready to lay down before me I had cunt I had cunt those Southern ones they'll show you ribbon fizzes I had some I had some No Dammit she'll come with me she'll be with me and I'll be with her all the time and Pop will have to shove it turn around that's the way it is he can whistle you don't make a previous arrangement for when you fall in love this is it I'll tell them and I'll stick by my woman till my dying day you can break my skull with an axe so what if she's American too she's not Italian like most of the women in this country so what even if she's been married so what they're supposed to meet her and welcome her in the family I don't care it's my choice and my rights I deserve that much otherwise it's out but that's the way it is goddamit listen to me listen she'll get flowers every day doing whatever she wants I'll be there I'll be her slave I'll do all the things she wants I'll oil my body she likes seeing my body and I'll give her a show just with my muscles and my dong I'll do some weight lifting for her and then I'll carry her around like she was a girl she'll know what I can do she'll know I'm big I wont hurt her it's all for her I'll lay it at her feet Helen Helen gold gold she's young we can make a go of it she's not old twenty-four the most we'll live together get old together it's only four years four years mean nothing after I'm making records playing clubs I'll look older the first time I saw her when she looked at me she was scared she saw me like those hoods and the cracks we made me and Charlie god forgive me all the jokes about all the women things we imagined about them but the night I brought her the appetizer somebody was coming for late supper I almost stayed I didn't care and told her then yes he'd have found me there all right I'll fight him I'll set it

up anyway he wants to anytime unless he wants to step
back like the old chidrool he is and gets kicks with his
money and the office stuff that just lives to lay these fat pigs
and their deals mockies they call them with grease stains on
their coats and shirts I won't live around here I know what
they'll say but who needs this fuckhole filling up with niggers and spics anyway and the lobbies of the apartments
have more piss in them than air you don't make a career of
this shithole dump of wops over there they have new things
going up and new restaurants and it's clean let the dumb
chidrools around here sweat in front of the candy store I'll
take those pools you get home from work you go upstairs
and change and you come down for a swim that's not even
so damn much either Mitchell's got his own pool and all of
them calling him Mitchell what did he do he took his doctor's last name that's not so hard and he's no better than a
hundred of them but these dumb chidrools think the only
way is you go out to Orchard Beach and fight for an inch of
sand well let the dumb bastards live in guinea heaven here
anybody that's still here they don't know any better they
like it well Pop and Mom you couldn't move them they
made it up to here and that's all they got Mom has the
church and Pop has the store you don't move bakeries
around but he wouldn't even go when I told him and Millie
told him and Al told him expand expand to make deliveries
in Westchester get the Mount Vernon market the supermarkets they all want Italian bread make some deal with a
bunch of markets no no I got enough whata you want Vito
go to school I got money college go go I got money some
think he grosses a neat number how the hell should I know
I still give him a share of my paycheck he goes around in
the old gray sweater and Mom in the black dress we could
be in East Harlem goddam how stupid are we maybe it's in

the brain it's wopized we're the wops we live under the fucking El tracks so let's act like they think we are with our dumb fucking gray sweaters and pointy black shoes on Sunday and pink shirts like niggers in Harlem sure let's be what they think we should be with our faces like Yogi Berra or some nose-busted fighter I saw her face even she was afraid of me at first afraid of me the first day she thought I was dirty like the creeps who walk on the West Side and she looked at my face and was about to say spics and she looked but now she sees me she knows me what I am and I'll be more I'll be better I'll show her the difference in me and these guinea heroes I can't take her back here in here to meet them all and let her see what is here well yes let her see let her see it guineatown let her see it what the hell it's not me but she should meet them and they can all see what she is my choice and let them all look and croak I'm twenty-one but I'm better than that Pop can shove it from now on in two months legal I can just take off and even if I came back I could make it like Frank Rizzo who works at Federal Savings all you do is take business courses at NYU accounting at night I can do that there's even her connections with lawyers and her family but I'll do it singing I know I'm as good as any that made it right now Agramonte has a falsetto that's all a cheap falsetto I can make it that good yes I can make it now Vic Phillips Vic Phillips Victor B. Phillips no Vic Vic Phillips Vic Phillips starring Vic Phillips.

## 🔲🔲🔲 12

Vito watched his mother walking about the kitchen; for the first time in his life he noticed that she moved with her head lowered, as though to avoid the sight of the kitchen.

Why wouldn't she, he thought: a whole life in the kitchen, a view of the back yards, somebody's bloomers, somebody's work pants, somebody's crumbs left on the table.

He had thought she got along in a different way, not like Tony Merola's mother or the other ones who were born in Italy, who choked on the language still, who thought they lived among thieves and dirty iron, who died of the cold in their heads every winter because it wasn't Naples. She had been born here; she had talked back to her own mother by dressing a little brighter, going downtown to work by herself, listening to the latest hit music, shopping at the supermarkets when everyone was still using the locals. But she was down, her head was down, like a beast of burden, the kitchen beast.

Yet she had pushed him for college, fought for his right not to follow in the bakery, made his father loosen his pocket once, and then even understand, so that he always offered money if it was for college: the one American magic: college: here is the money for college.

She stopped his thoughts by placing a dish before him. He looked at her face: she was smiling. God! She still waited for his words, as if he were learning foods today, as if this paste were new.

He ate a spoonful, his head down, away from the smile, the expectancy, like something of hers dripping on him. "It's good. Nice and warm, like a pudding. A little like rice pudding. What is it?"

"What is it? Oatmeal, silly. A new kind, with a malty flavor. Did you taste the maple in it?" She was changing mood, expecting him to dislike the food.

"Well, it's good, it's good." He pushed down to finish it fast.

He was like a boy these days, doing everything to please them — when he could, when he didn't blow. He was getting ready to walk in with Helen, and this was the only way he could prepare.

His mother went back to her work; he saw (as if he had not known it before) that she began to prepare for supper in the morning. His father and brother came from the bakery at odd hours, and the kitchen never closed: she was always soaking or washing or cooking: especially the tomato smell, that was too strong in the morning, a choking smell: once it had not even been there in his senses; now it spit like the acid in his father's voice.

Helen had her kitchen working for her, with washer, freezer going, a sweet smell, the room clean and light.

"Ma, listen. I won't be coming home for supper tonight. I'm going out."

Her voice came back, distant, out of the corner of the room. "Where are you going?"

"Well, listen. You know Bobby Agramonte offered me that break. They said they'd give me a contract. I'm going down to see about it."

"So you're going to try the singing." She came back to him and stood over him. "Did you talk to your father?"

"I will." His shoulders felt stiff already; the scar on his back hurt again. "But I'm the one who does it if it's done. I decide. And I decided that last night. I'm in it, now."

"Fine. Then do it." Mrs. Filippo had her daily transistor tuned to the small stations that played the hit records. "There's a lot of young kids making it. Terry Falcone's got a million seller. And Tony Bennett, and who's the new kid, Randozzo? I saw a new kid on the TV. On *Shindig*. It was his first appearance."

"I told you what it means at the start. You have to go wherever they send you. Little clubs in Ohio, and places like that. Pop's got to agree I go —"

She wiped her dry hands on her dress. "It isn't that your father's scared or wants to keep you here all the time. Well, he *is* a little hurt you never help out in the store —"

"I'm no bread baker —"

"I know it, I know it. But he's a little old-fashioned; he was born on the other side. He doesn't have much faith in a singing career; he doesn't trust a good thing to happen — it's not only to you."

"He does that to me. He doesn't want me to be anything — get anything." Vito was up, his chair pushed back, out to the small anteroom outside of the kitchen. But his feeling persisted. "Oh, he can go fuck himself."

"Shut up!" She came after him. "What do you got? What bank are you standing on you can talk so strong. Keep your mouth shut like that; keep it shut in front of your father, that's all."

Vito picked up his jacket and gloves. "All right, all right. But don't let me go on with one hand and then pull me back with the other."

She came to him and placed her right hand softly on his shoulder. "All right. You're my son, I don't forget. Do you have a date, too?"

"What if I have?"

"Nothing, if you *have.* I'm a mother. I like to hear about what she is —"

"And check her out. Right? Well, I'll tell you she's a nice girl. With money. With fineness. A woman."

"Is she Italian?"

"Who said Italian?" Vito walked along the hall, knowing she would follow. "Do you fall in love on things like that?" he said back to her. "Am I supposed to go up and say, pardon me, Miss, I just fell in love with you. Are you Italian?"

She turned back towards the kitchen, and Vito stopped. "Yeah, yeah, very smart. I was just like you. Very smart. I told them, too. My mother — may she rest in peace — you know she never spoke a word of English. You knew her a little bit, but you never seen her when I was a girl. Eighteen. Then it was Italian and Catholic, or forget it. I had a boyfriend down in Yorkville, Henry Kerner. We lived up on a Hundred Fifth. Well, they said it; they said it. And now I'm saying it to you. You go marry out of your people and you'll be sorry."

"You went through the whole thing just to tell me this from your own mouth."

She turned back again; Vito stepped onto the porch. "Yes, I *learned,* is what I'm telling you, Vito. I learned that you only could live with your own people, who know your ways. Look at this —" She had a wooden spoon in her hand; it was red with the sauce she had been stirring. "You're used to this kitchen. You couldn't eat no boiled potatoes and cabbage."

"That's what you know. That's the way you see it all. But it's different with my generation."

"It's different. Nothing's ever different. Things go back to what they were. That's all I learned."

"What can I tell you, Ma? You don't know how it is. You don't know *me*."

"Thank you. Chapter Two."

"Look. Imagine this. If I made it. If I made out in singing, I might marry anybody I'd meet, and it could be from any background; that's the way it goes; that's the kind of country we have. I didn't make it that way."

"I know all that, I know it." She was using her hands the way he had done, swinging before her, along with the words. "But if you want a piece of happiness, as you get older, as you go back to the things you're used to, then you don't want to end up with a woman in your house who's strange, who doesn't know what you like. Can't you see a simple thing like that?"

He placed his hand on the glass of the porch door and looked outside. "I could see that for around *here*. Here on White Plains Avenue. But not for me — people who get away. If I was in the bakery, I wouldn't even think this way."

"I love you, Vito. You're my son. I loved you best of all my children, may God forgive me. But listen once: you're not better than them; you're no better than them who work in the back of the store or your sister who lives right here."

Vito zipped up his jacket and then turned around: his mother's face was gray and dark, coming up from the schedules of the kitchen to assert her voice and think out of cold depths. He turned the doorknob.

"Don't walk out on the truth," she said. "Face me, Vito."
She stepped closer to him. "I'm afraid of you. You want to
hit everything head first. You don't even think there could
be failure someplace —"

Vito turned with a snap. "There's plenty of it for those
that sit and rot." He controlled his voice in front of her face.
"I don't want to be a CPA; I don't want to work in the
bank; I don't want to be a mortician, even though he has
two Cadillacs, or the insurance man — all that shit —
Knights of Columbus and Legionnaires and Holy Name
baseball. I don't knock it; I just don't want it."

His mother's face seemed caught in a net of shadow; he
became aware that her head of hair was dyed: the strands
were mottled with a dark red, some form of dye. Her figure
was still a woman's, but falling and flattening, not as bad as
the old grandmothers in their black sacks, but bulging and
uneven in a dress that hurt the eye.

He knew that he had reacted to this sight many times,
but now he drew his gloves on, though the day was warm;
the gesture was done to preserve himself.

She did not speak, and he let his own silence redden his
face, fill his neck hard, bring sweat along his back.

He opened the door and stepped off the porch. "I have to
go now. It's the big unpacking. I should be over there already." He stepped along the walk, then looked back at her
face. "I have to show you, Ma. I have to just show you."

She moved to the window and watched him go to his car
and drive away. He had gone to college this way and would
go into the army this way and maybe go for the last time
like this, driving off, his words not finished, her feelings still
not shown him.

His skin had no roughness; he was taller than all the
others around here, and slender, unlike the others you

passed in the streets. He could leave here and go among others outside. Whatever he became, they would let him come in and join them because he did not have the neighborhood marks: eyes, the darkness, the wrong voice — which like her own — kept one here in modesty and anger.

To be good enough was to look like a picture from a magazine, features and smile that suggested no street in no neighborhood, only an appearance that reminded everyone of other pictures. Vito could be that: he was her best, and he was almost not her own: she saw it now, for the first time, in the way he could throw away the bakery, the good job with cousins in business, offers he had here. He did not suspect the others outside, no matter what she feared or how much Armando shouted: Vito trusted them and went off to them. Alone, one day, they could nail him up, leave him to die in some faraway place.

The phone rang; she heard the tomatoes boiling at the same time and went in to obey both, losing her thoughts.


Vito drove along Two Twenty-second Street as the sun came up behind the new project houses: his outside mirror caught the first clouds turning from red to orange. The light made the car hood seem deep with color, like a lake.

Morning light struck the grass of Woodlawn Cemetery, and his eyes turned to it as he drove across Gun Hill Road to the West Bronx. The green seemed covered with a light yellow, the yellow ready to fly off the surface of the grass. This was the first yellow, that lasted only a few days. Herbie Waxman the bass player used to take him up the Saw Mill River Parkway every year for this first green of spring, the gold days.

He raced the car up the hill, passing empty sidewalks: he could see the pattern of small trees spaced among the storefronts and shapes he had never seen before. It was like the year of the blizzard, the whole street to yourself.

The last part of the ride was a small stretch of parkway, and he got the Impala up to ninety before his turnoff.

When he reached the store, he was alone and first to arrive, but the trucks had come already and dumped the big cardboard crates at the back doors.

Vito liked the mornings of big unpacking: he was the only one who liked to come. The new boxes always had a good smell, and the best feeling was tearing the crates open and seeing the rows of canned fruit or tightly packed boxes of cereal: it was as if he had never before had the knowledge of this abundance when he passed stores or before he worked here; he had thought that supplies could easily be used up, that somehow he himself could, in a dim day ahead, find that the supplies had stopped. And he would know no other place but the store to get food and supplies. But this unpacking was proof of the unstoppable flow, salving the forgotten but known scar of his mother's face of years before.

The other guys hated it. Charlie threw the stuff onto the roller, trying to break as much as he could. Brophy, his friend, called everything "the shit" and never looked at any of the stuff he handled.

Vito unpacked, set the roller up, and worked. He had reached the soaps and found some blue plastic bottles of bath soap for kids, each covered with clear plastic that fastened a blue plastic rocket to the soap bottle. Now it was even turning to toys, and the kids had that today. He heard Brophy's voice.

He stepped into the alley and saw Brophy in the parking lot, locking his Chevvy Two. "Stop thief," Brophy called out. "Hey, Muscles, stop already. Come here. I'm going to

buy you a cup of coffee for being such a good boy. You
*prick.*"

"Don't worry, I left you some." Vito laughed. "I left you
plenty." He walked to Brophy. "It's really almost all done,"
he said.

"Look, don't do that." Brophy walked towards the street
rather than towards the store, and Vito walked alongside.
"Some fuck of an accountant will come up and they'll say
we have to do the whole thing in such and such a time
less — whatever it took you. And we can't keep up with you
musclemen. But they don't care. They'll take the time, and
share it out, you know. Like somebody gets fired and we
share up his work. That's the way money is, kid."

Vito was pleased with Brophy, a big fat guy, but not
faggy like the other countermen, who had a little tea-for-
two with every lady customer. Brophy was a man with
them, and he always had his eye on things the old bastard,
the manager, was trying to pull off on them.

They crossed the street. "Vito. Everything they do today,
every nice machine they bring in with a smile, you can say
to yourself, some guy's getting fired someplace. Don't forget
that."

Brophy went silent, his face dour. Something more than
his words had affected him.

"Don't worry," Vito said. "We handle the deliveries just
right, don't we?"

Brophy did not answer but went in and sat down at a
stool in the luncheonette. When Vito sat next to him, he
leaned his head close and said, "There's only one rule,
Muscles." He came closer to Vito's face. "One cardinal
rule: the rule of *fuck off.* They will bust your muscles, too,
you know. There isn't a back wasn't made for breaking by
the man in the Seat. Ye are expendable! Remember

Brophy. He hath said it. They'll break your bones and come in with a little time-study hokus pokus and save a penny. Then he that sits in Scarsdale will fill his pockets again. Lest ye forget."

Brophy studied Vito's steady smile. "What is in you today? I give you the facts of industrial life and you smile. Do you musclemen love the world? You think it stands on your shoulders. Oh, you bloody Hercules. Wait till they put out your eyes."

Vito had been listening through the veil of inattention because the words of Brophy became familiar: they were like the sounds of his parents, of the neighborhood — the wail of the poor who stay poor. Vito would not listen to it; his anger was splitting in two, half to the *boss*, the rich exploiter, the other to the fool poor, who had no eyes on his own future pool as Vito had and built this wall of hate right up around him, preventing his own movement.

"Wait a minute," Brophy said quite loudly. "Something must have got *in* good last night."

Vito did not get it. "Yes, I'm feeling good today. I'm smiling at the English muffins and the eggs. I like to have breakfast out."

"Coffee, coffee. I only offered you coffee."

"No, I'm paying for it today. And yours, too. You always treat." Brophy smiled at the last.

"We never have English muffins at home," Vito said. "My mother never heard of them. Or *Danish* and stuff like that."

Brophy nodded but was silent; yes, he knew: for years he had sold many foods he did not eat, first because they cost too much, then because his family found them uncomfortable — they were not necessary; they were strange and went down hard and did not seem to be real food on the table, totally unlike the tastes that supplied the bodies of their fathers.

Vito sat and watched Sol cut the muffins, toast and butter them, then cut them again, adding two paper cups of marmalade to the dish because Vito liked it.

Vito ate and looked at his plate. It was funny he did not bring some of this stuff home from the store, but he kept forgetting.

The men and women from the other stores came in: the A & P girls in their starched white coats that pressed against their hips and breasts. They were all Irish girls, and Brophy knew exactly what to say to them, how to tease them.

One girl, Jo-anne Riley, used to banter with Brophy and come sit next to them on the stools while the others went to the booths. It was clear she liked Vito and had given him enough hints, but he had never asked her for a date, though he had joked about it ("When are we going out?" "When are you going to ask me?"); yet, something stopped him.

Bingo, and the Church. The neighborhood all over again. It was in her look, a kitchen in her face — like marrying a copy of your mother, with a few changes.

She sat down next to him. "Do you ever go to the big CYO dance at Mount Carmel?" she said after they had greeted.

"I used to go. Once, I even sang with the band that played there." His feeling towards the dances now were like those he had had listening to the disk jockeys with Charlie: an attraction that held him underneath while the face of it was stupid. In the middle of the evening, after dancing with a few girls and feeling his T-shirt cooling with sweat, he would begin to think, Is this all we do? Is this the end of our plans? Is this the big event of our lives?

Then he would notice the walls of the church, unpainted, wet, clammy plaster: he would remember resting his face against the wall to get cool during Sunday School after nine o'clock Mass: the kids would talk the whole hour while Sister Mary Joseph got louder and louder until she was screaming and calling them bad children.

Jo-anne sat with the knowledge of her curly black hair and her big body. Vito looked at her and smiled.

"I got some tickets," she said.

"Well, when do we go?"

"It's May twenty-second, if you're serious." She was uncomfortable and turned to order coffee before she spoke again. "Only you have to help me sell some raffle books. I'm supposed to sell ten books."

"Well, give me a couple of books to start." Vito reached his hands toward her body, very close: he was too fast, but she liked the fear of it.

"I'll bring some tomorrow. Are you really serious, now?"

"Bring me three or four. I'll sell one just with the guys in the store." He wished he would stop being so big. "What are they giving?"

"First prize is two Cadillacs."

"*Two* Cadillacs?"

"A his and a hers." Jo-anne allowed a little laugh.

"Well, you could sell one," Vito said.

"Or race your boyfriend down the parkway." Jo-anne was smiling, waiting for Vito to enjoy the joke.

Sol brought her coffee and she drank it quickly, while Vito watched her. He had been enjoying her eyes and her mouth until he saw how fast she drank, like someone pushed by orders to hurry; she could get no pleasure; she must drink up and get to work.

Vito saw her hands, the skin around the fingernails bitten

and red; it was a scar in her youth, a worn spot that gave her away as someone of dark kitchens.

"Come on, kid." Brophy was up. "You'll have to leave the colleen — before you corrupt her — and bring the hamburger to the kosher ladies on the hills."

Vito turned to Brophy's face, ready to hit him; he could kill him with a punch. Jo-anne was laughing behind him; Vito decided to let it go.

They walked to the front of the store; the sun was up high now, red for a warm day. The downtown buildings were clear, their tops in the blue haze of good mornings.

"Another day." Brophy was noticing the sky. Vito still looked at him in anger, ready to punch him if he spoke again about kosher ladies. "A good day," Brophy said. "Sometimes I wish I was in the truck again. I used to like it."

"Did anything ever happen to you, then? Did you ever meet anyone?" Vito said.

"Well, it was fun. And there was nice tippers. You shot the breeze with nice dames and wished you could just sit down and spend the morning and etcetera. Etcetera. But mostly I was out, *out*. Not confined. I get so I don't like being inside." Brophy began to walk, crossed the street, and approached the store.

Vito waited for him to say the rest; he did not know if it would come out of Brophy, but the thick Irish face was mulling a thought. Brophy started just as they reached the door. "And then," he said, "there's times I don't even like to go out on the street all day or at closing time. I'd like to stay in the store, forever." He paused on his words. "Now, what the hell is that, I ask you?"

"Well, the store's a clean, light place," Vito said, and he

was serious, thinking about it; he had had no intention of slighting Brophy.

Brophy looked at the boy and saw that Vito had said the words with serious intent. And he swallowed his piece of rage and let the thought of Vito's words come to him, and yes, the boy had said it so, yes.

They went in and Brophy disappeared in the manager's office. Vito went to the public phone in the meat storeroom and called Helen, but there was no answer. Angry with the ringing, he slammed the phone down and went out to his car where he had hid a Charles and Company gift box of jellies. No one else was around; he got in and drove to her building.

He went up the service elevator and rang her bell. Finally, he began to write a note on the box, but the door opened and he quickly stepped inside.

"Here's your order, Ma'am." Vito placed the box in her hand.

"You stupid jerk." She was in her nightgown, rubbing her eyes, but her tone was pleased. "What the hell are you doing here so early?"

"Had to leave you something good for your breakfast."

"Something for breakfast? Oh, you crazy kid. What is it?"

He placed her right hand on the box lid. "Look at it. It's nice stuff. Imported."

She lifted the box lid and admired the jellies. "Now, you shouldn't do this." Her tone was familiar to Vito now; he began to understand that she used the same words even when her feelings had changed. Vito caught the pleasure; she might have been saying, "I love you for doing this, for thinking of me."

She placed the jars on her kitchen table and while she

144

studied them, Vito placed his right hand on her waist. Quickly, she responded, moving close to him without turning. He lifted her body round to him and kissed her, pressing her to him.

The suddenness was like the wind, and when he let her down she was left with her mouth open and the gesture was like a secret wish of her own, exposed.

"I'll be back my lunch hour," he said, and moved quickly to the door.

"No, please," she said.

"About twelve-thirty," he said. "After I grab a quick lunch." And he left.

# □□□ 13

$S$HE HEARD the doorbell at noon and walked out of the bedroom: she had been putting on layers of makeup, watching her face, as if painting its replica in the mirror, stroke upon stroke, taking a long time, building her face for an event. She had done this before school dances and later when she modeled: the colors and aroma gave purpose to the night ahead. And now Vito's presence had started her at it again.

Vito rushed in, passing her so fast that she looked down and checked the doorlock: it was as if he had come through before she released the lock.

She followed him to the living room; he stood in the center of the room, under the unlit chandelier. "I love it here," he said. "Come on in."

Helen stood at the threshold and watched his smile: it was a big smile that absorbed the furniture, took it in and recognized it too well, for a later time.

"Come in, I said. I've got something."

She saw the space between his head and the chandelier: he was the tallest man she had seen in this room, yet when she had first met him, he had seemed short and squat.

"Take these," he said, and she saw that he was holding a bouquet of yellow roses. "Oh, how pretty!" The words rushed with a feeling set off by the flowers, not him. She came to him, and as her hands took the flowers, she was angry the emotion had been set off: he should not see this in her and believe that their meetings were starting long times together.

She stared at his rewarded face, unable to control her pleasure in the gifts of his eyes. "Why do you look at me like that?" Helen said.

"I don't look at you. You're inside me, already."

She brought the flowers to the kitchen, then returned with them in a crystal vase, the wedding gift of Aileen Block, used only once before. As she set the vase down on the coffee table, she heard Vito behind her, but as she turned to speak to him, he had gone.

"What is it? What happened?" He had jumped behind her. "You really scared me."

He held his arm up and tightened the muscle. "I just wanted you to see. It's my reflexes. They said I had the best reflexes in the Southern Conference. Here's what I did — with the team guys. I'll jump from in front of you to the back of you as fast as you can turn your head. Try it. Just try it. Come on."

"It's silly." This was childhood again.

But suddenly, she turned her head to the side, and as quickly, Vito had moved. "Oh, that is amazing," she said, but while he smiled, she turned again.

"Wait. You got me, but that wasn't reflexes. I didn't know you were doing it." Vito was angry with her. "It's not fair. You used a trick. It isn't strictly reflexes that way."

"No, it isn't strictly reflexes." Helen mimicked, but Vito

did not catch it. "You have the best reflexes in America, you big ape," she said.

"Maybe I do," he said. "I *could* have, you know."

For answer, Helen punched at him; Vito quickly took it as a game and began to shadow box around her. "Come on, come on, hit out," he said.

Helen stopped. "No, no. Come on, hit out. Here, look." He removed his jacket and polo shirt. "Hit me like a boxer. On the chest. Or the stomach. All your might. Come on. Hit me."

She began to punch at him, tapping at his chest with her open hands, the action not definite yet.

"Come on in, come on," Vito said, and moved back slowly, just out of reach; it led Helen on, and as she lunged, she reached him and struck hard.

She made fists and struck again. "Go ahead, all your might." Vito was taking pain and showing her his strength.

Helen punched again and again, forgetting her thoughts, enjoying the tight sensation in her knuckles when she hit his body.

Vito's skin took blow after blow; she moved around the room after him, unaware that his body was quite spotted with red welts.

Vito stopped moving to stop her, but she came on and in her forward motion ran into him — she opened both hands and pressed her nails into his back.

"Come on, now. That's enough," he said, but she did not stop, throwing blows harder and wilder.

He backed away again, annoyed now, uncomfortable with Helen, who did not seem to know him. He moved slowly and yet fell back as his heel tripped over the coffee table. Quickly, he regained his balance and jumped up to grasp Helen's arms and restrain her.

"All right, now. I said, come on. Let's stop. *Come on*."

She squirmed in his grip and hit his chin with her head, butting up at him.

"I came here to do something else," he said.

"What? What is it?" Helen relaxed and let herself be held.

"Let's go inside," he said.

"No," Helen said. "Tell me what it is. What you came to do."

"Should we do it here?" Vito did not understand.

"No." Her voice was not angry, but Vito felt her distant, talking to someone else.

"Let's cut it," he said.

"No, you must tell me what you came for."

Vito released her arms with a push. "Shit on you, dammit. I came to do what you do. Fuck." He walked towards the kitchen. "I'm going back."

She walked behind him as he went towards the door. "I didn't mean all that. Vito. I was teasing. Kidding."

"Kidding? Kidding? But Christ, I only get an hour. And that phony, make-believe stuff is bad. I hate faking out like that."

Helen smiled; his words were forgiving. "Will you come back and get me?"

Vito turned around and came to her, picked her up and carried her to the bedroom.

"Will you undress me?" she said when he had placed her on her bed.

He nodded but did not speak. "Will you pull my hair?" she said, and lay back.

Vito did not like these questions; she was faking into some dream again; she spoke off into the air. "And scratch me, too," she said.

"Stop it," he said.

Vito sat down at her side and gently unbuttoned her dress; he had never done this before, and the trust in her still body made his hands more difficult to use well.

In this manner, he did not understand the workings of her straps, her clothes with hooks, but she did not help him: he worked in the silence while the curtains of his thoughts slid up vaguely to disclose memory just beyond his vision, memory without the names attached: he had been in such a bedroom or he had wished himself there: he lay back in his bed and saw this before his eyes: this *had* happened.

Finally, he saw her and stepped back, standing: she was more than any beauty he had ever recognized, greater than paintings, lakes, rivers, mountains in the sun: she was something made of love.

He kneeled on the bed and bent to kiss her, slowly kissing all her body. Then he stood up, hesitant to touch her anymore; looking at her roused a different way of feelings: he was to look and play in his eyes and not touch.

Helen reached her arms up and brought him back down; the strange little world of feelings fell back from Vito; Helen placed her hands at the sides of his head and brought it down, directing it over her body. This touch, still new, was newest in the finding of her feelings in it, feelings more open and complete, so that from now, a gesture, any touch, the holding of hands, would never be a dutiful habit again.

(With Cy, she had been quickly met, embraced in darkness, quickly left. What was to open remained always dark and secret, and she felt wrong about the pleasure of herself; what they did had to come in acting little games. There had never been the slow forgetfulness of these times with Vito, the world forgotten — furniture and phone calls — a blankness filling up with herself, herself and Vito taking up the space of the whole world. And never this tribute from Cy, as Vito's mouth and hands had made the fields of her body large and clean, making pleasure clean in the expanding parts of herself known and enjoyed and therefore loved — shedding embarrassment that had begun to form in times even before knowing.)

After Vito had joined her, come down slowly upon her to mark the thread of time with their climaxes, she felt his body disappear and opened her eyes. He had leaped back and was dressing. "I'm late for work." She did not understand the worry in his voice: how could he fear the fools he worked for? "I'll have to run for it 'cause I left my car in the lot."

He was gone too fast, but she was still able to feel his weight, as if she had been pressed to the bed by it, still in the position that had supported his body, with legs spread as though she were pinned down: she thought of a native princess strapped to the grass — it was only a glimpse — a woman with long, white hair, her legs spread, her arms spread above her head, a stake near each foot, each arm, and a leather thong from the stake to the body, tying her down. Helen moved for a second into the enactment of that position and then forgot the dream.

But with her arms back, her breasts moved, and she thought of Vito's hands and his pressing — when he was wild and near climax, how he squeezed her breasts and hips and made them shake. Helen touched her breasts lightly, with her fingertips. Lost in those times with Vito, she might be getting damaged and not know. Vito ran down the halls of her body and at those times she lost the sense of protection: he was to have been something she would not think of as real, and his entrances were to be dream entrances.

Now, in her room, her own objects surrounded her and forced her thoughts: she turned on her side to shut her mind to the vision of damage; Vito came down upon her with the same motion as an arm and hand giving a beating — had she dreamed this — she was being beaten. Had she been, as a child? No, not by her father; he was soft, afraid, if anything.

She fell asleep and awoke with the thought again of damage: her insides, the insides of her breasts — whatever they were made of — had been torn loose by Vito's pressing and shaking and squeezing. Her breasts were like cups and in the cups (but she could not see) were the torn shreds of herself.

She lay, staring up, ready to cry for herself and her imminent death. The time moved through the silence until daylight began to leave the room; dusk made all objects in the room vague and unclear. And she sat up.

As she did, she heard footsteps and the sounds of the street. She touched her legs quickly for signs of what she had done. If it were Cy, she would say nothing; she would be ill with the flu, the curse. He would see nothing, and turn away, simply turn away. And good for him.

She had to be given a piece of new time, to think about Vito, had to speak to him; when he was present, walking through her rooms, they hardly spoke. And she had done it, avoiding his voice at first because he was young and simple, his puffed words embarrassing, a crowing, a swagger like the streets. Later, though the voice became familiar, she stopped her words again so that he could not know her when he turned against her, the thought she knew as the word *blackmail*.

Now, to the sound she heard or imagined, she was sleepy; she did not care to speak to any man and kept them outside, behind the locked door. Even Vito could come out of his silence and make this room his food, stand up and get fat, a pig like the rest.

He was good enough now, silent but moving, showing what he was. But she would have to speak to him, stop him, make him see the days ahead.

He was decent and had love in him and had given her a harvest of feelings. She'd help him on his way — his career — and they would close the whole thing with friendship, like brother and sister. And then one day his voice would come to her over the radio or from a record, from California, or some club, and she could enjoy what had happened, and his new success, and think of him.

Lovely as this weaving was, it made her angry; again, she was sitting back, in a chair while men danced up and down and ran the world; only them, only them with the handle to the doors, and she pushed back, left, with something missing out of her.

She placed her hands on the white telephone and took it off the bedtable to her lap. After she had dialed, she realized she had called Cy's mother.

"Hello?" She heard the older woman's voice, and listened. "Hello? Who's calling? Hello? Hello?"

In the semi-darkness of her room, Helen felt protected and allowed the fear to come up in Mrs. Steinman's voice, breaking through her usual brashness.

"Hello, Mother, this is Helen."

"Helen? Oh, Helen, thank God. We must have had a bad connection. I couldn't hear you good, and I thought maybe it was one of those nuts calling; you know, those people you hear about who call up a number just to drive them crazy. Have you ever had that happen? They'll call out dirty words or some of them just let it ring night and day. I tell you, I wouldn't mind if somebody was here. But all alone, I get terrified. I start to think so if they got my number, they know my address; they know I'm alone up here, and the next thing they're coming up to get me. Some kind of maniac."

"Yes, Mother. I called to tell you how much I liked the lunch. And let's get together again."

"Oh, you liked that place? Well, it looks pretty. But it's not as nice as the Hyde Park. Still, the atmosphere's around you — it makes the crap they serve look so good. And I'll admit, they have the desserts. Yes. They have good ones — didn't you have the Nesselrode pie?"

"No, Mother."

"I could of sworn you had the Nesselrode. Well, next time let me order it for you. But listen: I talked to Cy again last night. As if what's already happened is not enough, a mail-order house wants to make a fabulous yearly order, like thousands and thousands of garments. It's no Sears, but it's a giant. Yes, it's a giant and they do only clothing. Like the New Process Company. So, to make a long story short, the boys are stopping in Denver, and they can't be back sooner than next Thursday the earliest."

"But that's another week or so." Helen was angry; she would have known nothing of this from Cy.

"It never fails, like I told you. Once you make success, everybody wants to touch you. Gold makes gold, they think."

"Mother, what did Cy say to you?"

Mrs. Steinman caught the tone and rushed to defend her son. "Now don't worry, baby. When each week is another million, *you* can hold out. After all, this time you hit the jackpot."

Helen waited in the silence. Let her explain it, let *her*

tell why — the *boss*. Helen saw the image of Mrs. Steinman's big red lips, always red with bright lipstick, rising like curtains to show her uncapped teeth and then her gums as she curled her words and intoned them up and down.

"Helen? Helen, you know what I mean. I just mean worries. Kiss your worries good-bye. Now you can sit back for a few years, you know; now, a little bad luck could even hit you and you'll have a cushion. I wonder if you know what that means? Sweetheart, what *that* means, to *have it*, in the *bank*, to have, maybe ten, twenty years — se*cure*. Nobody can take it away from you. Oh, we all want that. I mean, the wish is inside us. That comes first — I mean, before fun, before anything. You know what I mean: it's a need."

Helen thought of Mrs. Pomerantz through the delicatessen window, her dirty wig changing color as it moved in and out of the colored lights of the neon sign.

"Helen? Helen? Listen to me, Helen, people tell me I'm hard, I'm cold. But what do you think I did? I only faced it, darling. I faced it. We *all* had to scratch and only scratching hard was going to do it, and I'm not living today in a dirty red brick walkup off Tremont Avenue where the lobby smells of everybody's onions and everybody's kid's you-know-what behind the stairs, and the others have written every curseword in the books on the walls. I'm *here*. I may be alone, but that's another proof of no matter what you do you get bad luck. So at least I got some pleasures. I got sunlight. Cleanliness. I got a doorman downstairs to keep out the *drek* that runs in the streets — Helen? Answer me, for Christ sake, answer. You know what I'm talking about."

Helen lost her anger; she thought the old woman would suspect it as part of something new about her and ask other questions. "Yes, Mother, I certainly appreciate what you did in your life."

"What *I* did? *Darling,* I'm talking about all of us, you and me and Cy. And even though Samuel and me we had it much worse, it was the bottom we started off, right off the East Side streets, it's not so different today, let me tell you, even if you got a freezer and two TV. The world's still here. It's what I'm trying to tell you. You're not so different and none of us are. The thing can turn around any minute — just turn your back. And that's why I'm happy Cy hits it this big. Big enough for your kids. You started like the others, didn't you, from the South Bronx, wasn't it? So you know. I wonder if you seen it lately. I see it from a Cadillac window, I see it. And let them call me anything you want — I mean anything they want. That's the only way to be seeing it. You understand me, don't you, Helen? The people who pointed the finger at me, they just couldn't scratch. They got what they did. They're happy where they are — they accepted it — and *I* don't talk about *them.* How could I get them to admit they got as much as they wanted to get? But I'll tell you one thing: I *can* resent them saying I don't have a heart because I made my own way. That is *my* privilege. What I had was energy. And want. Real want. I couldn't sit by the window, like my mother did — she was the old neighborhood through and through — and call down to the pushcarts. I was doing the books for stores in the area when I was fifteen. Well, I never got satisfaction in the home, anyway — But I told you this —"

"Yes, you were telling me at the restaurant."

Helen's voice came to Mrs. Steinman from a strange place; she had forgotten it while she spoke — her voice was a sound to go out over the multitude her mind made: relatives, friends, business associates as well as mocking strangers — and all Jewish. Yet they were a mob, for they all wanted something and none accepted the unity of Mrs. Steinman's purpose and idea.

Helen's yesses were like echoes; they meant nothing and gave no hint of Helen's opinions — whose side she was on.

"Yes, Mom. But right now I want Cy to come home. I bought new curtains and I had the rugs done."

Mrs. Steinman heard Helen go back to herself, into her little thoughts, always the same — this little *mammela*. "Mom, I just can't keep cleaning and cleaning. You don't live to *get ready* for life to start. Get this and get that so *someday* you'll start enjoying yourself."

Mrs. Steinman did not like the tone again; it was insolent and lazy. "Listen, Helen. You have time. You can afford to wait. What you need is something substantial to occupy you — more than you got now. I hate to say it, but it's the truth —"

"Well, then, I could start with a husband!" She slammed the phone down; the vibration entered her thighs.

Immediately, her face became hot, and she dialed again but heard only a busy signal. She kept the phone against her face as the buzz repeated itself, but Mrs. Steinman did not answer. Finally, Helen let the phone down, replaced it on the bedtable and lay back on the bed: it was an attitude she barely recognized: waiting for Vito to come.

Quickly, she rose to her feet and felt a pain in her left breast. She held both her breasts and looked at them, pressing with her fingertips, then stopped.

She went to dress; she would go out now; she had to walk: she would like to run, run fast along a lonely beach. She thought of her blue plaid slacks and got them out — she had bought them after seeing the Oasis cigarette ad in *Look* — the girl on the wooden bridge under a weeping willow.

Dressed, she went downstairs and walked out along the street; she passed along Riverdale Avenue, a wall of parked cars obscuring her view. The last red light of day, as the sun went behind the horizon, shone up at the rows of apartment windows. She stopped to watch the panes catching the color and light.

A woman walking a poodle passed her, the dog stopping to dig a hole right at Helen's feet; still, the woman did not seem to notice that the dog was going to drop its waste right on her; Helen moved away and had to go off the walk again as a group of teen-age girls in the green uniform of the Catholic school came by her, trailing thick briefcases they could barely carry. They walked to the bus stop, dropped their books and began to put makeup on their faces. The bus came and shot hot black fumes at Helen and she walked away, towards the river and better air.

As she passed the red brick housefronts, all new but somehow dingy already, she read the signs of doctors' offices and remembered the doctor near her she had called once — Seymour Berger's nephew. A block later she reached the house and went through the lobby to his door.

The nurse let her in. "Doctor Berger's just leaving. Did you have an appointment?"

Helen gave her name. "I'll go in and ask him, Mrs. Steinman. Sit down."

Berger came out with the nurse and led Helen back to his examination room. "I have to be at the hospital in twenty minutes, so if it's a checkup, let's sign you up for tomorrow or the next day. Could you come at two?"

"All right." Helen turned her head away from him. "Could you just check one thing now, though?"

The doctor had been packing his bag. "One thing now?"

He looked at Helen. "You mean right now? Something you're concerned about? Yes, sure."

"I have this pain in my left side, here, up here." She touched her clothes.

Berger nodded. "You're worried about a bump there? Well, let's check it right now."

Helen found it difficult to undress and Berger sensed it quickly. "No need to unclothe, Mrs. Steinman. Just loosen your bra."

It was brief. "All right. It's all over." Berger walked to the sink and rinsed his hands. "No, you're fine. No suspicious bumps, redness, swellings of any kind. Maybe it's only a little muscle strain; you may have bruised yourself by hitting something. It could be the onset of your menses." He looked at Helen. "Your period. You can get a little pain at those times."

Berger took his bag and coat. "I'll see you tomorrow. All right?" He held the door for Helen, and she went before him into the waiting room. "Sign up Mrs. Steinman for two o'clock tomorrow."

The nurse wrote it down, and Berger led Helen to the street. "Do you need a lift home?" he said.

"No. You're in a hurry. And I have all the time in the world."

He smiled. "All right. See you tomorrow."

She watched him walk down the street to his car, then turned and walked the other way. At the corner, she thought of continuing her walk, going down to pass Vito's store; instead, she turned towards home, angry for wanting to see Vito *this* way.

*Cy. Bastard. The bastards.* Her thoughts spit up quickly and she hurried her steps, to get home before they would come aloud and be heard.

# 14

H E HAD gone again; she heard the front door slam and thought of the doorman's red face looking at Vito leaving, then knowing that she was lying here, enjoying her nudity in the middle of the night.

Vito had given her this pleasure of herself, left her with it, but too often her mind absorbed some stupid, imagined face which looked and laughed down at her. Then she could no longer lie exposed, and covered herself, though she was always alone in the room.

The voice of her mind spoke to the faces; she argued — her inner shouts were hushed by the silence of the room: she would do this, show herself to her own walls, her own darkness at the windows, her own sun in the morning.

Helen squirmed on the bed and felt a fold of the rumpled sheet between her buttocks; she recalled Vito's weight and touched her breasts, then threw the thought aside and stroked her hips; she felt his imprint but it was in her thoughts and not a mark was on her flesh.

But if she were crushed in his threshing, she did not care: he leaped over her; he flew upon her with weight that was not his body but rather the force of his self driving up.

And she had even found that his words were clean; in bed, what he called was only the feeling inside him, dark and light, but at first she had remembered a bleak thought when he called out, of Saturday football games and the necking sessions in the locker rooms under the field at night, the couples on the wooden benches going farther than they had ever gone, the sickening shock when condoms had been found by the assistant principal, who got two girls expelled and suspended the whole football team.

It was there, though she had not been caught, that Charles Palella — or Panella — the name was three or four when she tried to pronounce it — had made her feel love. He was a *goy* — her girlfriends used the term going home on the subway and talking about the boys at school. A *goy* and more tempting because he could never be a husband; and handsome and whatever else she did not know anymore, but he had become her boyfriend, week after week, and finally they had done it as all the others had.

Then came the first time she knew about the fear of having a baby, and waited and waited each month, and had meetings with the other girls who talked about whether the curse had come, a group off from the rest, like outcasts who were special and better, superior to the girls who were afraid.

Some nights of waiting she would have a crying jag in her room and the times her father heard her and walked in, she would have to suppress the wish to vomit while he talked and reminded her that they always had had their talk before she went to bed, ever since she had been a baby. But then, she had the feeling that her father was looking at her legs and could not wait for him to get out.

Once she had thought of going into the old cathedral on the way home from school, just to see a Catholic church. And on those afternoons she always avoided passing the delicatessen and the sight of Mrs. Pomerantz, dried, under her wig in faceless grief, as though she had cried all her life for dead children while the limp, shriveled hot dogs on brown paper never changed, never moved.

*Oh, goddam them all.* Helen was standing now, about to go to the chair for her robe. She felt a dripping on her leg and ran for the bathroom, smiling, beginning to laugh. (She and Vito *had* been out: they had run for a Staten Island Ferry — he had made her run! They had run together down the steps at Yankee Stadium after the game to beat the crowds.)

She wiped herself and then walked to the sink and the medicine-chest mirror. "Hello, dere," she said aloud, in mimicry of a comedian they had seen together, and stared at herself, feeling again the newness of the pleasure. (Why had she been taught to undress so that she was not able to ever see herself, removing her underclothes only after her nightgown was on? Who ordered these things? Would Mrs. Pomerantz ever undress? Nude, would she exist? No one ordained the punishment: searching left her mind with the face and head of Mrs. Pomerantz looking out from over the hot dogs, cooking into death.

The sound of the doorbell came through her reveries. "Oh, go home, kid," she said aloud. "I'm all — I'm all fucked out." Her face became red and hot, and she ran from the bathroom and put on her robe and then started for the door. She was calling phrases, imitating the brusque, silly tone and language of Vito, laughing at the phrases as she said them.

She looked through the door peeper and saw Cy standing there and dropped her thoughts as she unbolted the door.

Her eyes filled with tears as Cy stepped in and embraced her. While he held her, she wanted to cry harder and fall on her knees and ask Cy to hit her.

She would tell him, saying it was a passing thing, a kid, a little excitement, a separated piece of lonely desire from waiting too long.

"Oh, baby," Cy kept repeating and kept her in his embrace until she felt a pain in her shoulder. "Cy, please."

She stepped back, leaving his arms hanging down. "Cy, why didn't you ever call me?"

"Call you? I wanted to surprise you, that's all."

Helen stepped back a few more paces. "No. Why didn't you call me up some other times? And talk to me. Or even a postcard you could have written — to your *wife*." Helen walked to the living room.

Cy removed his coat and dropped it on the couch and followed her. "We were too busy, honey. Just as we were winding up one deal, a phone call would come and some investor would come in, and *bam*, we got some more money. So I'd have to phone the subcontractors, the guys who live by the peas and chickens and get *their* price, you know. And come back and make a new estimate and then, bang, is it going to be fixed, here or there —"

Helen turned away from the office language, the office voice, and walked to the bedroom door.

"We were meeting all hours." Still, she would not show him her face. "All hours. A whole season's prices to quote. Big orders. It leaves you dead, money like that. You know, I'd go back to my hotel room with a stiff neck every night. So I'd take a hot bath to break the knots, and when I came back to my bed I'd fall asleep on top of the covers, right in my bathrobe. Night after night. I never got a chance."

"But you stayed awake long enough to call your *Mommy*. That's for sure."

"Come on, Helen. Dammit, let me get inside my house, already. And sit down a minute. I'll explain to you. I'll explain it all."

"All right. Make it good. Relax. And make it a good one." Helen turned and walked into the bedroom; Cy carried his suitcases into the room and set them on his bed to unpack.

Helen had forgotten the hours before as her anger turned all time into the present — it was that way with Cy, who made her wait and made her anger rise beyond her wishes. She must either shout at him or beg something of him.

Her mother had said it once: Jewish men. She, who had stood and swallowed the years, yet had turned in anger to Helen, trying to make her obedient in the same way, to know without words that they were better, more important. They looked at you with a bitter taste and in silence were able to bring out the sense of disgrace inside you, even while they made you head of the house and acted like boys when they were sick and put accounts in your name and loved to see you dressed up. Dressed like a queen, you were slave to the belief that they were all princes; they ascended from one to the other; they passed on thrones and you were beneath, regardless of what you had in yourself that deserved to ascend.

Her head was lowered again; she was staring at the sheets, which she had forgotten about. Quickly, she covered them with the bedspread and sat down.

Cy began to unpack, looking at her. She smoothed the bedspread with her hands. Slowly he removed pairs of socks and placed them on his bed.

1 6 4

Then he held up a shirt. "I had to buy some dress shirts. It's a new wash-and-wear cotton."

Helen looked up.

"The other guys talked me into getting these button-downs." His voice was soft, filled with the gentleness that always touched feelings of her love. "Can you just see *me* in a button-down?" He had changed completely; Helen nodded.

"But I still feel funny. What am I, a Wall Street broker? You know."

"I think it's very nice. I'm always telling you to try the Ivy style, instead of that Seventh Avenue white on white like a waiter and the jackets as long as a carcoat. Your neck is just right for those shirts."

Cy reached down into his suitcase and took a black leather case out of a pocket and passed it to Helen with a short throw. "Here's a little something *your* neck is just right for."

Helen hesitated; she took the case off the bed and stood up.

"Well, open it," Cy said. "Don't just stand there."

"What is it?"

"What do you mean, what is it? Open it up." Cy's hands were on his hips, his boss position.

It was a string of pearls with a diamond hanging at the apex on a tiny chain. Helen felt her face running tears.

"Ah, no." Cy came round to her. "No, please, baby. Don't be sad. Of course, you're miffed. I don't blame —"

"Oh, Cy. Do you know how long I didn't hear from you. It wasn't right."

"Yes, yes." He held an arm across her back, gently, aware he should not embrace her yet. "Just put it on. Put it on and forget."

Helen went to the mirror to look at herself and the necklace. Looking was Cy's order and she did it, but her eyes turned away, looked down at her neck — the necklace only.

"What have *you* been doing?"

She heard his voice behind her, with desire in it.

"What do you mean?" She felt her neck red and hot, beginning to swell.

"Exercises? Situps? Look at your figure. It's so tight. Trimmed down. Maybe I've been away too long. It just looks great."

Helen turned to look at him; his smile was crossing the bridge to his feelings, a bridge to carry them across to his mind. And it was always hard and slow for him at times like this, the quiet times, alone, that called for a few words.

"How about a little drink?" he said. "Just you and me and a nightcap? We'll celebrate that necklace. You know, it's a thing you could give to your grandchildren."

"How much was this, Cy?"

"Don't ask." He was smiling again. "But you got your first heirloom tonight. That's all. Now what do you want?"

She did not wish to answer: the drinking was not drinking, but Cy's setting-up exercises for desire.

"Come on. A little brandy? Or planter's punch? Something sweet and nice."

"OK, planter's." She lowered her head, and Cy walked to the living room.

She removed the necklace, placed it in the box and into her dresser. Then, as she waited, she touched her fingertips to her eyes and pressed the lids shut and sat down on her bed.

His footsteps shook the ashtrays on the coffee table inside; then the sound of ice and glass came to the room. Cy placed the glasses on his night table and sat down to remove his shoes. She looked at him: now he would groan and pity his tired feet.

"Ooh, these poor hoofs." His head was down. She shut her eyes again. "Ooh, my poor, aching toes. I better get a metatarsal thing. Don't you think?"

"Cy, do you realize what time it is?" Helen walked over and took her glass; Cy reached up to touch her, but she walked away.

He stood up. "Just this nightcap. While I'm unpacking. That's all."

"No, don't unpack." Helen sat down on her bed. "Lock them up and put them near the closet. *I'll* do it tomorrow. And do it right."

Cy obeyed, then came back to his bed, took his drink and drank it down. "Listen, get a case of Scotch this week, will you?" He shook the ice in his glass and looked down at it. "I drank a lot on this trip," he said softly.

"Oh, yes. And what else did you do a lot of?" Helen was smiling, holding her glass against her face.

"Oh, no. None of that. No dames and I'll swear it." Cy drank off the water melting. "Just drinking. I swear. It's Solly Chapman. Every time, *he* got me started. He's such a smart guy, the bastard. He talks to you like *now* is the only thing to live — there's no tomorrow and nobody cares what you do. So you drink and you drink. And forget what you're doing. Only Mom's calls got me. Boy, she'll do it every time. Like a rasp. You know what a rasp is, it's a tool that scrapes — scrapes your skin off. Well, she's got a voice and a way. So you give her the straight stuff — the figures — black and white, black and white. She wants it down to the pennies. And that even made me drink a little more."

"But look at you from drinking."

Cy pressed his fingers against his stomach. "Oh, you're right. You're *so* right."

"Liquid calories, they call it." Helen was stern and then pleading while Cy looked down at himself.

"You're Jell-O, Cy. Pure Jell-O. It's just too much. And you're going to ruin a whole wardrobe; you'll poison your body with fats — they cling to veins —"

"I got to lose. I got to." Cy finished his drink and looked back towards the living room. "You want another?"

"No," Helen said. "This one made me sleepy."

Cy went quickly inside; when he returned, his glass was filled. He paced along the rug, from his bed to the windows and back. "We got it now, Helen. It's real. It means a take in maybe six figures. Just for me. I can't even picture it, six figures. Then sometimes I think it's mine and I start to hate the government; I start thinking I better buy my congressman now."

"I know it's real." Helen lay back on the bed. "Your mother tells me everything."

"She told you? You know what that means? She really likes you. Yes. I always told you that. You never saw her cut somebody dead so you don't know what else she can be. But this here proves she likes you."

Cy was excited with his insistent feeling; he laughed as he thought about it. "See, she'll only tell someone she likes. And if she likes *you*, we're made. I mean, she'll cooperate with ideas I have. Because we have to extend a little and borrow. See, even retired, she has the say-so. She hasn't let it go yet."

Helen had shut her eyes and now Cy caught her face in his eyes as he went on excitedly. "If she'll just turn us over some power, we'll make the whole place grow bigger than anyone. Bigger."

He was noticing Helen and came to the side of her bed to pat her legs. He leaned his face close to hers and kissed her forehead. "Remember me, baby?"

Helen opened her eyes and saw his face; close to her, it held his warm, kind, expectant smile, his eyes bright and squinting with pleasure: she had liked them from their first date when she had expected a cold fish because Uncle Jack, who arranged it, had referred to Cy as a young *manufacturer*.

She puckered her lips and Cy gently kissed them. "Hello, kitten-little," he said, beginning the private phrases they had collected in their married years alone; they were words created in their bed: they had made up names for each other and for their genitals; they played a game of father and daughter; they played as if they were children or animals, and they would act their games until slowly, nestling against each other, permission came from their meekness and they made love.

Helen lay back, hearing the words and knowing what would happen as if it had already happened. It had no substance, but the liquor had made her drowsy and shook the desire inside her, a feeling that did not go down anymore as if dying. Cy sat down next to her; she placed her hands on his shoulders and embraced him. He smiled at her and began to touch her.

At each step, he paused. The time became too full of knowing: his touch and his pauses were caught in his expectancy of refusal. She knew this delicate fear and removed her robe, pressing her body to his, rubbing her stomach against his penis pressed between them.

She waited for his movement: this rhythm was always exciting and it abandoned the names of everything, of even the people involved: she rode into it and pushed her actions without embarrassment, with all her intentions unmasked, only for the feelings forming in herself.

She arched her back and let her voice make the sounds it wanted, then took his penis, placing it in her. Cy's quivering raced up quickly; then he lay quiet, fallen; had he done it like someone being chased? Helen turned her head to the wall; she had been too conscious. But she did not care. She would not cry: enough of her had responded, ready and unburied, so that the brevity had not hurt too much. And she could start again: she knew that now, start at any time.

She heard his dog-breathing near her ear and moved her body away. "Cy, would you please get off me now? And get me a Kleenex, please?"

# 15

"**H**ELEN!" Cy's voice was loud and mean. She turned her face into the pillow, away from the coldness that attacked. "Helen. *Don't* you have English muffins here? *Helen!*"

Cy came to the door; his voice was louder; it made demands with its damning sound. "*Helen,* I'm going downtown. Will you *please?*"

Helen sat up in bed, suddenly, and Cy was startled. "I didn't even *know* when you were coming home," she said. "Remember? Remember?" She was getting her own rhythm of anger. "I was not *informed.* Your Mommy tells me *everything.* And she said another week and a half. How long do you think English muffins *stay* fresh?"

"All right. So all right. For*get* it."

"Mr. *On* Time." One line in her mind was without control; it had to continue. "Mr. Always On *Time.* Johnny-on-the-*spot.* Always ready. Always where I *need* you."

"All right. So forget it. For*get* it. Shut up, shut *up,* already. I'm *late.*"

Helen placed her feet on the floor. "Oh, *why* didn't you

call me, Cy? I'll make your *damn* breakfasts. Just *wake* me up. Why, *why* did you sneak out of here?"

"Who *sneaked?*" Cy stamped his right foot. "I didn't *sneak,* anywhere." Cy watched her walk to the closet for her robe and put it on slowly. "Helen. What's the matter?"

"Oh, piss," her voice said, unaware of it until it was spoken. She walked past him, into the kitchen and he followed.

"Just tell me what's the matter, now. So I lost my temper. So I'm in a little hurry. I'm hungry."

She poured water into the coffeepot and spilled some on her robe; her anger had twisted her hand to turn the faucet on too strongly: the uncontrollable hiss of the water rushed longer than she wished it to, but her movements were still sleepy and slow.

"Nothing's the matter with me, Cy Steinman." She placed the coffee in the top and turned the switch to *on, medium.* "But maybe I did a lot of thinking in this *padded* kitchen. Sitting alone; among my souvenirs. And talking to your damn mother who calls me to drop hints. You want me to *work,* don't you? Get out of the house in the morning; go downtown and sell garments. *And* have muffins ready. And *what?* Hot *knishes,* too? I had a mother once, too, you know. Well, maybe I'll do it. It's the only way I'll get to see you long enough — by going downtown. Unless, of course, what you boys do down there, it's women not wanted."

"I don't have time for this now." Cy moved nervously at the door, unsure: he needed to go. "I'm in a hurry. I *told* you I'm in a hurry. But one thing I'll tell you. I asked you to have a little patience. While I'm getting set. I'm changing the whole business, maybe getting Mom to retire for real. The thing is in my hands — and *you —*"

He left the kitchen and walked to the hall closet for his

light topcoat. Helen walked to the kitchen door and looked at him while he examined the gray coat, held it in his left hand and brushed it down with his right, thoroughly, like a clothing man, then put it on carefully. He had placed his attaché case on the antique chair and was now picking it up.

"Then *why* did you wake me up!" Helen was shouting.

Cy opened the door; he turned to look at her as he buttoned his coat; then he took his case firmly. "For English muffins," he said, and stepped out, letting the door slam behind him.

Helen walked back and sat down; the red light of the coffeepot went on and she poured her first cup.

He has gone, she thought, without telling me about the trip. She sat and stared at the curved side of the pot: its automatic mind kept the liquid boiling, remaking the coffee, a mechanism too good for itself. She saw her reflection in the bright steel: though her face was distorted, she saw it as pretty, even untouched in early morning, her hair with waves already — she did look like a model, yes, but she knew that the reflection was elongating and that her glass mirror gave her back something fleshier, heavier.

In a moment the good feeling broke: thoughts began again, changing the face she saw, the skin under her eyes black and blemished, her whole face getting wizened, shriveled, small.

(She would go downtown, then, and see Cy for lunch — today. She would prepare a nice supper for him, a real kosher meal he'd like. She would call him first and arrange the time, like an old date, and make sure he'd come home on time and find it all just cooked. Yes, yes. She would tell Vito today not to come anymore. He must go off on his own now. She would even pay him — give him something,

something to start out. Even cash, a few bonds — anything; explain that to Cy in a few years; some trouble, trouble she had had. He would understand; every life has its rocky moments. Yes. She would get Cy to move out to Long Island — Great Neck, Massapequa, one of the nice parts, with the split-levels they advertise, Cape Cod Ranch, something you could add to later, a new wing, playroom, den. Yes. They would have to move. Away from here if Vito got bad about it. He couldn't make trouble. But they would divorce her. They would shut her out without a penny. They would kill her reputation. All right. She would have to go downtown and start work again. Call Cy. Yes. She would call Cy as soon as he got downtown. She would make him listen on the telephone, and tell him. No. She would make love to him tonight. She would give herself to him. She would buy a honeymoon negligee. She would get one of those sleeping bras. She would do things to Cy. Make him hot. Serve him. No! She would just call him and tell him what she did with Vito. She would offer to leave. She would take a furnished room over in the East Bronx and work as a secretary. She would not see anyone for life. Make it up in silence. Ask to go to his office and help around, do anything, and for nothing, no pay. She would model for him again if he wanted. Be *his* secretary. Whatever he wanted. Whatever he said.)

Her hands shook as she drank coffee: four cups; five cups. She had done this before, had sat in a kitchen and drunk for hours, ten cups, more. At that time — it was home — she had been unable to reach her thoughts: her mind was blank but full of whips for herself. At home she had stared at the sink, those old sinks that were half tubs, tubs we washed clothes in. And heard the Seventh Avenue train sigh and scream into the curves at a Hundred Seventy-seventh Street.

She was crying: the tears hit the Formica tabletop, as large as drops from a faucet. She dropped her cup and went to the bedroom for a tissue.

Noticing the clock marking ten, she went to the phone to call her order. She asked for as many different kinds of food as she could remember, offerings to Cy. And she knew that Vito would come and be told.

He came just before noon; she had spent the two hours staring. Helen watched him bring in the boxes and unpack them and, as though he had known the kitchen for a long time, begin to unpack and put the boxes away.

"No, no, I'll do all that, Vito." She smiled at his actions. "Now you just sit down. You still have to see something."

Helen sat down and waited. Vito finished and picked up a brown bag he had dropped to the floor when he arrived. "Now in here is not your order," he said, and opened the bag.

He placed a large plush rabbit before her; a red box of chocolates was tied to its forepaws.

"What's this?" she said.

"It's just a little thing I got. A bunny and some candy."

Helen held the rabbit, then rested it on the kitchen table; the wires inside it enabled it to stand on its hind legs. It stood higher than her head. She rubbed the plush of its body, recognizing the feel of Orlon. "Oh, Vito." She was looking at the rabbit. Vito walked close, leaned down and kissed her forehead.

"Vito. No. No." He stood up straight. "Last night my husband came home. After you left. I did a lot of thinking. We can't see each other now. And forget what's happened. I've done a wrong thing to you, you know. I'm sorry."

Vito did not speak; inside he heard the wish to roar in her face, spit on her, slap her across the room, knock her reeling off her chair. "I wasn't kidding around," he said. "There was nothing wrong. You hear. Nothing you did to me. Nothing I did. And I was straight with you. I gave you *honesty*."

"Vito. I'm married. You know that. And you're still young. You don't need me."

"You're young, too," Vito said. He stood his ground near her. "You are, you are."

"When you get married, you change. I'm not young the way you are —"

"Listen, listen, Helen." Vito was talking too fast, trying to stop the decision and the echo of other decisions. "I never talked to you before. I was waiting. I was waiting to do you an honor. Do something for you. See what it was — how you wanted it, how you would leave here. You know. I'll do anything. Anything you say. I'll run away. I'll go get that job on the Coast. I know I could get it. Those guys mean it *if* they say contract. And they said it."

"It's crazy to talk this way, Vito. It could never be anything." Helen shook her head. "We should stop everything."

"You want me to just walk away? Is that what I'm supposed to do? Hey, kid. Walk away with your balls in your hand. Just say jump on me again sometime, when my husband goes away and I get the itch. No. I am not *that*."

She looked at his angry face above her, petulant, stupid and strong. She was ashamed of it, that she had been equal with it.

He was clenching his fists and expanding his chest in his anger, like an actor trying out for Tarzan.

"Oh, come on," she said. "Please, let's talk simple sense. You know what we are."

"Talk sense? I'll tell you sense. I'm telling you I'll go to

the Coast and work there. I'll *marry* you. That's sense."
Vito leaned his face down close to hers. "I'll give it to you
short. Honest. You ask yourself why. Why did you like me
when your husband wasn't here? Ask yourself that. You
think *that's* going to close up and go away."

"Don't scream in here. Please don't scream in my
kitchen." Helen's head fell forward and the large tears she
had seen before, the new, strange large drops, came from
her eyes. "What do I do? Oh, you'll hurt me now. You'll
make trouble, I know it. Hurt me. Hurt me good. I don't
know what to do."

She felt Vito's hand on her leg and looked up abruptly;
he was on his knees, looking up at her. "Oh, no. Sweetheart. No, don't cry. Look. I'll go. I'll go right now. See.
Listen, please. I'll take off. Look. See. I'm going. Look!
Look!"

She stared at him, as though he were strange; he was
standing at the door, turning the knob. Her hands went up
to him, and he walked back to her. "I'll do anything for
you," he said softly. "And I'll show you I mean it. Even stay
away for good. If you want."

She took his hands in hers. She nodded and wiped her
eyes. "Vito. I don't know what to tell you."

Vito took her hands and kissed the palms. Helen stood up
and embraced him and kissed his cheeks. "Now be a good
boy," she said. "My good boy."

Her tone unlocked him; her body touching his, he did
not turn to go, caught in his feelings, from hand to mind,
from touch to strength, feelings that had thrown him on his
knees minutes ago. Now they were in his arms and body:
he turned and kissed Helen's neck, his lips sucking at her
skin for a moment, his arms tight about her, the energy of
his hard hands inside her quickly.

What was different today was the embrace and time; she had held him and then been embraced, and in the pauses thought of him there, of Vito, the godlike boy, becoming a lover after having been something else.

In the thoughts she felt his movements, her body light in his lifting arms, and she remembered that each night she had gone laughing under the blankets when her father had sat down on her bed to kiss her into dreams, his weight pressed against her hip fallen against his and felt through the blankets; and after he had kissed her and got up to leave, she would call to him and peek out, then go under again while he came to catch her, then held the blankets down tight over her head until she fought and broke out into the darkness —

She saw Cy's bags in the corner of the bedroom; her hands stroked Vito's face — it was a rhythm that came with feeling and began with the feeling of resistance — to stop him, to slow him, make him soft, change his size to something that would rest on her stomach or on her breasts, a small thing she could pick up as she wished.

She was silent: his arms, hands, his body and lips were like a wrapping, about her; they enclosed her; and her body soon lost the stiffness of day. She heard her slacks slide against her skin as Vito removed them with one gesture.

His weight at last made her arms move up and over her head — it was a position caused by Vito (and had been since the start); with it, she was graceful and weak, light and thoughtful, like someone in a dance.

When he stopped, she had finished for a time already, but she kept her eyes shut and did not move. She heard his steps and lay still.

"I have to go back," he said softly. "Do you want some water?"

She did not answer; his steps came towards her: her body, in surprise, twitched strongly as he kissed her stomach and her thighs and blew against the soft hair of her legs.

She brought her hands forward, to hold him off. "I'm going to finish the deliveries," his voice said.

It was insane to Helen and she let the words fall and fell asleep in the silence. At four, she opened her eyes and felt hungry. But first she had a bath and set her hair in a pigtail for some reason (it was a style she had not worn in a year). Then she wore her light-blue cotton dress, a yellow apron, and went to the kitchen to prepare supper: Vito had cleaned up the kitchen and put everything away.

Its cleanliness urged her on and she began the preparations, remembering the subtle things from her mother — how to cut, scrape, mix together. The doing took her mind into it, her eyes on the shapes she created and the stove that made the final cooking softness.

The feeling of feeding others came to her now; she remembered the recent pleasure of turning Cy's business friends into obedient, boyish things, while they sat and ate, thankful for being served.

She had the joy she had had before, downtown mostly, because they had not begun to entertain up here yet: that anyone who might come in would be welcome. When she cooked, she wished for unexpected guests, hoped for loud, smiling faces calling for food. And if they came in, no matter how many, she could not refuse them.

It was a crazy way to think, but she had let in some strange thoughts now in the midst of Vito never stopping and Cy returning. Both should be somehow chained until she needed them and could tell them when to act; but of course, both were welcome — and the reason was only that she lived the parts that opened her up, did the things that contained no refusal, no negation, no shutting out of others. The kitchen actions said, come, come, all. Where was the door that opened up? Where were the people who lived along the street, neighbors, who were always part of the rhythm that included yourself and your family doing something with the others every day, a place where others always moved and their presences controlled you and everyone else without a word, and there was always pleasure because there was never silence.

She knew she had been trying to put Vito into other feelings, blend the feelings for him into other places, change him to a shelf piece, or think of him as a spice, something to be added. She tried to think of him within her life, too, within the things she liked to do.

But that was wrong. Whatever made the judgment was hateful and cold, but she leaned back to accept it. Wrong and bad: the best wishes she had — the wishes and dreams that each thing she owned and enjoyed created. Actions with him created something strong, and *that* turned into a doom.

She had told him to go. But in the kitchen, her words were as soft as food, her welcome was the face and body she had taken care of, to be admired.

There was an argument inside; there was an argument inside all of us all the time. Who was the crooked old lady that hated some things and liked others; who made decisions that hurt you even for thinking the thoughts that wandered into your head while you brushed your hair or put on makeup?

At least, if she stood over Cy, handing him food, he would not cry out. She could hold him down, like a boy, in his own demands.

If this could be done with everyone, if it could only be done to the silent inner dead, whose orders clamped you shut at the craziest times, often just as you were ready to accept and relax.

Yet she could do it: with the excited power that came out when she took Vito and together found more of her; and also with the place in the world she would get with Cy. But that was wrong and bad; it did not go together, and she was left to prepare almost as an excuse, an apology, doing things for others, saying pleasant, passive things to others because she believed she was filled up with wrong.

# 16

Cy CAME home with daffodils he had bought from a man in the subway arcade; people came out of the hole and saw the yellow in bunches.

Helen was in the kitchen and had cooked his favorites: stuffed cabbage, *flanken*, potato *latkes*, *kasha knishes*, chopped liver and a strudel. "Get mad more often." Cy had given her the flowers and was over the table. "Yell at me. Scream. But cook like this."

"Cook like *this*. You talk as if I never cook you anything, you big horse." His filled face, with eyes open and staring, helpless, were good to her.

Cy began to eat before sitting down. Tonight, Helen held back and let him. "I didn't mean you don't cook," he said. "But this, you'll admit, we don't get much lately."

"Thanks to *me* you don't get it every night." Helen left the kitchen and returned with a large box, from which she took a new ceramic vase for the flowers. She brought the flowers to the table. "You know what you'd look like, Cy, if I cooked kosher every night. You'd be twice a horse. You'd have arteries they could sell to U.S. Steel. Lucky for you I make some sense at night after all that delicatessen you eat downtown."

She came to his chair and pulled it out. "Now sit down." Helen brought him soup, warming on the stove. *"Kreplach soup, too? Oy, gevalt."*

"Don't sound as if I never knew how to do it. You married me because you knew I could make it. Didn't you?"

Cy laughed briefly and leaned over the soup. "Soft as butter," he said after a while. "Look, let's have a party. We still have to warm up this place. Make a list; there's a bunch of people we want to see, and I can have two or three I want to talk to now I have these new accounts."

Cy began to eat. "That's nice, Cy. How about two weeks from now — the Friday after this one?"

Cy stopped for a moment. "A little more soup," he said, and while Helen went for it, he went on: "There's people, you know, I'd like to stick it to — gently — let them know what I did already. Singlehanded. *I* took the Steinman Company up the ladder. Let's get a caterer. Get everything! We'll sit down after supper. OK? And make a list — the people and the stuff."

Cy went down to his soup again. "All right," Helen said. "Just give me a date when you can make it. I said, how about the Friday after this one? How about that?"

"Wait, wait. Next Friday's May eighth. Then you have the fifteenth. Nope. Those we'll be busy. Then comes the twenty-second. How about the twenty-second?"

"The twenty-second. Yes. And no cancellations. Right, now, Cy?"

Cy lowered his head again to the buttery mounds of cream-colored *kreplach*, soft, always glistening with the wash of liquid round their surfaces; he sipped and munched, the little balls becoming softer and softer lumps in his mouth, until they were gone.

He reached for a roll while he ate, and Helen felt a shudder. "Oh, Cy, both hands," she said, and saw the wave of the quiver of his chest flesh echo on his shirtfront.

Cy looked up. "No cancellations," he said. "This one I'll be here with bells."

Helen removed his soup plate, then brought the serving plate of warm *knishes* and a clean flat dish. "Now don't eat all of these while I'm getting the stuffed cabbage. Little by little."

Cy sat back and rubbed his stomach. "Listen, I had *kreplach* all over the East Side. With *yiddle* buyers from the sticks looking for the old Momma taste, you know. And this much I'll tell you — I *eat*, tonight, the best I ever tasted."

Helen served the rest of the meal; at last, Cy struggled to the living room and sat down before the television set, picked up the remote box to switch on the machine.

Helen brought his coffee in on a new print metal tray from S&H stamps. Cy reached up and kissed her hands. "Fill their stomachs. Fill their stomachs," she said, and went to get her sewing bag.

"Salaam, salaam, Master," Cy called out.

"What are you doing?" he said when she sat down with the sewing bag.

"I am going to fix the holes in your smelly socks while we watch. Is that OK with you?"

"Any time. Any time. Say. Where'd you get that blue dress?"

"It's about time." Helen stood up. "I thought you wouldn't notice 'til I dressed in *latkes*."

"Oh, it's sexy, too," Cy said.

Helen lifted her skirt above her knees.

"It's a high waist," Cy said. "Like the empire line translated to a street dress. Hey, that's clever. Who made that? Let's see?"

Helen came to him and leaned down while Cy looked for the label. *"Oy, gevalt.* It's my own. It's mine. Well, that shows to go you. What's happening is I can't even keep up with my own numbers." He sat back and blew out air.

"Look!" Helen called and stepped away and spun round, twisting the skirt in her spin, so that it whirled high and showed her bare legs.

"Nice. Very very nice." Cy smiled. "Dance, ballerina, dance." It was the line of a song Tony Martin always sang: they had heard him in Miami on their honeymoon and then again at the Concord.

Helen stepped out of her shoes and spun across the rug. At the end of the room, she caught her skirt and held it high for a moment, showing all of her legs.

"Hey, hey." Cy clapped his hands; Helen let her skirt fall back, then slowly raised her skirt again, until her panties showed.

"You've been taking dancing lessons." Cy was distracted by the sound of television voices coming louder. He turned from Helen to the picture, then back to her again, looking at both.

Helen watched his head rotate and turned and walked to the kitchen. "Where's the *TV Guide?"* She heard his voice, but did not answer. "Helen! Did you get the *Guide* this week?"

She waited. "Helen! Anything good on tonight? What are we going to look at? What's *on?"*

"I'll be in after I clean these dishes," she said.

When she returned, Cy was staring at the set; she looked

at him for a moment: he had been silent while she scraped and rinsed the plates and placed them in the washer; she had listened for his movements but had heard only the noises of television: the tinny voices and music and the feeling that no one was there. She had begun to hate the gates of loneliness for herself and had begun to break out (these last weeks at least); and now she resented Cy inside there: it said that she made nothing good out here. But then, no, no; Cy ran to the set from other things, deeper down, and washed out the stupid buyers sitting at the set, and forgot an afternoon argument with his mother or one of his partners. No, no, no, no.

"Cy, we were going to make that list. For your party." She had stopped her thoughts.

"Yes, sure, right after this, Hel." He could not leave the picture and his face twitched with the two wishes. "A minute, just a minute." He caught her face, to hold Helen, but she turned and walked into the bedroom.

She undressed, put on her nightgown, and sat down to do her face with cream. She studied her hands against her face, in the mirror, and thought of the party and the trip Cy had promised. She should get the tickets, simply get the tickets, like a bossy *yenta*, and they'd go. Then Vito would have some time to think and stop coming, after all.

She began to twist her hair around her new large plastic curlers and while working, dropped one; reaching for it under her dressing table, she remembered Vito, on his knees: it seemed a crazy thing at first, but it was almost a pretty thing, a gentle thing.

Cy was at the door behind her. "Helen? Listen; will you laugh? Look at this."

Helen turned to see him holding a large layer cake, covered with white buttercream icing. "I put this down in the foyer to unwrap it and bring it in to you, but then I smelled your cooking and I saw the meal you made and forgot all about it. It's banana royal. Come on in."

Helen finished her curling and came to the living room. Cy had brought in a tray with cups and the coffee that remained from the evening pot. "But how do we eat this?" Helen said, looking at the tray. "In our *hands?* Go get plates and forks, *stu*pid."

Cy went back and returned with forks and large plates. "Don't you know the difference between cake plates?" For a moment Helen's anger was beyond Cy's mistake; it spilled into her fingers — a little moment: she saw her nails and the wish to scratch at Cy's face; but the feeling left as Cy went off to the kitchen.

He brought salad plates the second time. "All right, that's good. Bring them here, Cy. And sit down before you'll get egg cups."

Cy sat and watched her cut two large slices; he took his to the TV chair.

"You're not going to *watch* now, are you? 'Cause then I'm going inside. I swear."

"No, no. Look, I turned off the sound. Now, what's the matter? You're on my back all the time."

Helen watched him wolf the cake; his cheeks were puffed and his chewing made him nod his whole head, as though he were agreeing with her, with whatever she would say.

"Cy, look, we haven't had even a *small* chat since you came back. You mean there's nothing to tell me. I'm a moron who wouldn't get a *thing?*"

Cy swallowed and swallowed. "What was it? What was it? Here or there, it was talk and talk and talk. You want to know that?"

"Well, then — Nassau. When do we go, or do we go? *I* wanted to go. And *you* promised, if you'll recall correctly."

Cy had finished his slice and came back to the coffee table to cut himself another; he did it quickly, then went back to his chair.

"Are we going to finish a whole cake all by ourselves? Cy, that *is* disgusting."

Cy ate.

Helen watched his face. "Well, what about Nassau?"

"Swell. Make the arrangements. Any time after this month and I can take two weeks. For sure."

Cy looked at the remainder of his slice of cake; he had left the iced top and back of it for last: he cut through it with his fork, licking the icing that oozed out, pushing with the fingers of his left hand and bringing the forkful up with his right.

"After this month. See." Helen turned her face away and looked down at the remaining cake. "After two weeks. After this month. After. After. We'll never go. You know that, Cy."

"I know that, *shit* I know that. Helen, I got a business to keep going. You forgot that. Look around here, sweetheart. I'm the one has to bring home the *shekels* to keep this place filled up. And that *is* the way it is."

Helen looked at his face again. "Well, then please don't *yes* me, dammit, and then say you can't make it. All right? Just give me the truth, if you *please*. *Yes* is not *no*." She suddenly turned on the cake and cut herself another piece and ate it rapidly, stuffing large chunks of the soft slice into her mouth, chewing very little and swallowing the barely chewed lumps with a sound in her throat that drove them along.

"Go get the tickets. *Get* the tickets, will you?" Cy was

sitting up nervously, looking at Helen, trying to get her face to return a good feeling.

"And just *don't* back out." She caught his eyes. " 'Cause if you back out, that's the last thing I'm doing, Cy Steinman. And just *remember* that."

Cy stood up and stamped a foot. "Dammit, Helen, don't blame it on something like *I made it up* to bug you. This is the only business I know. I got hooked very young, you know what I mean. Now it's mine, you know. And I have to run it. It doesn't run alone." Cy felt his hands — they were hot — and rubbed them on his trousers. "And *this*, I might *remind* you — it's been damn good to us."

"And you better come *with* me. Or *I* go alone and I'll stay alone. Cy. I'm sick of it; I'm sick of things."

"Helen, please. You can *get me* so damn mad. What's the matter since I came back here? You talk like my business is a plot to get *you*. What *am* I? I am like all the rest of the men around here. We have jobs and we have to go different places sometimes. So we have to go. We just have to go. We work, baby. We work to last. Nobody's so far ahead as you think. And sit back in Miami on the coupons. I got to survive because nobody's going to be there to give a damn if I go under. Too many people in this country forget you can go under any day; the credit cards turn to shit in your hands." Cy was sure of this. He had walked slowly as he spoke; now he stood across the coffee table, leaning towards Helen. "So I ask you to show me how I can stay downtown less time than any — *any* of the other men you know in my business, and *I* will follow that lead. So help me, Helen. I'll follow. *Just* show me one. *One*."

"Look, Cy, all right. I'm not standing over you with a whip. Please believe me. You don't have to explain to *me*. I'm here all day. All day long. Sometimes I feel stuck like you. I feel stuck — oh, maybe you'll say that's not true — I can get up and take off any time. But I get nervous and I get restless. Alone, in here. A person gets thinking. I get all sorts of kinds of thoughts in my mind. And what am I doing? What am I doing? I'm sitting most of the time, and I wait for you —"

She stood up and packed the plates and cups and forks on the tray and went in to the kitchen. She returned to find Cy seated again, watching TV. "Everybody gets to worry they won't survive." Helen spoke loud enough to rise above the voices. "Don't you think that, Cy?"

Cy turned to her and nodded.

"When you were gone, I didn't even know where to go. A person will do crazy things to feel they'll be alive again when they're stuck, alone in a house. Things you'd never do. Things that sound terrible if you heard about someone *else* doing it —"

"I know, I know," Cy said suddenly; he was sure she meant his drinking.

"A person's mind will get stuck with barbs, like knives, alone too much, being scared — scared — first for protection. For protection you'll go at something to help you, to cover you with protection; even the craziest things you'll go for."

Cy snapped off the sound and turned to Helen. "Oh, I'm going to cut it out. It was just nervousness that got me, and Solly got me going to cure it with the booze. The whole thing was too much — it was too big, you know. I had nightmares I was shrinking. But it'll be different now because — well, the thing's established; it's a corporation, so none of us have to take it all. Even a bankruptcy we'd have a little —"

Helen nodded, with nothing to say. When Cy turned

back and snapped the sound on again, she went back to the kitchen, rinsed the plates and stacked them in the washer, then turned on the water and the motor; she listened, never sure the machine would continue until the first two cycles were done. While she waited, she saw Vito's rabbit, picked it up and took it to the bedroom, placing it on her dressing chair. Then she got into bed.

Now the other thing came back, the stain or light of Vito. She had talked as if it had not happened, had been able not to think, yet it had been the reason behind her words. It would come up; it would come up like lumps of undigested food; it had to be shown, but the thought of telling was stupid, like saying, *I'm a bad girl,* little simple sentences: *I'm naughty: hit me; spank me.* The punishment was the shame of falling back like that into a simple, uncreated thing before the hands above.

But something else fought this, a force, like a piece of energy, a chunk of it that sent the knowledge of Vito and herself as a private matter, not done against Cy but acted for herself. It could rest in its own past; it was done and had not been unpleasant; it was an act of two, only two. Why should it grow to take in all the other anger, resentment, thoughts of Mrs. Pomerantz's face looking sour, nights alone, even the thought of blaming others? It should stand still, like a moment enjoyed at the ocean, where the first sight of the waves and sand and sky beyond make a feeling you cannot lift into words. Sleep was allowing these thoughts, but now sleep began to cut them off.

She heard Cy's voice after she had fallen asleep, still lightly falling. "What is it?" she said.

"I was just thinking." His voice moved closer. "The kind of a big party I'm thinking about, you don't just ask people on a plain night. It should be a special time. Somebody's birthday; anniversary. Our wedding anniversary's June tenth."

"But that's another two weeks after the *whole* month of May." The words made her tired, as if she had spoken a long time.

"Yes, yes. But then we can do so much more. The caterer can give the party a theme. It wouldn't look like we're showing off. *Our* anniversary, it would be."

Sleep had taken some of her consciousness again. "Go ahead, go ahead." Her face smiled; she heard her own voice. "Do it, do it," it said again.

"Do what?" Cy looked down with a smile for her, but Helen seemed asleep. He watched her for a few moments and then began to undress, quietly, feeling a moment of anger in his chest when he bent to remove his trousers; the anger fled as the chest feeling became something like heartburn, a hot stone, something sick.

*Helen,* he wanted to say: *help me.* Instead, he lay down, waiting for the pain to leave, holding his hands one upon the other, as someone had told him long ago would take the pain away.

□□□ 17

IT WAS the front door; Helen looked at the electric clock across the room, over the refrigerator, but could not read it clearly. The clock face was a ceramic plate, on it a sun face with many gold lines; it had seemed ideal in the store, but from any distance now it was ambiguous: she guessed it to be ten or eleven-thirty.

Vito stood there: his body seemed afloat as she stared through the front door's peephole glass that gave a double image, like a TV ghost.

Her first reaction to Vito — to his clothes — was one of fear. He was dressed wrong; something was wrong: she noticed the little white buttons gleam at the collar of his blue button-down shirt; his jacket was casual but very pressed — newish and stiff — a Shetland, in checks.

Not seeing her, he placed his mouth near the peephole: "Helen? Open up. Helen. Hello. Hurry up."

She opened the door quickly. "Come on in here. Inside." She took his jacket sleeve and pulled.

Vito was in before her force could feel resistance. "Look," he said. "You got to come. Right now. Just this one day. You got to come with me."

"What is it? What happened to you?"

He took both her hands. "Look; please. Just today. You come out with me. It's a ride. Just come along this *one* ride. It's all I ask you."

"Didn't I tell you. Oh, Vito." It was easy to remove her hands; he was not squeezing tight. She began to walk, but stopped herself from going further into the apartment: she paced tight steps in the foyer. "I can't go on any ride with you; I can't go anywhere with you. It's changed now. I told you, I told you. It's a changed thing. With the new change, the change."

"I want to go over the East Bronx. And we'll ride up the Hutchinson River Parkway. It's perfect out. Perfect. You know. You just get a day like this a couple of times a year. And everybody's working. The roads'll be great."

"Why aren't you working?" Helen asked from a fear. "Did they do anything?"

"Don't tell them, will you?" Vito had misunderstood her tone. "And don't call that work. The bastards. That's for horses, that job. And when the niggers wake up, they'll be plenty fat white asses to get reduced. Oh, the hell with them. You think I need their shitty seventy-five cents an hour. Shit on them. I *need* a day off. I'm not like them — they don't even want a day off anymore."

Vito's anger had rushed up too fast; he tried to feel it towards the right object, but there was only Helen to shout at. His hands had become fists while he spoke and he would have hit a face to punctuate his feelings, any face in front of him. He turned from Helen and looked down at his hands.

"I didn't mean that, Vito." Helen began to speak and Vito felt the wrong of his fists. "I mean, I don't care what you do to them. If you take a day off, or whatever. You shouldn't be working there; it's just not for *you*. I only asked because I'm so used to seeing you come up from the store. I got worried, like somebody died."

She looked at his face and his clothes; his new appearance had come to the back of her mind: he was not a delivery boy. Singer or athlete? She did not know. But something different: he was that. The expression she always saw looked beyond the neighborhood. Looked back at it. But it was not calm, not assured (this worried her). It was the *nerves* in a runner before a race, or a soldier, pent up, and turning fear to hate to save himself from dying in his own mind before the fight.

"Please, please." Vito had come close to her. "Please come with me. Please! You got to."

"Vito. Now, listen. I can't walk out of here, as much as I might want to. I can't walk out the door downstairs. And I can't keep seeing you like this anymore, and then in a few hours, Cy comes walking in. I'll go crazy. And then — sometimes — I want to — want to hurt both of you for doing this, making this."

"I'm not ashamed." Vito's shoulders were up, his chest expanded, the cock's pose that he needed for certain words. "I'll tell the whole world what I did. And fight for it. And defend you —"

"Stop it, stop it! I'll get sick." Helen went to the antique chair and sat down. "I'll get sick. I'll get really sick." She placed her hands across her face. "I sit here, and then Cy comes home and I have to start talking to him. And put you out; but what goes on in my mind; what runs in my head is like a thing that's ready to scream."

"Tell him, then; tell him and send him away."

"No! Vito, you're being a baby. It doesn't work that way. You don't throw yourself in the street to scratch for bread. And Cy is my husband. Do you know what that means?"

"Look. Come with me. Let's get out of here right now. I'll talk about it while we're driving." Her tone had cast itself down on him, and partially in anger he took her hands and pulled her up and towards the door. "No," she said. "No. I can't go out like this."

Vito held her arms, carrying her along. She was in the maelstrom of his strength and began to let herself move, though she was afraid. "Let me get my purse and a jacket." She spoke in a quiet tone, as though others were near enough to overhear. Vito smiled his gratitude and his power, able to bend to her, the politeness given to held prey. He watched her go to her bedroom and return, more dressed, wearing a white blazer jacket, a soft sweater underneath, and a new short plaid skirt. The pride came back to him in the softness of the clothes, her red shining moccasin shoes, her blond yellow hair puffed and waved, her clean long fingers and the perfect fingernails, long and glistening with color.

On the elevator, Helen thought of the doorman in the lobby: she *should* pass him and laugh and spit at his feet; the thought made it hard to prepare herself. When the pink steel doors opened, she strode out very fast, three steps ahead of Vito, taking no notice of him.

She walked to his car, let herself in and did not look back. Vito stepped into the driver's seat, and they drove off.

They drove down, away from Riverdale, to Broadway and the elevated stanchions and older cars and cramped gas stations, the gutters dirty with paper cups and sheets of newspaper rolling along out of Van Cortlandt Park. It was the dividing line.

Vito turned the car into a station for gas. While they waited, he thought how he would introduce Helen to his mother and sister first, go right in on them before they could fancy up the house, let Helen see it honest and clear; then he would go around to the shop and introduce Pop and Vic.

He faced the tracks and his eyes looked at the hills beyond, the golf course and then the clustered houses of the East Bronx, closer together, rows of roofs under the hundreds of TV antennas.

"Do you know Gun Hill Road and around there?"

Helen had fallen into silence, waiting. "No, I don't," she said slowly. "I came from Bronx Park. You know, down around Fordham."

"Gun Hill's a big Italian neighborhood," Vito said.

"So is Fordham."

The attendant appeared at the window. Vito paid and drove on, up over the hill and a sight of his whole neighborhood. He saw his mother bending to shake Helen's hand; he saw Helen's blond hair and her gold skin in the dark rooms of the house, like a shaft of light.

The smell of the alleys came in memory; the odors wafted to his room upstairs, to all the rooms. When he had come back from college, the smell had made him sick to his stomach the first week. In a few months he was not aware of it at all and forgot that he had walked away and down along the Bronx River for hours just to be away from his house.

Now Helen would come from outside and get it right away; it would stink to her as it had to him that night he came back from Durham.

The odor was like the remains of the grapes crushed for winemaking and thrown into the back yards in cold October, steaming for days and looking like cowshit. It made an air of vinegar, heavy and sour, that rose first up the back doorways and seeped through the cellars where the families lived most of the time, in makeshift kitchens and sitting rooms furnished with old chairs to protect the good stuff upstairs in the parlor.

He saw his parlor where they would all sit with Helen as guest. It was like a storeroom, packed with stuffed chairs from Ludwig Bauman, a high, quilted couch, glass coffee tables with legs carved in curves and paws at the bottom like eagle claws clutching round balls. And even though the furniture was untouched, it was old in its way and the fabrics dark in a strange way, as though they could no longer receive light.

He felt the dust and the darkness of the house as he had found it after living in the college dormitory where the windows were large, the walls painted white, the halls wide and light. The smells were the darkness and the darkness hid the smells and gave them off, as though bits of decomposing things had settled in the corners. Yet his mother and sister cleaned all the time and mopped the floors and set the sheets out on the long clotheslines strung to old poles in the back yards and rubbed the piano and the legs of chairs and tables with rags and polish. Still, the inside air, the stripes of it you could see in the sun, showed the collecting dust rising all the time.

All that. All that. He saw the back of his mother's hands, the flesh over the veins (the topographical maps in high school would remind him of her hands, the ridges, the streams running off, the eroded land). The first time he saw it and thought the flesh would tear, he shuddered: and then he wanted to touch the skin, loose, the veins beneath ready to break through with blood. And he had: she had winced, let out a small cry. When was that? Ten?

Helen's voice roused him. "Please don't go so fast. It scares me. Vito! Please."

198

He had been weaving through traffic, passing cars suddenly, cutting them off at lights. Helen looked at the faces of drivers and their mouths opening.

The car passed the peak of Gun Hill Road. Below were the small houses of the East Bronx, the old El tracks like caked dirt, the crooked TV antennas like webs in the air. Vito saw the look of it enter himself, the wooden, unpainted streets; he saw the meeting happen again, his mother and sister shaking hands — Helen in the house; it exploded. The rage came up in his forearms, his hands on the wheel. He could not smack them around; he could not bow down and let them stare at her, curse at her. They would spit, jealous she had made it. Helen would not sit down. They were all running, everyone running out of the house; he could only scream STOP. Stop. He could not stop them. The idea was a joke. Who was he? Coming in with a blond. Coming in with a blond. They'd say it and say it. Who was he? He could do only these: leave them or beat them all down, with his own fists, even his brother: he could beat them all now.

He lowered his head a moment, away from the sin. His foot let the car go slow, be passed by other faces. The neighborhood came up and he rushed along the rim of it, to reach the Hutchinson River Parkway before being seen; near the parkway, he went faster still, but Helen had become silent, her fear greater than her anger, looking at Vito and the road ahead, back and forth.

On the highway he was especially careful, and stayed in one lane and held the speed at the limit. In Greenwich, he turned off and drove towards the water, finding a restaurant after a few miles and turning into a wide parking lot with a small cluster of cars parked around the brown building.

Vito stopped farther out in the lot; in the silence he was

embarrassed now, sitting with Helen, and he did not look at her.

"Should we go in there?" he said.

"Yes. Let's eat." Helen looked at the low, square building, its roof supporting a wooden lobster, painted red; from their position they could see it was a cutout, with no body, twice as high as the building, but without shape when seen as plywood fastened down with metal supports.

Vito now turned to her; the noon light touched her face, and she was no longer frightened. A wind reached her hair and blew it back; Vito thought of her face as it was on the bed when it was lost, sinking back into her feelings. He loved her; he was sure of it. Her features picked up the sun; he felt he would cry now, cry to look at her.

"What is it?" Helen's voice was pleasant. "Tell me what's wrong."

"I have to tell you something." He turned away from her face. "I'm going to leave you alone. What I did today. I dragged you up here. I do that. I drag people all the time. I drag people around too much. I can't help it. I can't stop. To me, you're *all* too slow."

Helen touched his right hand clasped around the steering wheel. "I know it's bad to push people around." His words came out above the sadness; beneath, a wound had shown. Helen felt the pity that enlarges: now she could cradle his head and hear his last words.

He looked at his own hands, then out over the water at the end of the lot. "It's this. I was going to take you to *my house.*" He watched a small boat docking beyond the lot, and he was quiet for a time. "Hey, look at that blue! That's what I came for. Look at it. That *gets* me — like the grass along the Saw Mill in early spring when it's still yellow, before it goes all green. It's only a few days when it's yellow like that." In his excitement he turned to Helen again. "I drive slow — all alone — all the way up the parkway to the end of it."

She smiled, and he remembered what he had begun. "But today I was taking you back. I was going to make you meet my family — before they could prepare — both of you. I'd make them greet you, welcome you. And you'd see them. Oh, Christ." His hands rocked the wheel and the steering column shook. "What a fucking gas!" He hit the wheel with his right hand, flat; the vibration could be felt in the seats. "Shit! What the hell am I daydreaming? Look. Look. Forget it, will you? I'll take you right back now. Tell your husband some story; tell him you went for a shopping trip. It's the last time. And then tell yourself you're an old lady. Right? That's what you said. And I'm a kid. OK?"

Vito turned the ignition on; the engine ran up, roaring then hacking down in quick deceleration.

"Let me buy you a lunch," Helen said. "I owe you from a long time ago."

He turned the switch off. "You mean that first party, don't you? When I brought you all that food and those little appetizers."

"Now I have to buy you a lunch. All right? A farewell."

Vito turned away in the emotion of the word; it had echoes, like a song's words.

"Just a lunch, then." Helen had begun to comb her hair. "Come on. Vito. Look at me."

She placed her hands on his face and he did not move. "Come on, let's go inside," she said, and opened her door.

Vito followed her in, and they sat for a meal; he ate slowly, unsure of which fork to use — there were three; he placed his torn rolls on the tablecloth until he noticed that Helen had rested hers in the small butter dish, then copied her.

Helen told him of her plans for a trip to the Caribbean and of little things she never had mentioned before — her rugs, new lighter drapes for summer. He was silent and looked about at the other tables and carefully at his food while he ate.

She reached forward a few times and squeezed his hands; during dessert she touched his knees with hers and watched him blush, and said, "What is it?" but Vito only smiled.

When they left, walking across the lot, Helen said, "Yes, I think I'll go home now." But as she approached the car, she stopped and looked towards the bay. "Let's go see the boats first," she said, and walked that way.

"You have to go home," Vito said.

"Plenty of time." She threw her purse into the air and caught it. "Come on, baby," she said, and kept walking quickly.

Vito followed, caught up, and walked beside her to the dock. "Vito, let's take a boat out for a while."

"Take a boat?"

"Yes. We'll go for a ride to the end of the water."

"Wait. I'll go down and ask the guy about renting." He jumped down to the wooden slats of the dock. "No, no!" Helen called to him, and then laughed. "I'm only kidding. We're not dressed for a boat ride. Come on back."

Vito came up and stood beside Helen while she looked out across the water. The shore wind whipped at her skirt, and men below, on the dock, looked up occasionally; Vito started to feel anger: he wanted to place a hand against her skirt but knew he would be laughed at.

Helen stood and turned her head slowly up and down the

coastline, unaware, it seemed, of the men watching her. But abruptly, she turned about and walked back along the parking lot to the car.

She slept on the way home and made Vito find a radio station that played quiet music. Vito did not mind, except that it was night music to him, the kind you used to cover other sounds.

She awoke as they drove along the hilly driveway to her building, jumped from the car as soon as it stopped, slammed the door shut and began to walk away.

"Thank you!" She stopped and called it, her purse swinging. "Be good!" She went up the steps and through the entrance, smiling at the doorman holding the rimless glass door.

# □□□ 18

O<small>N THE</small> third morning Vito did not come, she heard the bell, near noon, while she was dressing to go downtown to Altman's. She went to the kitchen door dressed in her suit and opened it slowly to see again the Negro boy who rode in the truck with Vito.

"This the order," Charlie said. He had just placed the box on the painted gray concrete floor near the door. He was leaving and looked back at her face. "The order from the store." Charlie tried to explain to the stare. "Didn't you order?"

"The other boy used to deliver."

"He's not here," Charlie said. "I do it, now."

"Oh, yes, I see." She had said something stupid. "Wait a minute, will you?" She went back for her purse and brought Charlie a dollar, then shut the door and went to the bedroom, leaving the box unpacked.

She imagined Vito had been hurt, in that white convertible with the spinners on the wheels — he had been speeding, missed some turn and crashed into some river.

Her anger towards Vito seemed to float; he may have

gone to the Coast and this meant that he would return unexpectedly. Yes.

Or he was down there, still in the store, sending the colored kid instead. She would have caught a look on the other
one's face, but no, no, he had not blabbed.

Something happened in him. Last time. He would not
come again. And that was right. He had a little class.

Helen dressed as fragments crossed her mind; his absence
was like his presence behind things, hiding, as though in
wait. When her coat and hat were set, she was annoyed at
Vito's dishonesty and walked down to pass the store: she
would show herself to this bastard kid.

Twice she passed and then crossed the street and went
into the luncheonette for coffee, waiting there until the
truck returned. Through the window she saw young boys
along the street, not much older than Vito. They stood near
the curb, never moving far from the door.

Their existence was only their long high slender legs in
tight jeans, and their long hairdos — they were bodies, only
bodies, and far from her in their play, in their vacant minutes milling: they did not want anything.

She went to the store as soon as the truck returned and
passed by: a counterman noticed her, waved, and she had to
walk in.

"I forgot a few things," she said after he greeted her.
"Could you send them up later on? I'm going downtown
right now."

"Why, sure," the counterman said, and Helen slowly
thought of items to buy, looking around the store and ordering luxury things, things that Cy would eat.

As she signed the receipt for her order and was about to
leave, she looked up at the counterman. "Say, whatever
happened to that nice kid who used to drive your truck?"

"You mean Vito. Vito Filippo who drives the truck." The counterman seemed pleased. "He's not with us anymore. He quit. When was it — just a few days, maybe a week ago. They say he's going to some music school. He's going to be a singer."

"Music school?"

"I'm not sure — but something with music, it is. He was a singer, you know, Mrs. Steinman. A good singer."

Helen did not like the counterman's eyes; she turned away and walked quickly out of the store, to the bus stop nearby. In a few minutes she became impatient and took a passing metered cab to the subway.

At four, when she returned, the second order was at the kitchen door and it set her to making a large dinner.

When Cy came home, she was setting the living-room table and explained that she was tired of kitchen eating. "What are we saving the rest of it for, I ask myself."

Cy saw her cheerful. "Listen, Baby. Listen. I just got a little set today. I can tell you, let's go down to that place right away. I can, I can make it."

"*Now he* wants to go. What happened to you?"

"What do you mean, *what happened?* Sure I want to go. I have been *saying* I want to go. Let's just get on that plane and go, go, go."

Helen went to the kitchen and returned with serving dishes. "Now what is it?" Cy asked.

"Take off your coat first and stay a while," she said.

Cy went to the bedroom to change and returned sullen. "Sit down," Helen said; she had been waiting, standing over the table.

"Cy, I was talking to Rachel and Manny's wife, Rose, and I got a new idea. It's so close to summer, you know. So why not just take a season at a Long Island club."

"All right, all right." Cy sat back and pointed his hands at her. "But. But just note here, my dear, that I am saying let's go and you are changing it. Should I say you can't be satisfied?"

Helen had been holding a fork and dropped it so that it struck her plate. "Should *I* say, how the hell hard have you tried? Satisfy? Should I say, what the hell do *you* know about satisfying? When do you *practice*? Should I say you're thirty years behind time in getting started?"

Cy looked down at his plate: words to the deepest part of feelings; they came down like blows.

"Answer, Cy." Helen's voice still above. "Answer. Defend yourself. You won't answer back as soon as I say anything. Maybe I'm wrong. Say your side of it; we'll face the facts that way."

Cy shook his head but let it hang down. Helen waited for his voice, but he did not move, his position like a found one of peace.

Helen stood up and walked to her bedroom; her eyes were wet, and she went to wipe them and stare into her mirror: the flesh below her eyes was beginning to darken and come through the makeup.

She paced the room and slammed the doors of her closet; she removed her dress and placed it in the closet next to the suit she had worn to Manhattan. Then she removed her slip and took her quilted housecoat, and stopped. Something made her remove her bra and panties before putting on the housecoat.

She came back and sat on the bed, facing Cy's new insistence: two hurry-up weeks, it would be, a bad burn, a strained back. Oh, let it be Long Beach now and get away from here from June to September.

No, no, no. She would sit and wait. Let Cy do something, once in a while. Let him get the tickets. He has the mood, *finally*, well, let him go downtown and let him get the tickets. The big arranger, the wheeling dealer, who eats at Leone's: let him call *his* friends and arrange it. One hand washes the other. Let them wash each other and come home with tickets.

She lay down, her face against the pillow, her mouth a bit open to breathe. The clean odor of the starch came to her: the pillow seemed to breathe against her: it vibrated with her breath, her heartbeat, like another presence, human, but not Vito, not Cy — someone like herself.

The pillow became wet after a while, her eyes unconscious of it again. Vito had let this sadness escape from inside her; it made her feel that something was wrong with her, feeling things so much. She cried, when everything was here to have; she cried for him and for Cy.

It was something to tell: she had thought of Doctor Berger, even of Mother Steinman, but you could not tell them of something closed, without words you knew, of a language you could not find.

It was ignorance. She had not been to college; Cy could not use her for anything anymore. Could she model with the pads collecting on her hips? A perfect *balloon* twelve. What could she *do*? What act that would show?

Her mother came back to her: whining, to placate that weak fool, her father, always waiting for his stupid approval of food, or something else she did for him, waiting even after she knew he was worthless, and had lost his hard-earned money on investments that fell through. Her mother, who told her to get ready for her own man; you did everything for them, worked on it all the time, but you would always be a badly scratched picture next to them; in them was always the seed of surgeon, lawyer, owner, judge.

The tears helped her fall asleep. When she awoke, the apartment was silent; she stood up and walked to the door, not knowing what to expect and afraid of the silence in the living room.

Cy was sitting in his chair; the TV was going, and he had fallen asleep facing it, his body curled up but his head facing the screen.

He awoke when he heard her removing the plates; she stopped and noticed the uneaten food and then Cy, looking. "I'm so sorry, Baby," she said.

"That's OK." Cy spoke with a quiet voice, tempered by sleep, and then smiled while she stacked dishes.

"Will you get the tickets tomorrow?" she said.

"*Me?*" Cy was confused. "You mean for Nassau? But I'm not sure I'll get the time — to get out — uptown."

"Send a secretary," Helen said. "All right?"

"Send a secretary? To talk over a trip *we* are taking? Someone should talk over the reservations, the kind of place. Couldn't you do that, Honey?"

"All right. Then I'm elected again." Helen went to the kitchen with a stack of dishes and returned. "But just listen to this, Cy." Cy turned and looked at her. "No questions asked. You'll go where *I* arrange and you'll shut up on the kind of hotel I pick and the room and so forth —"

"Whatsa matter? Whatsa matter?" Cy used his bluff, downtown voice. "I'll go along with anything you pick out. Just *pick* it. Don't we have the same tastes — in things like that? Whatever hits you right, I'd go along, too. We're the same."

Helen did not answer; she continued taking the plates away, lowering her head, intent and careful in her work. She would not agree, yet she had no other wishes than Cy's. Still, by saying that she could choose only what he would choose, he was wrong. How could his head, full of business, be like hers, too? She was not his double, but if she were, she was nothing, while Cy could make anything by wishing it and not even moving.

"What did you say?" It was Cy's voice, and she looked across the room to him: he had leaned forward in his arm-chair to speak, struggling to sit at the edge, his stomach affecting his balance.

"I say we better get down there and get in the sun," Helen said, "and work up a sweat and get some of that fat off you."

"Forget my *weight*, already, and tell me." He stood up and sucked in as much as he could. *"There,"* he said, then blew out his breath and walked towards Helen, stretching his arms, one of his preliminaries to sleep. "Say, Helen, what's this Nature Boy stuff? What do you want me to get like, some *Tar*zan of yours?"

"Just what the hell do you mean, Cy Steinman?" Helen's hands shook, against her will, as she held the coffeepot and creamer.

"Take it easy. Don't get mad." Cy smiled. "I mean you got a crush on some Rock Hudson, Tab Hunter, movie-star image you want me to turn into?"

"Oh, go to hell." She carried the pot and creamer to the kitchen, set them down on the pink Formica shelf near the sink.

Quickly, she began to rinse everything on the crowded shelves on either side of the sink, packed the dishwasher, filled the soap cup and set the machine going. Then she stopped and leaned over the sink, seeing her face in the steel pot's curved side, red and flushed. She had expected Cy to burst in.

She turned away from her burning skin, took the pot and

rubbed it with a scouring pad and watched its thick dry suds accumulate; then she ran the hot water and leaned over the rising steam while she rinsed the pot.

When she went to the living room, Cy had gone. The set had been left on, soundless, though. She switched it off, then folded the tablecloth, left it on the table for morning work and went to the bedroom.

At the door she heard his snores. Cy was in bed and as she entered and saw his face on his hands, cradling his cheeks, he seemed small. His body was pulled up tight. His forehead furrowed, as though feeling pain, was white, shiny: he had not washed. His legs were pulled up, a protective position. It was two different people: his face open and welcoming, a nice boy, but his body hunched, ready to ward off imagined blows. Poor Cy.

# □□□ 19

M<small>RS.</small> B<small>ERGER</small> had told her about this place, La Belle, after Mr. Fred had closed down suddenly. It was owned by Miss Mimi — you never got their last names — and her partner was supposed to be the lady who did the tinting, a friend of Mildred Berger's from Intervale Avenue, the old old days.

Mimi was tall and very pretty, her hair cut short, and crested with brief curls; it had probably been blond, but it was fixed with highlights of white-blond now. Helen was seated, watching her, and liked the look right away.

"How is Mrs. Berger?" Mimi said. "I think she said you were new up here."

Helen talked to the mirror, keeping her head straight so that Mimi could examine it and comb it out. "I had been going to another place. Something I just picked out of a hat. Did you know Mr. Fred?"

"Wasn't he the place with the white front? What did they call it?"

"Ezio of Rome."

"Ezio of Rome. That's right." Mimi's smile was a large

one; she seemed happy, like a person celebrating, having walked out of a prom. She did not seem to be thinking about Mr. Fred; the smile did not gloat. "You know how it works? A couple of guys get together in a partnership. Three or four hairdressers with a lot of dreams. They get themselves an expensive location — usually too expensive." Mimi turned to look at Helen and smiled. "The overhead is always too much. *You* know. About a hundred space-age chairs. And people go running for just about a year. Then bang. They're out of fashion. And they go broke in two months. Did you by any chance know Francesco's?"

Helen had been noticing Mimi's dress, a simple sleeveless polka-dot sheath, in blue and white, and then her toeless pumps, silk-covered: the look of it reminded her of midtown, of long summer afternoon luncheons, of the people at the Tavern. "Francesco? No, I never knew it," Helen said.

"Well, they had the place near the bank. Gigantic. I think he really *had* about a hundred chairs. And a Lincoln Continental to pick up his customers. Oh, he had everything. Somebody said he had Mitch Miller or Arthur Godfrey backing him. I really don't know. Nobody ever found out. But they went broke. That overhead. It must have been unbelievable."

Mimi combed in silence for a while and they began to discuss the style. "Well, it should be something quite dressy," Helen said. "I'm going down to Nassau."

"Oh that's wonderful. My husband used to work there." Mimi looked at Helen again. "The Carleton Arms. You're not going there, by any chance?"

"No. I don't remember the name. But it isn't that. This is only my first time there."

"Oh you'll love it." Mimi seemed happy. She reached for the large pink rollers and began to set Helen's hair, humming from *My Fair Lady.* "Don worked there for a few seasons. Then we came back here when he got the spot at Southampton. Oh you're going to like it."

Mimi shuffled away for more curlers. A smiling man came back with her, carrying a large open box. "Mrs. Steinman, this is Carmen."

Helen looked up, but the handsome face came down to her. "Hello," he said, with a young smile. "Always happy to see a new face." Carmen began to laugh; he brushed his blond hair back and bowed and stepped back. "Eventually, they all come here."

"He's happy today," Mimi said in a low, calm voice.

Carmen straightened up and did a little happy tap dance, hugging his black silk work coat around him tightly. Yet Helen noticed that he was not effeminate, but rather excited about something. He leaned down again to talk, but did not. Helen saw him nod, back away and move towards a customer who was coming from the tinting room: the woman smiled at Carmen and Helen and Mimi.

"He just made good again." Mimi had spoken softly and Helen turned to her face in the mirror. "Carmen's got a way with people; I don't know what you call it. I mean, he *is* a nice guy. Good at the work. There are customers who come in here and after a while they've got to have him in their business. He just went in with another woman and this woman's husband — their business — I don't know, about four or five months ago. This morning he told me how much he made out of it."

"Do you think he'll open his own beauty parlor?"

"Carmen? No. He's a free spirit." Mimi laughed. "Oh, he might go in on a coop deal. Like one of those Ezio of Rome's. At least he *would* have once upon a time. But he's nice. He wouldn't knock anybody. Those places, they start to knock each other and then their help. And that's the beginning of the end."

Helen smiled at a young woman in a white silk uniform who came from the back and began to set up her box of curlers at the next chair. "Mrs. Steinman, this is Ninette." Mimi turned to smile at her. "She came back in with me last winter when I bought the place again."

Ninette smiled at Helen and said something Helen did not understand. "She's a painter," Mimi said, when they had turned away. "And a good one. She *shows,* downtown." Mimi laughed. "We're all free spirits in this shop." Her eyes met Helen's in the mirror; the smile was slight, but her face held it, as if it were part of her. Helen liked the confidence of it, the care it held.

Mimi was like her place; it was a pleasant blending. The other dressers she had known were isolated from the room around them, which was *decor,* made up, pretty or fancy or fake, but something you accepted as a salon. Helen felt that she would come back here many times. She looked at Mimi's eyes: they were blue, with lines underneath that were part of her constant smiling. "I suppose I'm talking about myself," Mimi said. "I've been away three years. I sold out and went home." Mimi was shaking her head and smiling at Helen. "But I couldn't last. I came back last winter. I have to move around all the time."

"Do you live around here now?" Helen said.

"We live in Pelham. South Pelham. I grew up right around there, in Eastchester. My first shop was over in Eastchester. I'm an old hand in this business."

Mimi was working Helen's hair as she spoke; her hands were very quick and deft. She sprayed the hair, combed and set the shape while her mind had been wandering, her voice in a world different from her hands.

Helen was ready for the drier, and Mimi leaned down to remove the curlers in her lap. "Yes, it's a long time," Mimi said. "And I learned hair. And I *know* hair. Those overnight shops that come and go, they don't even have an idea about hair — how it grows and the different patterns of different heads, and diseases of the scalp — they wouldn't recognize them if they saw it." Mimi laughed again. "*Listen* to me. I'm giving you the whole history today, Mrs. Steinman. I should be on the couch."

Mimi looked to the back; it was early in the day and most of the driers were free. Helen stood up carefully and walked back.

Miss Evelyn said hello while Angie set the machine on Helen. Miss Evelyn sent regards to Mildred Berger and returned to her customer. Helen watched her while the drier worked.

The woman getting the dye was short and heavy, not as fancy as the ones she had seen at Mr. Fred's, and she was having her hair tinted black, which meant covering gray. She was clearly an old customer, and she laughed aloud with Miss Evelyn, who was heavy and busty: the two of them made the place homey and old and established.

Carmen came over while she was watching and leaned down to speak to her under the drier hood. "Mimi told you about me," he said. "The big businessman."

"Yes." Helen smiled and nodded that she had heard.

"I'm not the executive type," he said, and laughed. "But some women, they suddenly come in one day after a few years of coming in, and they're sure that *my* personality is going to make them more money." He stopped smiling. His eyes were up, an attitude of thought. "If I am in their business, everything's going to go. I'm *all right* music. *Now, now* they're going to make it and *enjoy* it. That's the story to them. But I always made a place. I worked. I really work."

Carmen smiled and went into the back room for coffee. Helen watched him through the open lattice door; he poured a cup from the silver urn and looked up and offered it to her. She shook her head. Carmen nodded and sat down, looking at Miss Evelyn pulling strands of hair through the holes in the plastic cap on the old woman's head.

When Helen was ready, she walked back. Mimi was standing with a young woman. "Mrs. Steinman, this is Irma."

Irma shook Helen's hand, then pulled back quickly. She kept her hands in tight fists close to her body, a tense woman with the body of a girl, a thin long body with small, pointed breasts that pressed against her tight nylon dress.

Irma's hair was very short, so much so that it seemed unnatural, cut that way because of something in her nature; it did not make sense on a beautician who had all this around her: the back was shingled too roughly, like a hairdo of the thirties.

"Irma was with me when we had this shop the first time." Mimi was speaking, and Helen looked towards Irma after she had sat down. Irma had turned to her own customer, a quiet, tall woman, and began working silently. "You know we three are the old-timers. Irma. Ninette."

"Irma seems so young," Helen said.

Mimi turned her head towards the mirror and looked at the hair's mirror reflection, studying it in preparation for the final combing. "I met Irma, oh, about ten years ago. From Sweden; she was right off the boat. She's about the best dresser I've ever known. She could go anywhere. But this shop is steady; it's always been a moneymaker. And thank god we all get along."

Mimi seemed to be thinking; her hands were held over Helen's head. Helen looked up at her, then out at the street: through the small space between the drapes she could see busses and cars, all silent behind the glass.

Mimi combed her hair up, shaping two swirls on top of Helen's head. "Is that the idea?" Mimi asked, and Helen nodded.

Mimi finished the shaping: it was almost too dressy, but slanting and graceful. Mimi caught the pleasure in Helen's face. "We're going to make you just right for Nassau," Mimi said. "Maybe somebody down there will remember my style." Mimi laughed, then stopped herself. "How long are you staying?"

"Oh, about two weeks, I think."

"Second honeymoon?" Mimi laughed at the thought.

"Well, maybe we *should* call it that? My husband wants to celebrate. He's so happy. It's his business — he's made a very big merger, and we just keep talking about this trip. He's been asking me to go, asking me what I want: he keeps wanting to buy me things. It's crazy, but it *is* fun. You know."

"Oh that's good." Mimi had stepped back to listen. Now she took the spray set and used gentle bursts as she arranged the final stages of the hairdo. "He must be a happy guy these days."

"He *is just* like a kid. And now I'm excited, too — especially me. And I hardly know what's going on, except that it's good. But we both wanted this trip so much. And secretly, I've been wanting to see him get down there and open up and have a real time to enjoy himself."

"That's for you to do, Mrs. Steinman." Mimi watched

Helen's face for a reaction. "Or maybe I'm just quoting myself. Don, my husband, always says that. When I get out to Southampton, he'll always ask me to plan the night. Pick out a place to go. He wants me to set the mood."

Helen watched her hair becoming moist and shining, softening and moving into graceful curves; she could not believe her own hair had become this. "It's so nice," she said. "But isn't it going to be a bit too formal for day wear?"

"Oh no. Not while you do this." Mimi reached into her marble drawer at the base of the mirror. "Do you have a pin like this?" Mimi held a large bamboo Japanese hairpin.

"No, I don't have anything like that."

"Then take this. Look. For daytime, you just let down the sides like this and pull them back. See?"

They looked into the mirror and watched it. Mimi showed her the two styles. "I see it," Helen said. "Up for night."

Mimi put the two locks up again and fastened them with a twisting motion. "Yes, up like this for night."

"I like that."

Mimi smiled again, let the strands down and pinned them back with the bamboo pin. "I'll return this pin," Helen said.

"No you don't. You keep that for Nassau." Mimi stepped back and dropped the used curlers into the big box. Angie came to take them to the washroom. Helen had caught Mimi's face: she did not call any of her help, but merely looked around until she caught their eye, then signaled them with a look. That was why Carmen had come over, and Irma, and Angie. "You have a lovely place," Helen said.

"Smooth-working." Mimi laughed; it seemed that she had guessed Helen's thought. Mimi removed the plastic apron and followed Helen to the coat closet near the entrance. When Helen went to the cashier's desk, Mimi sat down on the semicircular couch in the waiting alcove. The couch, like all the furniture, was coated in dull ivory, darkened at the edges like Mother Steinman's antique tables.

When Helen had paid, she went to Mimi and gave her the tip. Mimi smiled and offered Helen a cigarette. "No, thank you," Helen said, and sat down. She did not wish to leave the atmosphere of Mimi's smile, and it seemed that she should sit with Mimi for the duration of the cigarette. "You're a good boss," Helen said.

"I leave my help alone," Mimi said. "It's the only way. Whatever they do, they do. I have no comments."

Mimi had relaxed, looking at her cigarette; she leaned over and let her neat legs spread: Helen saw her thighs: black, unshaved hair; it was a shock because Mimi had seemed so light, Scandinavian. The black hair was a sign of something else, of something without elegance, a secret neighborhood made before blond Riverdale. And Helen suddenly sensed the disclosure and moved her eyes quickly to Mimi's face.

"Sometimes I feel like an actor," Mimi said. "I mean, sitting here, I think I'm between the acts."

Helen saw that Mimi's eyes were directed to the chairs behind them. A short, hunched gray woman had come in: she was seated in the chair Helen had used, and Angie was gently dressing her in a plastic smock.

"Now you see I'm going to be talking about grandchildren and the awful condition of the streets. I'll be completely different." Mimi pressed her cigarette into a glass ashtray. "Excuse me a minute," she said.

Helen watched her greet the old lady and quickly begin on her hair. In a short time Mimi had rolled the gray hair into many small tight curls, on tiny rollers. After spraying the hair, she saw Helen and came back, holding a roller. "Remember these?" Mimi said.

"It's the old type of permanent, isn't it?" Helen looked back at the small gray head, its reflection in the mirror, looking globular and silly, the work of time. "Oh, I remember when everybody looked like that," Helen said. "Walking around with those little pin curls. Remember the curling irons?"

"Everybody sticks to her own look," Mimi said. "I look in that mirror every day and I know I have to change; it's my work to look different. But I know when a customer looks in the mirror, she wants to see what she looked like at a certain time. *You know.* The best time. Whenever it was she was satisfied. Like the night you first heard 'The Music Goes Round and Round.'"

Helen laughed at the dead time, though it was a song before her own days: she nodded politely to Mimi.

"I remember," Mimi said, "those were the days when this kind of set was all we did."

Helen looked into her eyes. "In Eastchester?"

"You know where that is, don't you." Mimi watched Helen for recognition, and Helen gave it, discreetly, offering the knowledge that both shared the East Bronx as a beginning, that it was not unspeakable but only needed a little hiding at certain times and in certain places, at La Belle, where hair was a preparation for Nassau or charity affairs where Sammy Davis shook your hand.

"Over there," Mimi said, "all we had were permanents, permanents. We all had those little frizzled heads. And lousy bleaches. Don't you like this new soft look today?"

Helen nodded. "I grew up on Bronx Park South."

"That's way down, isn't it? Did you know the German

neighborhood around Evander Childs? It's all Italian now."

"I graduated Evander," Helen said.

Mimi laughed. "Well, here we are." Mimi looked at the old lady, who was being helped by Angie towards the driers. "Is your husband from there?"

"No. Cy's from Manhattan."

"Don's from Mount Vernon. He's been a golf pro fifteen years." Mimi looked down at the glass table between them and nodded.

"Cy's family had a big business built up. He's made it bigger, too. I told you. He's always talking about moving here and there, getting a big house."

"*You* want a house?"

"Oh, I don't know. It's up to him."

"We got a house once. Lawns, the furnace that breaks when you go to work. You're always calling some painter. You find yourself spending more money on the shingles than yourself. It was going to be *our* house. You know, with a little white fence around it, which it had, and black wooden shutters. New England style. Cape Cod something." Mimi was shaking her head. "It was awful. We never could get away from it."

"I'm not sure Cy wouldn't really be happier in a house."

"Well, *that* you know. I mean, you know *him* — if it's the thing for him. Now Don, when he works at a place like Southampton, he's at his best. He's not a house type. But they say men are. They fool around with lawns and cellars, playrooms. And Don *did* like the house. But he liked it better when we sold out."

Mimi laughed and looked up, over Helen's head. The front door had opened, and a heavy young woman, wearing slacks, had rushed in, leaving the door open. Mimi went up to greet her.

222

"I'm double-parked," the woman said. "Look, we're going away this Friday. My hair has grown out. Can you *do* this?" She raised her right hand, which was holding a full hairpiece, lighter than the woman's hair.

"We'll lighten it all," Mimi said. "Just leave the piece and then come in Thursday and we'll match you."

"OK, OK," the woman said, and looked at the wig, which she had placed on the cashier's glass desktop.

Helen then noticed a small girl in shorts, whose thighs were very thick, pressing against each other, pink and red. She was about six, and already had a shape like her mother's and a face beginning to move in imitation of her mother's nervous twitches. But she did not have the same speed yet and was bewildered by her mother's pace. The child was moving towards the cashier's desk, looking around at the chairs and the women facing mirrors when her mother slapped the wig down as a gesture of acceptance to Mimi. Then she walked away quickly, grasping the child's hand as she moved to the door. "I'll be in Thursday about noon," she said to Mimi, and pulled the child out with her.

Helen stood up and saw herself in the mirror over the desk. Her hairdo was familiar already, as if it always had been on her this way. She turned her head to look at the pin Mimi had given her: it was pretty, the bamboo lacquered in stripes of brown and black that complemented her blond hair.

"Good-bye," she said to Mimi. "I've got things to do."

"Have a good time." Mimi walked to the door with her. "Enjoy yourself." Mimi opened the door. "Nice to have met you."

"I'll see you when I come back," Helen said.

"We'll want to hear about it," Mimi said.

## □□□ 20

$S$HE HAD finished the packing, gone down for resort clothes, arranged for the girl to come in twice a week, taken valuables to the bank box, even secretly bought Cy some new cabana sets and a swimsuit in case the old ones did not fit.

The luggage was waiting at the kitchen door: its readiness for flight had brought back Vito. But he was away, placed in a handsome compartment, in his job, his club. Now it was necessary to settle him there by knowing where he was. If he were out of work, betrayed by the music people, he could come back to penetrate this apartment because he had left from here.

She thought of her bonds, cash from the special account in her name, money she never touched: she would invest in him herself and keep him away with her money.

She tried to find the checkbook, giving up finally in the bedroom, sitting on her bed, unable to remember where it was kept. Her thoughts went to the day of the ride: blueness and wind; they were outside: Vito had been unraveled, torn up by something not her fault. She was not the cause.

But she had used it to drop him, stepping on the weakness with her tone, her laughing. An hour after he had gone she had wished him back; the flippant good-bye she gave him seemed filthy.

All week she had spent the mornings dressing and making up; she had gone down to the avenue and passed the store, like a fool. On Thursday, Cy had asked about her appearance — did she want to go out — and she had answered that she felt shabby in slacks or housedress day after day.

She was going to say good-bye to Vito; each morning she touched herself with that resolve, groomed herself for the meeting, adding new eyelid color, new eye lines at the edges, new pale lipstick shades, a matching polish for finger and toenails, tan pancake for her legs; she wore rings from her jewel box, and necklaces; on Friday she wore her pearls.

She was going to offer him help. If he were going to the Coast, she would give him the names of the lawyers; then she would tell Cy about this nice kid who had helped her and his lovely voice (she had the record to play). Cy would like that, would take him in: he went for young talents and had invested in one musical already.

But Vito never appeared. She had sat in the luncheonette, aware of the counterman's facts about Vito's quitting, watching the street and the store. She must ask them more. But each day that she imagined herself at the counter asking, she saw the countermen laughing at her: she had fallen down and was beneath them, those red Irish faces (all like policemen). They were large and mocking, liking nothing better than a chance to knock others, and let's face it, on Jews, as they rode them in Bronx Park, as they stoned the Hillel Center and left Learsi Goldman sitting in blood.

Only the Negro kid was possible to talk to, if he could understand, respond. But he was in a trance when she spoke to him. He came in with the order; she had talked to him, had let him into the kitchen, but he had stood and blinked his eyes, waiting for her to go on. Helen spoke in short phrases, waited, then spoke again to the placid face. It did not react as if it heard.

Today, though, she would ask him directly; she had called in a last order, all canned goods and paper stuff that would keep, and waited for the boy. He came just before noon, and she told him she was going away. "And you see, I've still got this demo record Vito lent me just to hear — his singing voice — which I'd like to return to him."

Charlie's eyes went up; Vito had been getting some of the grits around here. Charlie looked into the living room, packed with things and empty of people, like a movie room, the apartment that is always waiting when the chick walks in.

"So I wonder if you could just get hold of Vito's home number?"

Oh, that boy. The quiet MF. Right under my nose. But did he lay an egg in here or did he take a few little jams himself?

"I said, I wonder if you could locate his *address?*"

"Well," Charlie said, "Mrs. Steinman, he live up in the East Bronx. Around White Plains."

"Yes, I know that." She was presssing her hands together. "But what is the street and the number?"

"I don't know the house." Charlie studied her face: this bitch was jumpy. "See, he asked me, but I didn't go up. But I got a friend — O'Gilvie — who goes up there a lot. Maybe he'd know."

"Would you ask him for me?" At least, the voice was clear enough to understand now, out from under the trance voice. "Soon?"

"Yeah. I have to see O'Gilvie. My friend. I have to see him, and I'll ask him. When you going away?"

Helen lost patience. "Thank you very much. I'll see you when I get back. Thanks." She placed a dollar bill in Charlie's hand.

Ten minutes after he had gone, the front doorbell rang, and she was sure that the boy had called Vito, who was now here. But it was the pickup truck to take the bags to the terminal.

While the man was tagging the bags, Cy telephoned. "I'm going to have to finish up here, so I'll meet you down here — at the East Side Terminal. Now remember, it's six o'clock. And take one thing for me, will you — I forgot my electric razor."

She returned to the delivery man, tipped him and watched him carry the suitcases through the kitchen and out, smiled at him, then shut the door as he waited for the service elevator.

She went back and walked through the apartment, pulled the shades and blinds, closed drapes; she found Cy's razor and put it in her tote bag. She did not want to touch the kitchen now, though it was early; if she ate she would leave some crumbs no matter how she cleaned, and they would attract roaches. She decided on the luncheonette for a sandwich.

While she ate, she watched the store across the street; at one-fifteen she left and stepped out into the sunlight, pleasant and warm. Rather than go back to nap, she walked away from the closed apartment. Crossing Johnson Avenue, she stopped as a yellow meter cab passed slowly. She called to it and made it stop in the middle of the street; the driver backed up and she got in. "Go down to Gun Hill Road," she said, "and across to the East Bronx."

The driver leaned over and dropped the flag. "Anyplace special?"

"I'll tell you when we get there."

At White Plains Avenue, the cab slowed down. "Isn't this the Italian neighborhood?" Helen said.

The driver turned around. "Yeah. Up White Plains here. Fish stores, pork stores, anything you want."

He parked and Helen paid and left the cab. "Just walk straight up that way," the driver said. "You'll see it all." The driver was smiling at her — it was flattering, and she smiled and waved to him.

The avenue was shabby, the same dingy, colorless ugliness as her old neighborhood, the sidewalks gritty and paper-strewn, the sound of trains overhead and the shadow of their tracks and pillars perpetual. It was like a return to twenty years ago; Riverdale had made her feel that there was newness and improvement and because her parents were dead she had forgotten, as though her neighborhood had been closed down, like the TB hospital that couldn't get enough patients. But there were always more poor, a greater number ready to take the old places.

She noticed the little rows of apartments over the stores. And looking into shop windows she saw that some color and life and shape was there.

Then she turned off the avenue into a street of small houses. Dark, wooden, tar-shingled or of dull red brick, they seemed worn by too many hands, rubbed out of life, not grown old nice; their windows were gray and hooded, empty of light or movement.

Helen paused occasionally to notice the yards and the alleys between the houses. Children were all around, white, black, and all shades: it reminded her of El Paso, where they had stopped over for two nights.

228

She walked through it all, passing new houses going up, the same dull brick with double windows, but just like the old houses. On certain streets there appeared clusters of stores — bakeries, butcher shops, fruit and vegetable stores, a grocery with paper advertisements covering the whole of the glass window and neon light coming down like red dust.

Near one cluster she saw an empty store with a sign in the window advertising it as a taxi service. Inside, four young men sat on bridge chairs and looked out: they could have been Vito's brothers.

The sound of bells drew her to a church of orange stucco; she stood and watched the bells swing in the wooden belfry, big, black iron bells, the largest she had ever seen. The vibration filled her body and she thought of going down the steps that led into the church.

But she turned, embarrassed now; the bells meant it was late, and the vibration was disturbing. She walked back to the taxi service and arranged to be taken back. Two young men argued over who would drive; they tossed a quarter and argued over the results, then did the best of three. Finally, the winner came running to the car at the curb, where Helen stood, watching.

"Here we go, here we go, Miss." He opened the door and after she had sat down, ran around to the driver's seat and removed his driver's cap, combed his hair, and drove off.

Going back to the west, he passed traffic so fast that Helen shut her eyes. But when they reached the apartment, she had him wait while she went up for her bags.

"Now take me to the East Side Terminal," she said when she came down.

"Gee, I wouldn't know how much I should charge you for that." The boy turned to speak; he had black curls on his forehead.

"Charge me whatever you want," Helen said.

"Wait! Wait! OK. OK. Let's do it. Let's see how quick we can make it. I'll tell them I stopped off for a Coke. Then I can do it for nothing."

"Not if you're going to get into trouble."

"Don't *worry,*" the young man said, and they drove to the West Side Highway.

After they had passed the toll bridge, Helen felt Manhattan coming and wanted to talk, to tell the boy where she was going and all she planned to do there. But she sat silently and looked at the wide river, blue and brown, catching the flat clearness of the sky and crests of shining from the sun. They rode under the bridge.

"Don't you love the Washington Bridge?" Helen said.

"What's that, Miss?" The driver spoke after a pause that suggested the daze of his thoughts.

"I wonder do you know a Vito Filippo in your neighborhood?" Helen looked at the back of his head.

"What was that, again, Miss?" He did not turn, but kept his head stiff and straight, intent on the road.

"I said did you know Vito Filippo. Sometimes he goes under the name of Phillips; he lives in your neighborhood. That's why I wondered."

"Vito? Vito Filippo? Yes, I know him." He turned his head to the side, a polite movement which gave Helen his profile, showing that he was speaking for her. "Vito I think lives over on Two Nineteenth. His family has the bakery."

"Do you know the address?"

"You mean the *number?* No. It must be in the six or seven hundred, like six something something East Two Nineteenth." The driver was silent for a while. "Vito. Yes. He graduated with my oldest brother, Robert. Did you know him when he played college ball? They say he was a star. Written up a lot in the papers."

"Yes," Helen said, and turned to the window.

"I only knew him slightly." The driver did not know the context of Vito and this blond woman, and he could not understand her abrupt silence. "Vito used to go with a different crowd of guys — older than my crowd; they go downtown a lot. So I don't see him too much. But we all heard of him. In the neighborhood. He's well-known."

"Yes," Helen said. "Well, if you *do* see him, tell him Helen says *hello*."

"Helen says *hello*. That's it?"

"Yes. That's the message. Helen. He'll remember."

"He better remember," the driver said, and Helen smiled at the tone.

They had reached the Twenty-third Street exit and drove off the elevated highway into city traffic. Neither spoke while they rode through the noisy streets.

At the terminal, a porter came and opened the door before the driver could help her. The porter took her two bags; Helen leaned forward on the seat. "Don't forget to tell Vito," she said, and gave the boy a five-dollar bill.

"Yes, sure. But this here's too much." The driver held the bill near her.

"Not if they don't believe your story." Helen stepped out. "If they do, remember to find Vito."

"Vito?" The driver was distracted. Cabs were rushing by, honking behind him. The porter slammed the door and slapped the side. "I'll look around," the driver called.

She looked into the car once more, leaning down, and studied the boy's face: it had big eyes, and his hands and arms bulged with hardness. She found herself smiling, a smile she did not control, not polite or grateful: she *knew* this boy, his humor and his wants and urges; she knew his simplicity and the kind tone of his bigness. She turned away in a blush of feeling and walked to the escalator.

# 21

A**T THE HOTEL**, they were greeted on its wide porch by a concert for incoming guests, a steel band playing. The guests clustered together, impatient to get to their rooms, looking at one another. Waiters came round with drinks; Cy took one, but Helen refused, sensing the silly discomfort going through the little crowd from New York stopped by the director or manager, to enjoy themselves here.

But the nice part of it to Helen was the way the ocean breeze took the sounds of the instruments and blew them back and forth, out over the water and back, like riding echoes. And upstairs, unpacking, she mentioned it to Cy, who went to the window and looked down at the lawn that led to the beach. He was quiet for a long while and Helen continued unpacking.

"Yes, there it is in the air," Cy said. "You can't see it. But it just fills you with something."

"Are you happy you came, now?" Helen was placing his swim clothes on the bed.

"I look out over there and I wish I could just stay right here." He turned from the window and looked at Helen, with an expression of hope, as though he wished she would change into another being and he himself another with her. "You'd get a tan here, and you slim down and go to work on the boats. You know, once one of my gym teachers said I could be a champ at shot-putting."

"Really, Cy; you did sports? You never told me."

"Well, look, I'm five ten and a half, with an extra-wide build in the shoulders and chest. My shoulders and chest is a size forty-six, you know, and the rest is a forty-two. I have to get special cuts all the time. Stands to reason; I was on my school team."

"Maybe you could start up again. You know, start some one thing —"

Cy came to his bed and looked down at his trunks and picked them up. "You can't start *anything* again, Baby. Don't you know that? Once you're screwed, you're screwed —"

"Oh, Cy, no! Never say that. We're never finished. There's always a new start."

Cy removed his shirt and trousers; the sight of his stomach was unpleasant: he rubbed it gently, then removed his undershorts. "The body, I mean the body," he said. "I can't climb two flights of stairs. You don't get breath back. You don't make your muscles again; look, even your own arms are beginning to hang. But not as bad as me. Look." He squeezed his arms and thighs, pressed his stomach. "Every day you feel them turn to Jell-O in the hand. That's what it is to make a buck. And then, even take those guys who go to a health club — how long do they keep it up: six months? Ahh — forget it." He took his swim trunks and tried to put them on. "Helen, look at this."

Helen laughed. "Well, I've got a little surprise for *you,* Baby."

234

Cy put on the new bathing suit, thanked her for being smart, and went out to swim.

He swam back and forth beyond the breakers and came in to rest occasionally and then went out again. When he was through, he felt tight all over and came back for a drink.

Then he changed, dressing in the Bermuda short set Helen brought for him and walked out along the beach for a long stroll alone.

Helen watched him from the terrace; she was pleased to see him in the shorts — his legs still shapely and his hair blown by the sea breeze: he had not looked this way in so long.

When he returned, they had supper and Cy was quiet, unwilling to talk. "What is it?" Helen said, but he shook his head.

"Just when you're feeling so good, you get depressed." Helen placed her hands on his in concern, to stroke him with care.

"I'm tired," he said. "I unwind and I get tired. You know what I think about?"

"No, what?"

Cy stopped as the waiter brought coffee; he watched the tan hands, long hands, move the cups, saucers, plates, so deftly.

When the man had gone, he did not wish to say. But Helen asked, "Please tell me, Cy. I am your wife."

"Oh, it's not that," Cy said. "It's just that it's a little stupid, that's all. I suddenly hear my heart. Well, then I think I'm going to get a heart attack."

Helen caught herself; she would not repeat the same warnings. "You look swell," she said. "Really good. I think you have a tan already. Did you use the new Tanfastic cream?"

"Do you mind if I went to bed right away?" Cy had taken two sips of his coffee and pushed the cup and saucer away slowly.

"No, no, I'll come up."

"No, don't make yourself come up. I'll just go alone. You can stick around. There's the band."

"But what am I supposed to do, sit alone and *drink* in there?"

"You never know." Cy was smiling. "You might find a little romance."

Helen looked at his face, his eyes; Cy could not exchange the stare, and turned away. "Yes, thanks a lot," she said. "I'll pick up some nice, handsome, skinny rich man."

"Good, good," he said, and stood up. "Are you coming?"

"Why? You told me to stay and fool around."

"All right, all right. Have a good time." Cy walked off, through the dining room towards the elevators.

Helen sat for a few minutes, feeling insulted and then embarrassed, as though she had done something bad to him. She stood up and looked around: no one came; she turned and went out through the terrace and walked along the back gardens of formal green hedges. The night was too good to stay hurt in or to be alone; she longed to go up to Cy.

She went to the room; the lights were out, and moonlight made a light-blue cast of light over the large bed and the bureau and night tables; the floors were specked with this light. She undressed and slid into the bed next to Cy, placing her back against his; he murmured and pressed himself close to her, but as she waited, his body turned itself further into the crouch of his sleep, and he slept without moving. Helen placed her palms against his legs and stroked them, but he did not move: she did not go on, but waited for Cy, who did not come out of the cover of sleep.

Next day, Cy went for the water again, and later took a boat to row and then found a man to play badminton. At night, his back growing tender under the sun, he nevertheless dressed formally for the big costume *dansant* and came down with Helen and danced; the evening was excited by the loss of an evening skirt by a British woman, whose dancing partner had stood on it unknowingly while she walked away; the woman's leopard print silk panties had suddenly flashed up, and a few dancers had applauded to take away the embarrassment.

Cy could not stop talking about the moment, and it inspired him to drink a great deal. Later, in the room, he tried to ask Helen to come to bed wearing her panties, but he could not find the words.

On the third day, Cy rested on the beach, taking brief dips and lying on a blue blanket and beginning to eat in earnest. The waiters came out to serve the bathers, and Cy ordered four different baskets of fruit and later miniature pastries and sweetbiscuits and tea.

Helen looked up from time to time, feeling hidden deep behind the darkness in her sunglasses; the baskets pleased her: a sight and shape that meant vacation to her, the food all about, ready when you wanted to reach out, more than anyone could hope to finish.

But Helen did not eat much; she soaked up sun most of the day and found herself *dreaming off into space,* as she called it: her eyes would stick on a point far off, waiting for thoughts and words that never came.

Between times she brushed her hair, and the movements took away the agitation near the thoughts that would not tell themselves.

She did her nails with a new color she had found: Key Largo Pink. The place made you want to do all these things: you barely contacted the people who were all around after greeting them briefly at breakfast, people who came down on the plane or ate while you ate, faces you saw in the embarrassment of chewing. And when you looked up to stare at them, they were looking, too, from behind their large black glasses, but no one needed to nod or smile.

That night Cy drank heavily again and because Helen knew what he was preparing for, she drank, too. He hung his lust like a little light, and she had come to hate it when it was obvious because it was so public.

It had been hateful, but that had changed in a few months. Cy was tiring but not hateful; they sat facing each other.

Cy began shaking his shoulders to the music as he drank: he was getting himself hot. Yes, she would go along, keep up in drinks, for in the past two years, as everything he did in bed speeded up, being drunk helped her to be close with him and to feel some thrust inside her when he whined his ending.

She did not like her own examining: sitting back, she could see him working up his plans, building a world inside him. His speech would gradually change; the respectful tone, the politeness he was known for, would drop away. "Hey, puss," he would say, and look up from reveries over his glass, "how's about it? How's about a little pussy to-night?"

Helen at first responded with anger and talked to Cy as if

he were shouting to the crowd; he would be spurred by her anger: "Whatsa matter, whatsa matter? Everybody knows about the nookie here. Everybody's looking for a little nookie at the end of the rainbow. Look at some guys; want a little bit of yours, hanh? Just don't give it away. Don't give it away. Just show it to the boys. Show it to the boys."

In a short time Helen knew the words: she accepted Cy's game, and what he said did not need apology although Cy would come with remorse the next day and say he forgot what it was he had said but that it must have been awful.

She did not care tonight, nor even begin to explain it to herself as a duty to her husband, these words, and later his body in bed, his mumbling and his awkward pumping about, like a schoolboy excited yet made drowsy with a tricky drug.

She was enjoying it; she wanted Cy. He was wearing his formal white jacket and looked handsome; all men were handsome this way: they shone like pictures from the Saturday movies, standing in the center of white upholstered rooms, with white telephones on the plastic tables and white and black diamond-shaped floors and windows that looked out on a painted scene or nothing.

She had forgotten how many drinks she had had and barely saw the waiter; her view passed Cy in brief, short glimpses. Cy had suddenly decided on a rum drink made in a pineapple and had ordered two, and they were there on the table, blocking pieces of Cy.

His head roamed in the space before her eyes; it went about, as though he were looking for her among the other guests, his Helen who could become a stranger he would meet and immediately possess.

His head rocked; his shoulders moved up and down in

exaggerations of the orchestra's rhythm; he was not merely Cy, and he took Helen up to dance, twirling round her, daring to bend his knees and move about in a crouch, even calling to the band in his ecstasy.

At four, they left the dining room; only a young crowd of couples remained — college kids, Helen thought, and envied their big party and their sureness, as though they owned the room. They did not look back at anyone who looked at them.

Cy's sweat was beginning to show through his jacket; his arm on Helen was wet, his hands were wet, his shirt collar, like a choking chain, had become gray with wetness.

"Unbutton yourself," Helen said, and Cy's fingers went up to undo his collar button, but he could not do it while they walked.

"Upstairs," he said, and began to dance in the lobby. Helen disliked the dancing most of all: his body was so thick, clumsy: in it was the little fat boy who always had to work, kept away from dancing by it except for the night of some affair, and then, if he *could* dance, fresh from some lessons.

He drummed against the elevator walls with the flat of his hands and the operator smiled at Helen, a much worse reaction than anger. In the smile of the West Indian, they were reduced; they were items, looked upon indulgently for whatever they did since they were driving inexorably to the end of their vacation and the paying of the bill.

Cy pushed his body against hers as they walked along the narrow hall to their room and pressed his fingers against her dress, in the space between her buttocks. She let him come on, and they fell into their room, Cy sitting on the bed.

But, as Helen undressed, he jumped up and pushed her

down upon the bed. "All right, Cy. But let me get ready first," she said.

"No, no, keep it on, keep it on." It was his love of lingerie, and she smiled now and lay back and let him rub her. Cy murmured along with his hands, and it was pleasant feeling the sensations of herself coming from outside, from beyond the surface of her flesh.

She lay back on the wide bed and watched the last stars and the blue Caribbean water of light morning. The wind was mild and cool, and she felt it all. With Cy, with anyone here, she could make love. Here it was like eating the many fruits, natural, more natural in this warmth and light than at home where the silences were always broken, even late at night — the squeals and farts of the busses loud in your own room, the fire engines on patrol every hour, the police chasing some addict who just robbed an apartment, sirens going, and the constant highway traffic.

Here, there had not been a sound of machines in four days, and her mind went along that passage as Cy stroked her and kissed her.

*Oh why can't we live down here in the sun where you can feel clean inside and out and everything you do is the whole of you, felt without the world shut out of your self, where you're not just a mouth that eats or a mouth that talks or a hand that gives out money, part of a human instead of a whole one complete with the one you know and you're sure of like love that enters you both a living thing you take and you give and forget the rest the pieces of you that stand for you in the cities.*

Cy's mumbling grew too loud and ran through these thoughts, but his movements were slowing down. She placed both hands on his penis and rubbed it very quickly, to bring him back. His voice became louder, rising up the scale. She had wakened him; now she stroked him until his penis became stiff and then placed it gently between her thighs while he mumbled the words of some adventure in which he was not being led but rather was striking like a thunderbolt.

THE APARTMENT seemed new when she returned. The perfumes and lipsticks she had brought back started her on a shopping spree; every day she found some new things for summer. She came in off the downtown limousine and modeled the stuff in the bedroom, the big paper bags on the bed, pins rolling on bits of white label, sheets of tissue falling on the rug as she unfolded blouses, saleslips blowing across the room.

She dressed in the clothes, put them away, then modeled them again later. She tried on lipsticks and eye makeup and the powder blended for her at Saks. She did her nails and worked on the new bird's nest she had had done by Mimi.

There was no response from the mirror, nothing for thirst. Nothing was good after a day, nothing changed, nothing traveled to a smile. She stared at her face until the image seemed to be a real person, strange as the mirror's truth, looking at her.

The sun of June bore itself into the apartment day after day; even high up, over all of Riverdale, the air brought wetness to her skin; her armpits were wet soon after she sat at her dressing table to do herself, and she used deodorant pads all day, even though they were expensive.

In the late afternoons she would start her wait at the windows, watching the homecoming cars roll up, increasing in number as the hours went along. She would have a supper prepared and be dressed up, her face wet under the makeup, the powder getting dark in spots.

Cy would return tired from the heat trapped in Manhattan. He welcomed the meals, and they took in a few clubs, still in the mood of Nassau. They met a few new people and were invited to three parties, then an art opening (a niece of Cy's, who had just finished at Bennington).

Helen sat at these parties in the pleasure of the image she could recall in her mind from her dressing mirror. The prepared face made her speak slowly, as if she listened and spoke from behind a painting of herself, her lips becoming stiffened on words. But she did speak as men came to talk, her voice softer than usual, back in her throat. The men watched her face and asked about her days in the city, where she went, where she might be met; she began to understand that she looked like someone else, someone who was on the town, who went to restaurants and museums every day, living some pattern the men suggested by their questions.

A man at the art opening asked if she would be at the Cézanne exhibit next day at the Modern Museum, and she said yes and went the next day, taking three hours to dress.

She met the man, Mr. Russell, and walked through the white rooms next to him and went with him to a Sixth Avenue bar for a drink. There she saw that he was bald, that he had crooked, greenish teeth, that his neck was soft and doughy like her father's. The following day when he called, she said that she was leaving the city for three months and shut the phone.

Cy escorted her with his own pleasure, looked at her from across rooms and smiled, fell into the times of holding drinks and exchanging a few loud words; then they went out for supper and movies: he was excited by the nights and, with a flourish, called for late-night cabs to drive them all the way home. Riding back he would rest against Helen, his head on her shoulder, and in the apartment would make his last drinks and donate his portion of love, culled from the evening. It was as if June were an amnesty, and in two weeks he and Helen enjoyed each other's bed, the warmth of the nights allowing love, and then sleep, light, slow sleep, speckled with dreams that fell in and out of his mind.

In July the city began to shut down; the heat grew distracting. Helen bought the plastic covers to fight the sun and kept the drapes drawn through the day. The apartment became dark and still; there was sadness in the sleepy silence, and she lay on her bed in the afternoon, in shorts and halter.

Sometimes she became aware of herself stroking her thighs and was suddenly very embarrassed. She would get up and go to the living room to watch TV. But the machine made her think of the kitchen, and she walked in to prepare suppers.

Cy came, and when he had eaten began to notice her. "You don't eat."

"It's too hot, Cy."

"Why don't we have somebody up? I keep asking, but we never get around. Even the boys have hinted — you know, because we have this new place. Why don't we make an evening. You'll feel better."

"I can't even talk in this heat." Helen heard herself say this, yet she had been thinking of Rachel and Sarah and Rose and their husbands, and a summer party, with gin drinks and a cold turkey; she had cut an ad out of the *Post*, of a catering service that delivered the whole party to your house, tables, plates, sandwiches made, desserts in pretty arrangements.

But she did not carry it out of her to Cy. She was waiting; she waited for the day that would unite her wishes: Cy could do it, Vito, even Mr. Russell, if she had met him again and shared new moments with him.

"Then why don't we get out of here? They're all taking places out in Long Beach." Cy was studying her face as he spoke. "You're too hot in this place. Even though we're so high up — I expected it would be nice and cool all the time. All right, so we'll go."

She looked at Cy and his presence; if she touched him, he would stop talking.

"Sol and Manny rented out there already," he said. "And it's not so expensive. I'll come down weekends. You'll get a change."

"I'm not doing anything here."

"So?"

"I feel worthless. Do you know what that is. I want to do something for you.'"

"I'm not going to hear all this. You're just tired." Cy stood up and walked the kitchen; he wanted to attack her for being able to have the day here, all time hers, no phone voices yelling. "Maybe you think it's me," he said. "Is that the story?"

"I just want to do something for *you*." She felt tears on her face, feelings beyond reason.

"You want to *do* something for me?" Cy came and placed

his hands on her face, then took them away from the wet tears.

"Yes, yes —" Cy held up his hands and stopped her: "We *do* things. We've been going out. Now let's go to Long Beach and enjoy the ocean."

Helen rubbed her face and felt the makeup. "What? For a week or two?"

"All right, take a month. Take two."

"I'm not talking about *me*. Don't you understand? What about you?"

"I'm coming, I'm coming. I want my free time, too."

Helen moved away from him. "You want a half hour under the sunlamp, *you*. Half-hour man. Like those contests where you get a half hour in a supermarket, to grab anything you want. That's your prize."

"Well, some of us got more time on our hands." Cy left the room, and Helen knew the tone: the prince had been wounded.

Still, she followed him to the door to apologize; on the threshold she saw the whole living room and his body settling in his chair. "You wouldn't know time if it hit you in the face," she said, and walked through the living room into the bedroom.

She waited, but he did not come; instead, she heard the TV going, alternately loud and soft, voices and crescendos, gunshots, women's voices singing, whistles, explosions, screams of agony, trumpets, bits of melody, weights dropping, the sound of motors. Her image of the living room changed, and Cy was gone.

When Cy came in, she had been asleep for an hour. He looked down at her in the low bedlamp light, prepared to speak. The sleeping face frightened him: it was too still, as if death covered it. He turned away and walked to the bathroom, thinking of her, his thoughts changing from the pictures of her dead. She had spoken before through a web of trouble netted to her face, and he must help her, yet he could not find the right words to explain that what she thought about was unnecessary. She must stop her own torturing, yet there was no way, except to order it, as his father had done to him when he was a boy, walking into the bedroom at eleven o'clock with a single shout, "Sleep!"

They went out the next Friday, Helen having packed for five days. On Monday she was left with Sarah Chapman and Manny's wife, Rose, and the good weather and the beach. But Sarah and Rose had children on their hands and could not focus. Whatever Helen started was interrupted by one of them going off to a child, down to the water or off for food.

The children were like electric signals that switched on and caused responses in their mothers, but each to her own child only. If Rose's child ate sand, Sarah did not become fearful; if Sarah's son, Gregory, went near the waves, Rose did not become hysterical.

Helen watched and became a stranger; she could not understand the unseen signals sent by the children: she only saw Sarah or Rose in a changed state, screaming, laughing, kissing a child's face or pinching and slapping in a sudden, vicious rage. It was like a pageant made by a madman, but even the show of hate began to tire Helen after a few days.

She found an excuse to leave them, saying that she was going to take long beach walks to improve her muscle tone. Rose and Sarah admired the plan very much and in the evenings would ask about the general success of her body:

248

was she getting more solid; did the walks tighten the hips and thighs; did they pull up the seat?

Helen went further along the beach each day and finally found a jetty of rocks where she could sit and be alone; the next day she noticed mussels clinging to the rocks and walked out towards the end of the jetty until a voice called her.

It was a young lifeguard, in an orange polo shirt and brown swim trunks. She let him follow her out. "We don't like to have our people fall off these rocks, Miss. See how the waves strike down there. You could get an awful knock at high tide."

Helen looked down at the wave force and did not move. For a moment she thought of jumping in to answer this man: her face smiled with the secret and was stiff.

He offered his hand, impatiently grasping hers; then he led her to the sand. "Are you a resident, Miss?"

She saw that he was eyeing her. "I'm staying down there."

"Oh, the Bayberry Club Estates. That's a nice area. Your family down with you?"

"I'm by myself for a while." He responded to this as she wished: it was too easy to start them.

"I hope you don't mind — I mean, that it's not being rude, but there's a beach party here tomorrow night. The lifeguards. We're sort of looking for girls who can come."

His face had the youthful seriousness that was still untouched by the appointments that crowd life in; he asked, but he had time and hope combined; he was trying to discover her rather than make an appointment.

"It's going to be right here," he said. "We're cooking out, and we want to get a crowd up. Could you come for a little while?"

Helen now began to walk, and he kept in stride at her side. She saw his legs stepping out in rhythm with her: their walking was so fused it was like a dance. This man brought up all men and all feelings of them, like green, entwining vines grown together in one thick plant.

"What time?" Helen asked, and stopped.

"Oh, around eight-thirty. When it gets dark." He looked towards the nearby cottages. "Where do I pick you up?"

"No. I'll meet you here on the shore." She began walking again.

"All right, then," he said. "We'll meet around here." He offered his hand as they walked. "My name is Peter Miller."

"I'm Helen Steinman." She had almost said another name; she lost it, then caught it again: Helen Phillips. It was Vito's stage name that had come up. She walked silently, feeling the wind off the water, the heat in the sand.

"Don't you like this weather?" he said.

"Oh yes, one day after another like this. I love it. I feel wonderful —" She caught her own enthusiasm, heard it, stopped; she turned to watch his face react to the heightened feeling: he was smiling, looking down at her body.

"Have you sat out on the beach these warm nights — when it's clear?"

"No," she said.

He nodded but did not speak as he walked along. They were almost upon a string of rope and floating barrels that marked off the beach sections. "My station ends here," he said.

His hand was out to her again; she would have taken it, embraced it on herself, but stopped in the thought of the people behind her: the space behind held them, filling the sky, outside and still within — Cy, Rose, Sarah, Father, Mother.

She turned and walked away, not looking back until she reached the beach before the cottage. He was still there, tall, a broad-chested man with blond hair, who stood so straight it seemed he was always pulling in his breath. His legs were brown, and their curves stood clear against the light sand; his raised arm (he had caught her looking back) was long and dark against the blue. She waved quickly and walked to her cottage.

Inside, she walked restlessly; she wanted to go out again; she thought of play, of the tennis courts across the road, the players running back and forth on the soft green; she wanted to do that now. She reached her arms towards the ceiling; it was a fine movement, that felt perfect inside, but alone it had nothing to accompany it, no rhythm, no harmony of others.

There was only the kitchen, food for the night, eating, talking with the girls when everything was done. She would do anything now, anything, anything with anyone.

She went in and prepared a supper, an aluminum-tray dinner, but when it was ready she did not eat it. She took the ice cream from the freezer compartment and ate a large plate of it, then went to the bed.

She met him at dusk, while Sarah and Rose were fighting to get the summer kids to bed. She stood in the darkening light and listened to the sounds of the children: they were laughing at their mothers: it was a chase. "Get to bed, goddam you." It was Rose, who never swore.

The cottage behind her glowed as if she were in it, and the front door was shut, the agreed sign for privacy in the colony.

251

He was wearing tight white slacks and a wash-worn sweatshirt; already he was distant and unreal because of the perfection of his looks: she did not know what to say.

A portable radio was playing "Mood Indigo" when they reached the fire; she tried to name the band in her head while she stood next to him, watching the fire and the people around it. "What is it?" he said. "Don't you want to join the others?"

"I was watching the day disappear. There's a rim of light on the edge of the sky."

"Do you live on the Island or in Manhattan?" he said. "Hey. Helen. Remember me?"

She had turned away from him to avoid the others. Now she turned back and looked at him: he was like day, visible as light, warm as the line of sun turning its last red. "Would you mind introducing me only as Helen?"

He was silent, kicking the sand. "All right. But let's go over."

After she had met the others, she sat down with him at the back of the group. "You look cold," he said, but she shook her head.

She saw that his stare knew her, her lies, a husband hidden behind her, away in that darkness, her shame in her posture, knees up, legs held close with her arms, a knot apart from him at this threshold of friendship.

She could not release her hold and lie back on his blanket and look up at the sky getting its clear stars. The film in her throat began to tear, quietly, working its betrayal —

She lost the feeling as three of the men played guitars and sang; she heard his voice, but she could not sing; she was lost to it as she had been on the day she finally danced and lost her breath.

He brought supper to her, slices of steak, corn in tinfoil,

and a can of beer. The eating forced her to come to the young man; she released her legs and sat closer to him.

"What's wrong?" he said.

"What do you think it is?" She was pleased not to have told a lie.

"Probably us," he said, and smiled. "You don't look like parties on the beach."

"What does that mean? What *do* I look like?"

*"Don't be alarmed."* He smiled at his phrase. "I think you understand." He tried to get her eyes. "You're used to parties with a little more dash, and a little more dough."

She put her plate down. "Is that supposed to be flattery or insult?"

"It's flattery, I guess. A little of both." He moved closer, leaned on his elbow. "You're a hard woman to know. As soon as you like it here, you want to go. You back away. I can feel it."

"That's about it." Helen looked down at the paper plate on the blanket. "This corn is delicious. Does it get steamed in the foil?"

"I think so. Charlie Brian's the cook."

"Do you ride those long surfboards I see?"

"Yes, that's the way we patrol. You couldn't do it in a boat out here with the breakers."

"Of course you couldn't. You'd get seasick." She looked towards the water. "What are the rocks like at night?"

He was up. "Come on. I'll show you."

She went with him, away from the fire; in the darkness, she remembered time: if it were late, one of them might check her light.

They reached the rocks and walked out. "It's much calmer now," she said. "The water lights them up."

253

"It's low tide. I'll go out and pick you some mussels to take home."

"No!" She said it too quickly, and he turned to look at her.

"There you go again." He began to walk back. She reached for his hand, and he stopped. "Helen. I'm slowly getting it."

"I'm married," she said.

"Oh no! Is that all?" He stepped closer, their hands between them. "You should have told me yesterday. Because I was sure it was something about me. You had me sniffing my sweater all night."

"Is being married nothing, Peter?"

"Well, no. I don't mean that. But it isn't jail, now, is it?"

Helen touched his sweatshirt. "The smell is not so bad."

"Come on down tomorrow. I'm even headier in the daylight." He released his hand, and they walked back along the beach until the lights of the cottages made them stop.

"What's your husband like?" he said.

Helen smiled. "Why do you ask that?"

"Well, I mean, is he old or tall or fat?"

"Does it mean something to you?"

He sat down and pulled her down. "I just want to know what he's like. Like, what are you faithful to?"

"You mean, is he as good-looking as you. Is that the question?"

He leaned over, kissed her cheek, and stood up. "And you don't think that's a question, do you? You love him for his brains." He lifted her up as he spoke. Helen stepped away and went quickly back to the cottage door. When she turned, the beach was dark; if he were there, she could not have seen him.

Next morning she did not go out; at two, Sarah knocked at the door. "I saw your light on till late. You must have been reading or something."

"Yes," Helen said. "I read."

"No wonder you look tired. Can I get you something at the store?"

"I'll shop myself. I want to stretch my legs."

Sarah left her, and she waited a few minutes before going out. She reached the A & P in the midafternoon quiet.

She walked the aisles looking for new foods she had not planned for, food that would change her feeling. And the big store and the packages changed her mood; it was all newness after a while of roaming the shelves. She went back to her kitchen with the packages, then baked a new mix cake, which would be waiting for Cy on Friday.

He arrived at the usual time, with Sol and Manny, and had supper with Helen and his cake; next morning he went down to the beach and lay in a chair. Helen came and sat beside him.

After he had divested himself of the week in New York, Helen tried to change the subject, but he was stuck on a subject this week: the shortage of young executives, people you could trust when they were a thousand miles away. "We can't do it all alone," he said a number of times.

Finally, Helen changed it. "Cy, look up there. I've been watching those tennis courts. Let's try it."

"I'm just working up to button-down shirts," Cy said. "Give me a couple years more for tennis, will you?"

"You remember all the things we were going to do when we moved to Riverdale?"

"Oh, please, Helen. I'm enjoying myself. I really am." He lifted his head, unable to answer in a relaxed position.

Helen saw the stiffness in his neck. "I'm sorry, Cy," she

said softly. "I don't mean to bother you. I wanted you to have some fun. There's all kinds of people who play, all ages, young and old."

Cy leaned back and held her hand. He did not speak; his eyes were shut, but Helen knew his emotion. That it was good for him, she did not question, but it held her down, it kept her in soft chairs, depending on the stillness of dreams, the reveries of TV or the winkless calm of the A & P.

"I'll get you a cool drink," she said as an excuse, and when she came back, Cy asked her if she wanted to stay until Labor Day.

"No, I'm ready to go back on Monday."

"They've got room here. We could get another place if this one's being rented."

"Do you like it here, Cy?"

"Oh, I like it. But I've had enough."

"Then we'll go back Monday."

Cy left early on Monday with the men, and she went back at noon. Though she was relieved to reach the apartment, the city heat had made it sour, and Cy had left gritty remains around and left the windows open. Exhausted and sweaty by four, she called the TV shop and ordered two air conditioners.

Next day they were installed, and Cy noticed the first in the living room and was pleased; but when he found the second in the bedroom, he was surprised and called to Helen, "Hey, what is this, the Fedders' plant?"

"Can I camp out in one room all day?" She came to him to drive him back. "I have to move around. You want your supper when you come home, don't you?"

Cy agreed.

With the windows now shut, the remaining weeks of August barely filtered through to Helen; she was trying to decide two things: to go to work, or see a specialist once more, start her hope again, ask about new drugs, some new pill that could make it happen.

And if it were impossible, Cy would have to sit down with her and talk future, some other way to be.

The thoughts of a baby came up at odd times and with different feelings; since she had been through the days with Vito, the feelings had become stronger: a baby would be hers and then be her again, would help fill the house with beautiful things, and even keep out men. There were hand-made Italian dresses, gorgeous and light, with hand smocking and embroidery and the whole feel of the child in them already.

And if it could not work out, then work. Work with new people, something for others, not just for money. Liz Klein did three days at Montefiore, saved all her coffee cans, was always carrying things to the patients. Meeting her, Helen saw someone without impatience, who never had to talk about it.

☐☐☐ 23

THE FRIDAY before Labor Day weekend Cy went downtown late; she took the elevator with him and stopped off
for the mail. One envelope had a return address from a record company and she opened it first. In it was a note from
Vito: he had started his first job; would she come to hear
him on Sunday? There was a smaller envelope: she peeked
in quickly and saw two tickets.

During the day she imagined conversations with Cy, and
when he came in and she mentioned the tickets after supper, there was no break in her story, no weakness in word or
tone. Cy came up with a smile.

"So this young guy has got his first break." Cy paused
over his food; success was good to talk about, but it made
you stop and stare, as though some thought wanted to come
up but was embarrassed. "Is he Jewish?" Cy said.

"No. No." Helen was speaking slowly. "He's from an
Italian background. But he's quite fair. And tall. Really an
awfully nice kid. Someone you could imagine investing in
yourself."

"Well, that's an idea." Cy was staring, slowing his eating.

He pushed his plate back and looked up for coffee. "Well, why don't we go? If you think he's got something."

"Yes, I would like to go, Cy." Helen had poured the coffee and pulled the plug so that the rest of it did not boil again.

"Let's see the tickets." Cy picked up the envelope and read the name of the club. "Someplace on the Island," he said. "Well, OK, I'll hire a cab for the night. We can have some fun."

Going out, on Sunday night, the limousine passed over the Triboro bridge and slid into the lanes of traffic: the Island parkways were all a bit of the same, twisting into each other, bounded by the same patches. Cy began to think about the club they were going to, who the boy could be, what he could say to someone who had been a deliveryman, had received tips and kindness from Helen. He smiled; it was a good story, one everybody liked: the kid who made it big.

The rows of car lights, the suggestive marinas as they passed, strung with lights and showing up a few white prows and glimpses of pink-lighted cabins and people at parties began to build his mood towards the stranger. Lights came by along the roadway, fast; there were house lights up in the green low hills behind the road — he imagined the club, with a porch, saw his hand shaking hands.

"Helen, you said he delivered for the store?" Cy spoke in the middle of thoughts, but looked out the car window.

"Yes. He was very nice to me when we first moved in. Remember the night Siegal first came?" Helen turned to Cy, who did not look back. "Well, he's the one that night who brought the dinner. He's a really fine person."

"So how did you hear about this? I mean, do you know his work?"

Helen wished to tell Cy too much; she was too pleased in the night herself (it was the mood of bringing them both together, both men, making what she had done natural). "No, I've never heard him," she said. "He just dropped out of sight one day and then Friday came the tickets. But I bet he's good. He has such determination."

Cy was silent for a few moments. "Ever notice how many Italian kids have voices?" Cy rested on the thought. "Could it be hereditary? In a people?"

Helen did not answer.

"What's this place called, again?" They had driven off the highway, away from the green-tinted lights, now along streets that passed neighborhoods of copied houses, rows of white gables, thin rows of red brick round picture windows. At last they turned into a main boulevard, looking like the Bronx, with Chinese restaurants, square white stone bowling alleys, very bright drugstores and big delicatessens. The car slowed down as they rolled by.

"What is all this?" Cy said. "Could this be where a club is?"

"How would I know?" Helen squinted at the storefronts; she was embarrassed for Vito.

They stopped at a canopy leading from the street to a blue wooden door. There was a doorman. Cy stepped out: this would be a bust. "Look at this." He began to scold Helen.

But inside, the place was huge: it had been an old movie house, renovated now, with heavy black drapes around the walls and large red-glass chandeliers. There were no foot sounds — the rugs were red and thick.

"Hey. It's all right." Cy felt the good feel of a big club, the whole world cut out.

A headwaiter came up and Cy showed him the tickets.

260

"You are Mister Steinman?" He read a note from his clip-board. "I have your table."

Cy turned to Helen and smiled and took her light wrap in his hands, removing it as she walked before him. When the headwaiter stopped, Cy watched him seat Helen, then reached in for some money to rest in his hand.

"Oh thank you, sir." It was the big reaction. "You are friends of Vic Phillips. You are his guest. Everything."

Cy ordered drinks for them and the man left. "That's very nice of this kid," he said. "The royal treatment. I hope we're going to meet him."

Helen saw the envelope that had contained the tickets, noticing that it contained something else. She removed a newspaper article. "I didn't even bother to look," she said. "Cy. Read this. It was in with the tickets."

Cy read the article aloud. "He's got a great review here. That's nice. He could hit it big. The papers will do that. Lift you right up and put you on Easy Street, before you know." He looked about. "Maybe we'll *have* to invest in him."

The waiter brought drinks, and Cy sat back in smiles. The waiter reported that Mr. Phillips sent his regards and would see them after the first show. Cy took the words with a nod and smiled at Helen, who was relieved by every pleasure they gave Cy.

In a few minutes, the show began, with an MC, then a New York comic, a dance act, and then the boy.

Helen was only aware at first that his face was smooth and pink, unreal, like another person's. Its texture hid the touch or the recognition that might be so great in her eye, a light to catch Cy. If she let go, the feeling of Vito pressing her to run might touch her; but up on the stage every part of him was unknown, though familiar. To go with him now

261

would be to go as someone else, to not know herself as she traveled in his car.

His gestures were like all the good crooners, but still she was embarrassed: to her they were learned tricks and unlike Vito. But Cy smiled and enjoyed it: Vito was succeeding: his voice was expressive and large, could change into a light falsetto, was full of what Cy expected but which made Vito turn false.

As he went on, she was saddened. He had gone away; he was locked in his act, timed from start to finish, even to his little quips said in a different voice. He had gone away; she could not imagine him talking with her.

But enough of Vito was there to be possessed; she knew him behind the makeup, angry and pleading, kneeling, uncomfortable, beside her. She had pictures of memory, of sight, voice and sound that she could present ahead of all the others staring up at him now.

When it was over, Cy waited impatiently, had two more drinks quickly before Vito came out. Cy jumped up when he saw Vito. "Mister Phillips. Over here. Hello. I'm Cy Steinman." He shook hands. "We enjoyed the show. Very nice stuff."

Vito smiled at him, then sat down and shook hands with Helen, pleased at their faces watching him.

"Oh, you were very good," she said. "Really very good. Do you go on again?" Vito nodded. "Will you do 'I Have But One Heart'?"

"Sure. Did you like that?"

"I like them all." Helen was glancing at him, then quickly turning to Cy.

"We just now read this review. It got lost in the envelope until just before." Cy held it up. "It's just terrific."

Vito reached into his jacket pocket. "I have a couple more

good ones, and last night I was called for a TV spot. NBC, nighttime."

"Let us know when," Helen said. Cy spoke right after. "Sure. We'll have all our friends up looking. You're from the neighborhood, right?"

"Well, I'm originally from the East Bronx." Vito looked at Cy's smile and smiled: he had done something in meeting him, had cleared it out of his mind and won something too; yet he was sweating, more than being onstage, as though an ax overhead would come down and cut his head off. "But I'll call you," he spoke to the smile. "You can tell the whole neighborhood."

"Well, yes. Now, how long is it you've been here?" Cy rubbed his hands, having found the next subject; he waited for the face to respond and noticed the tables around looked his way.

"This is my fifth week. I was held over because the papers got me —"

The waiter came with more drinks. "You drink now?" Helen said as she saw his hands on the tea-colored glass.

"After a show. It relaxes me." Vito turned to notice Cy.

"I thought you didn't drink," Helen said.

Vito was nervous and smiled, looking at Cy's face. "I didn't use to drink," he said. "But five weeks here and I drink."

"Nerves?" Cy looked about. "I had them a little while ago when I was fixing up a merger. Boy, did it get me in the nights. Right on the chest, like a stone."

Vito shook his head slowly. "With me, just learning what goes on here. Just that it makes you a little sick. So I take a drink."

Cy leaned closer to him. "You mean rackets and stuff? Unions?"

"Everybody's racket." Vito sat back and played his fingers on the tablecloth. "I mean all the money that's floating around. And these people who live around these clubs; you get to meet them — well, you don't meet anybody else. They *live* here. Do you know what I mean?"

"It looks like a nice joint," Cy said. "It's got a name in New York. I see their ads in the *Post*."

"There's people here who think I got magic words because I work up at the mike. They'll tell me all their lives, start to finish. It's one thin stream, right in my ear."

Helen spoke: "Isn't it nice that people trust in you?"

"Trust in *me*? You think so? How could they know me? I'm a voice at a mike. Why should they trust me — what did I do for them?"

Helen's face was stiff; she was afraid of Vito going on, but he did not notice her. He looked about at the tables, noticed the attention he was getting, aware that keeping the makeup on helped.

"Vic?" Cy said it hesitantly, and Vito turned to look at him: Cy was looking around, too. "But it must be nice," Cy said.

"Sure it is." The simple statement had broken through. "I'm lucky. What am I saying? I know I'm lucky. I don't jinx that." He faced Cy directly. "It's only that I'm not used to older people crying in their beer for me. You *know*?"

Cy was pleased; he had drawn Vito close to him with his truth. "Well, how many of us really come to drown our sorrows?" He wanted to confess; he looked up and saw pretty women. "I guess any life, any job — has the good and bad sides. But you're not going to be here all the time. You'll get around; you'll travel. You won't be stuck here."

"No, I won't." Vito saw that Helen watched him, but he

264

did not look at her. "They have a date for me coming up in LA."

"See?" Cy was riding along with him. "I just got back myself. We've got a new bunch of shops on the Coast. Say, give me the name of the place in LA. Who knows, I might be out again soon and drop in."

Vito wrote his name as Vic Phillips on a menu and the name of the California nightclub. Cy took it and put it in his inner jacket pocket. A dance orchestra had started to play, and Cy turned to Helen.

"Why don't you two dance?" Vito said.

"I don't want to dance," Helen said.

"Oh, come on." Cy held out his hands. "One little dance."

"No, I don't want to dance." Helen looked at Cy, who did not understand her eyes, except for embarrassment: something about himself, perhaps: he was being too loud or too forward with the boy. He was showing the boy too much.

He turned away from her and began to talk with Vito about his own business — the new shops, the biggest merger the industry had tried in ten years; the towns on the Coast he had seen. "Oh, you'll fall in love with it. I could gladly settle in Beverly or Palo Alto. Gladly. Just wait till you see it."

"It'll be better than the Bronx, I'm sure." Vito smiled. "Better than that craphole."

"We all got to go up." Cy rested a hand on Vito's sleeve, in the friendship of the young.

"I've got to go back a minute," Vito said. Cy stood up. "Will we see you after the show?"

"I don't think so," Vito said. "I have to get back to the

city with my manager. But why don't you come again? Give me a call, will you? Just call here and I'll make them send tickets again."

Vito was standing next to Cy; he shook hands, then looked down at Helen, who smiled. "Thank you, Vito," she said.

"Vito? Is that your real name?"

"Not anymore. You can forget it." He smiled at Cy, and felt the blush as he did, but knew it could not be seen under the makeup. "That's only for the people who knew me *then*."

They watched him walk away, and Cy sat down again. "I'll dance now," Helen said.

Cy stood up again and walked to the floor with her. "You're a funny girl," he said. "What, did you think you'd insult him?"

"No," Helen said. "I didn't think anything."

They danced, then sat down for the second show, then left in the limousine. Cy was full of the boy. "I really liked him," he said again and again. "Did you ever get that feeling, *this one's going someplace*. And I'll also tell you this: I'm a little sorry for him. Didn't he seem a little lost?"

"As lost as a man in a gold mine," Helen said.

"Well, he ought to *hit*. Maybe I'll see him on the Coast. It doesn't hurt to keep a friendship like that."

"Why?"

"Why? What do you mean, *why*? Because it's nice to know people like that. You think I want to spend my whole life only talking to Solly Chapman, your cousin Manny, and the foreman?"

"I know, I know."

"Helen, you're funny. You take me out here to meet

somebody you got to know and you liked. Now you're all sour grapes."

Helen looked at him. "No, I'm not sour grapes. I'm just Helen."

"So what is it? He's got a little light shining on him now, and it makes us shabby? Do we have *nothing*?"

Helen did not answer. "What'd I say?" Cy looked at her, and she took his hand. "I said I'm just Helen," she said.

"I know, I know. But you don't have to live in the glow from somebody else's spotlight."

"No, only in the glow of money."

"What does that mean? He's got more money?"

"Nothing. Nothing."

"All right. Have it nothing. Everything ends with nothing, nothing."

# 🔲🔲🔲 24

Next morning, early, when she wanted to sleep, the phone rang. She hoped Cy would take it, but he did not move: it was Mother Steinman, announcing that she was taking a boat trip, a sudden decision, and telling them to come see her off.

Cy awoke and took the phone, got the information, then put the phone down. "How do you like that?" He was being cheerful for Helen's coming reaction. "She's found some kind of private yacht — a big sailboat — that takes people on a short cruise."

"That's nice. Say good-bye for me." Helen got out of bed and began to dress.

"What do you mean?" Cy said.

"It's very simple, what I mean. I'm not going out in this heat." Helen went to the bathroom, returned to Cy still lying on his back. "She doesn't order *me* up and out," Helen said.

Cy watched her finish her dressing, then followed her to the kitchen and sat down for breakfast. "But Helen, tell me what I'm going to say. What are you doing today?"

"Just say I'm sick."

Cy waited for more, then became sour with her silence; yet it seemed more familiar than her other moods, especially this new way of spitting out at him. He arose, with his face set and stiff, as though he had been hit, and went silently inside.

He dressed as if it were a business day, though he knew it was not necessary. Putting on his tie, he felt the sweat on the back of his neck, but smiled, as if his punishment were a bleeding that would show up all those who made demands and those who did not comprehend.

He came out of the bedroom and found Helen sitting in the living room. "Well, here I go," he said. "With a chain around my neck again. It's Labor Day." He walked to the door. "A national day of rest."

Helen looked up at him and smiled, at last, and waved a hand. She was swallowing her thoughts, messages to his mother, some which made her begin to laugh. Cy misunderstood: "Bye, bye," he said happily. "Off goes the slave. Can I bring you something, Cleopatra?"

"Go, go." Helen waved, and he went out the door.

Two hours later, she was making the beds, having first changed into shorts and halter, then at last turning on the conditioner, which she hated to start in the morning. The phone rang, and she made ready to talk to Cy, but it was Vito.

"I'm up here visiting my family," he said. "I thought I'd give you a ring because you don't have my number. Thanks for coming last night and I hope you liked it."

"I want you to come up here." Helen waited for the response.

"If there's any time. It looks like we're having an all-day

Italian meal, the way they're cooking. They're going to eat out under the grapevines. They're celebrating me. How about that?"

"Come over," Helen said. "Who knows when we'll ever see each other again."

"I'll see what I can work out." Vito hung up quickly.

Helen went slowly back to the beds; she rubbed her hands over the risen folds from night tossing and pulled weakly at the sides of the sheets. She was weak with the anger that turned like a rock rolling back on her while she had to be alone.

She left the bedroom after hanging up Cy's robe and pajamas and went to the living room; she had decided to wax the coffee table because it was a seated job.

As soon as she began, the phone rang again and she walked to the bedroom to get it. It was Cy. "It's all right," he said. "I told her you got a bad headache from the sun. But look. The stupid boat can't leave yet. They're giving us all a lunch on board. And listen: it might not leave till eight o'clock tonight — some kind of permit they need."

"But Cy." Helen was pleased and annoyed. "Do you have to stay all the time and hold her hand?"

Cy's voice came through, whispering. "She's all alone here. Right on a dock. I'm calling from a booth right in the open." The voice became deep; he had cupped his hands over the speaker. "Can I leave her alone on a dock? I can just see her standing here. It's a damn dock on the Brooklyn waterfront. You know what it is down here. And everybody's got someone with them."

"Well, I'm up here. And you know what it is up here." Helen dropped the phone in its cradle.

She lay down on the bed and took a copy of *Mademoi-*

*selle* from the night table shelf; she turned pages of pictures until she fell asleep, her skin beginning to feel cool.

When she awoke, the bell was ringing. She stood up and saw that she was in her sunshorts and halter bra, but she went to the door. "Who is it?" The answering voice said, "Delivery, Mrs. Steinman."

She opened the door for Vito, smiling. He was standing, with his arms touching the door: she thought he would have flowers.

The wet heat of the hall pushed against her skin; she stepped back to let him come in: he was wearing tan slacks and a yellow polo shirt.

"Anybody home?"

"Come in." Helen stepped back and Vito was in. "My husband's downtown with his mother. He won't be back for a while." She had lost the awareness of time in the nap. "It must be after lunch." She said it for herself, then walked to the living room.

She smiled at her bare feet, then turned to Vito. He was looking around the room. "Nice and cool in here," he said. "I was over there in the shade, but it was hot. We ate for hours and sweat our guts out, you know how it is when you eat. And my mother, she made all my favorites — *lasagna, parmigiana* — that's eggplant — And *bracciole* —" Vito smiled. "You probably never heard of these things."

"I'll bet they're all good, too."

"Oh, that's my weakness. Italian food. It's the one thing I really miss. I told my mother she could send me CARE packages to the club." Vito walked back and forth. "And do you remember I used to tell you how they all tried to stop me. Yes, yes. Well, now they see the color of the green. They got milder, you know what I mean. Now, it's like I took the road to Paradise. There's even a story about one of the execs in the record company — my father knows him from way back. He's had a shady thing or two. Well, my father was saying what an old *paisan* he was and how they were old buddies on the other side. When before I started, this man was a thief. Oh boy, don't let me get started on hypocrites."

Even though Vito was again locked for a while in the family he spoke of like chains or stains, Helen saw his voice and tone were new and were the action of what had been the dream; the voice was full of breath, urgent with his doing; it was not part of the stage voice and face, the planned tricks she had seen last night, but it was new.

She studied him for the clues of the change: his complexion was smoother and had lost the grime and blemishes, the skin of hard work in trucks, with no time to wash or think of himself.

And his head no longer moved in quick, tentative, darting actions; its rhythm was slow and trained, as he moved, without fear of attack: there were no bosses in the back of his mind.

He sat down now and rested his head on the chair pillow and spoke out of his thoughts. His words had once been simply responses; he had reacted, his language like grunts, following what she or others said. She had to order her attention to keep up with him: it was perhaps these days on her bed in the square of cool noise: she had become her hair, fingernails, lips and lashes, existing in these and the thoughts surrounding them; the thoughts were all; only they had strength.

"Are you owned by a record business?" Helen said.

"Well, it's all tied up together. It makes sense that a record company will buy or push somebody they can sew up with the records. Records are the money now. So what's the answer?"

Helen sat down; she was aware of her bare legs but went ahead, leaning forward to talk. "Aren't you ever afraid? They'll just leave you out in the cold some day if you don't have hits."

"Well, I don't know." Vito leaned forward; his fingers rested on the glass center of the coffee table; his brown muscular arms came forward, covered halfway along the upper bulge by the smooth, expensive polo shirt. "As far as I can tell, it's a big tieup of record and club and juke-box people. They've got all to gain. And there's plenty of my own *paisans* in it, too."

"Do you get paid right? No commissions going out every which way, cuts here and there?" Helen used her questions to keep Vito off, so that she could watch him, take him in. Her interest in these matters was not strong, and they expressed themselves more as worry about herself than of him.

"Oh, they do it right, don't worry." Vito looked at himself as he spoke, examined his fingernails, pressed his polo shirt into place tighter. "Remember, they've got all the dough. So my dough is their dough. And nobody's out to shaft me because I'm the talent. It does them no good to squeeze *me*. You should see the crawlers, the guys who come up to you trying to squeeze another buck; they say they've got an idea for a big hit, but they're little guys who crawl around. They're nothings, and you see that right away. They're different from what I'm in. I'm in a system; I'm riding along, and they don't want to stop one of their trains." Vito stood up. "And whatever it is, they don't ask me to take a Saturday night delivery for an extra quarter." He dusted at his trousers. "These people are all together, for themselves. And I'm with them, now. It's my own crumbs."

"But you must stand up for your rights. And be brave." Helen barely understood the words or the reason for them.

"Brave? What does that mean? Brave men are in the river, too."

In the same feeling she could not explain, Helen left her seat and stood before him. "You mustn't talk that way." She was struck in some pose, some way of being, but the feeling that started it was true.

"Nobody should talk this way. But it's only what it is." Vito followed her legs, her exposed stomach and her shoulders, shining with tan: he lowered his voice. "If you drive a truck, you'll never have to talk this way. But if you want some of the money going around, you do it the way it's done. Like the way it's done all over, and even college ball. They had a system."

Helen turned away and walked towards the kitchen. "I'm getting some lemonade."

Inside, she prepared the drink, a frozen can and water and cubes. There was a box of cookies from Strikoff's, a bit soft in the box and smelling of paper already, but she set them in a mound on a pewter plate, a wedding gift she had used before.

Carrying it in, she remembered that Cy would be back at eight. Vito had remained silent and she came back, curious to know if he were angry at something.

He was smoking and leaning back, like a relaxed guest, an old family friend. "I just started smoking these filters; you can't taste them." He was responding to her face with a little discomfort. "I decided I better give up Camels because of the voice."

"I only smoked a little, but I gave it up," Helen said. She

274

set the tray down. "I don't know why. I mean, I like the smell of it. Cy's like a chimney; that's my husband."

"I know. I met him last night."

Helen laughed. "You did, you did. What did you think?"

"Seems like a good man." Vito looked at the cigarette burning, then at the tray before him. "If you want to know the truth, I got scared. That's the truth. Me."

Helen gave him his glass and a red steel coaster. "Have some of the cookies," she said. "You know, you've gotten too thin."

Vito looked down at himself. "I don't get a chance to sit down and enjoy a meal anymore. Do you know what it's like to grab a bite all alone —"

"Do I know what it's like? Oh, Vito, you don't see what you don't want to see."

"That's right. *You.* I forgot." Vito nodded over and over. "I work right near the supper hour, so I don't eat before. Then, when it's late, I only take a little bite. And that's how I started to hit the bottle."

"So I noticed last night. How bad is it?" Helen had said it like a nervous mother, and she heard the whine.

"Well, I mean, what is it with me. I have maybe two Scotches a night at the bar after I sing. I have to do that. Then maybe somebody buys me a drink. Then sometimes they do a little business in the bar — an A and R man comes up, or something. That's all I mean." He drank his lemonade and stood up again. "Well, I better go. If you want to come again, just call the club." He turned to her. "And you can tell me what you think of it."

Helen sat and looked up. "What makes you think I can tell you the truth?"

"You?" Vito pointed at her. "You're honest. I know you're honest."

Helen watched his face, grown serious and expectant, a way that always made her smile, the child in the man, and began to feel excited, pleased with the innocence, the softness in the force.

"But I'm prejudiced." She smiled and leaned over, took Vito's glass and refilled it. "No, please," he said. "That's all."

"Do you think you should meet my husband again?" she said.

"Well, no, not really." He picked up the lemonade and drank, then moved towards the door. "What's he going to say to me? I mean, no, it's a bad thing. I'd better walk out that door."

Helen felt a shaking in her throat. "He doesn't know anything about what you're worried about. But I feel so good about your career. And he's got friends who could help, who could give you a push here or there."

Vito stepped away. "No, no, it's crazy. I don't want to get to know him." He walked towards the foyer.

"No, wait." Helen came after him. "Don't go. It's nice and cool here. You used to like it here."

He turned around. "Sure I like it. I liked it. Don't worry. I didn't forget anything about here. I'm just trying to do it right. It took me a long time to come up here today. I drove around three hours with a dozen roses on the seat — and I was even ashamed to bring the roses up —" His head twisted from side to side. "Oh, let me get out of here."

Helen went up to him. "Say good-bye. Say good-bye." She placed her arms on his and leaned up to kiss his lips.

Vito took her arms and held them down and kissed her. Helen pressed herself against him: some rich aroma, a good men's cologne, came from his body: the store had completely washed off him and now he had the smell of night-time Manhattan, the hotels, the clubs.

Vito had met no one else in these weeks, and his singing had intensified feelings ready to take shape at the touch of a woman. Yet he had not gone out to act upon them, but had only sat at the bar in the club, sitting still like a model posing, as people noticed him and spoke about him: he had been two people, a second one watching himself sitting, as if he were one of his own admirers.

Now he could break out. Helen was unlike any of the women he met at the club, who were as fake as the decor. She was still now, her thoughts stopped. He knew that she asked for his strength; he was uncomfortable with the force she wanted. He slowly kissed her shoulders and arms; his head leaned down to kiss the flesh of her stomach; he lifted her halter, holding itself to her with the elasticity of the cloth: her breasts came out, larger than the flattening covering had made them appear. Vito lifted her and carried her to the bedroom.

He stood over her while she lay back and smiled. "Never go away," she said out of the dream of the touch of the bed. Vito did not answer, but came down on her body with his face.

Beyond him the gray air conditioner shook muffled sheets of metal and hummed within. Knowing her movements, the reactions of her hands and legs and head, helped him and led him. Helen's body rushed up to him like a greeting, stronger than all the other days they had found themselves; she fought and then held him, and became slowly soft as the blond shape he had first noticed, that outline of a dream.

Later, when he awoke, the sunlight was taking the redness of evening. He looked to his side and saw Helen's breasts throbbing with her breathing.

He placed his lips upon them, drawing on her nipples until they were erect and she awake. Her lightness, her shape, always in light, took him out of grimy places where he was part of the others; her color and softness made him touch like a child feeling flower petals.

He heard her panting and ran his lips and tongue along her body. Her arms took him to her again, bringing him down upon her, slowly but with her arms strong for this. He rose up a moment; he would enter into the quiet.

"That was the best." Helen spoke first.

Vito was silent and sat upon the bed. "It's good when you give more than you own. More than you have of yourself." His face felt red: words were unsure and often untrue. "When you love somebody, you love them more than yourself. You get to know them when you — when you — fuck."

"Those words still embarrass me." She turned her face aside. "They're so ugly. To me, they're ugly."

"Words aren't ugly. They don't mean anything bad. I'm trying to say what I feel. Who cares about the words anybody uses? When you mean your feelings."

Helen saw the darkness coming. "What time is it?"

Vito leaned over to the clock on the bedtable. "It says seven-thirty. I'm late."

"I'm going to get dressed now." Helen sat up and found her robe on the rug. Vito watched her go to the dressing table and brush her hair. "I'm coming out to hear you to-night."

"All right," Vito said. "But listen. Is it safe to take a quick shower? Then I'll only have to get my suit on when I get to the club."

Helen watched him through her mirror as he held his clothes in his arms. "Go ahead," she said, and he walked to the bathroom.

She thought of getting him a towel, but she did not move; she waited; she knew that Cy would come.

She heard the soft, hissing sound of the water and lost her thoughts in a blank reverie: her hands began to apply makeup. After powder base, she did her nails with stick-ons, wiped her face and rubbed on more powder.

Before lipstick and eye liner, she went to the closet for her new white cotton dress and hung it on the outside of the closet door and studied it, to decide what color slip would match it best.

Two things went on at the same time: she was going out and she was going to have Cy come in and catch Vito. It was impossible.

She selected a slip, put it on and sat down again. Her nails were firmly in place, and she leaned over and made the green lines over her lashes to the edges of her lids. Her face was changed: it was the new one of parties, the heavy face of the woman who had returned from Nassau, grown closer to her mirror.

Vito came into the room, but he was only movement in the back of the room, at best a stranger, but not a presence in the room.

Then her name was called by a voice and of course she knew it was Cy. She had been waiting; she had made it happen; she had moved her head under the ax.

She heard the sound of Vito whirling on the rug; in a moment he had moved to the wall at the right of the door; at the same time, Cy appeared in the doorway.

"Well, she's gone," Cy said, and stopped. "Helen! Look!" He was frightened at first. "What is this?" His voice was slow, low, surprise and discovery clipping it. "What is this? Who is this?"

He stared at Vito, noticed the polo shirt worn outside the trousers. "Helen? Do you know this man? Are you OK?" He stepped in. "Did he take anything?" Cy was fumbling on disbelief, on the obvious.

He looked at Vito, whose hands moved before him, preparing to fight. "Cy!" Helen had seen Vito. "Don't do anything. Let him go."

"Who the hell is this man? Don't you move, kid." He turned to Helen. "I'll kill him. I'll kill him in here."

He stepped towards Vito, who crouched low. Cy looked at the position, the arms moving slowly up and down, and became frightened. He turned to Helen. "You *know* this man? Helen? Do you know this man? What are you doing behind my back? Oh, you filthy pigs!"

Cy was shouting now: fear, hate, the nightmare of the stranger within your door, were locked together, piled one upon the other. He looked at the young face and the chest and stepped further into the room, on the white nylon throw rug, closer to Helen, who stared at him.

His face was hot; he wanted to cover Helen in her slip. The man looked at him. He could not unravel it. "Whore bastard," he said to her at last.

"Let him get out of here," she said. "And I'll tell you. I'll tell you!" she said. She sat at her dressing table.

"Dirty bastard. Bitch. Fucking whore! Fucking shit!" The words were like phlegm spit down upon her. "You *talk*, or I'll kill you." He was turning from Helen to Vito: "Helen, goddamn you. What did you do?"

Helen stood up. "All right. Shut up. They'll hear you all over. Yes, I *know* him. What did you expect?"

Her voice was loud, but not excited. She held up her

hands, to show her red bright fingernails. "Look. Look at this. Look at me around here. Look around this place. Open your eyes a little. Look at my hair, the clothes in the closets. Did you think it would make me look like your *yenta* aunts locked in their girdles like Jell-O? Look around! Look at the rugs, here. Nice. Nice and soft. Look at these soft rugs you gave me. Look at the lamps, the silk spreads, the striped sheets, the quilted headboard, the stall shower with the Sherle Wagner special brass taps of nudes — the dressing room with neon lights like a movie set. What did you expect I should do here? Knit? Sleep all day and feel like your grandmother inside because I got a new sweater or a new suede jacket? Wait for the night you could make it while I'm made ready for it night and day? Cy, what do you think it makes me feel here? Calm? And it's you, you too. *You* made it with me; *you* told the decorator you liked dusky pink. If it looks like a good place to have fun, remember one thing — I didn't make it all alone. I only lived in it alone. This comfortable cathouse!"

Cy was struck and went silent, as if he had fallen. Helen's breathing had speeded up, and she looked into his eyes.

Cy turned to Vito. "All right, all right. Go. Get out of here."

Vito heard the high-pitched tone, the stumbling hate in the whine, ready to crack, ready to run at him: he backed out and stepped backwards into the living room.

As he reached the door, Cy had his anger again. "Wait a minute. Stop, kid." He walked after Vito. "Who are you? What's your name?"

Helen screamed behind him. "I said let him get out! Did you hear me?"

It came so loud that Cy stopped and remembered the

hearers outside, upstairs. He paused and watched Vito getting close to the front door; then he rushed after him; he ran through the living room, shaking the ashtrays on the coffee table.

It seemed shocking to Vito that they might touch, though Vito had thought of Cy's presence each time he came, and after leaving the apartment, whose chairs and tables became only Helen's. He moved away quickly, but Cy reached him.

Vito stopped to prepare himself, and as Cy came directly at his stomach, he thrust a two-handed push, like a defensive block. He watched Cy fall backwards slowly, strike the coffee table and come to rest on his right knee. Vito was concerned that he might have hurt him and now felt a curious affection for Cy and his fallen body.

But he quickly walked backwards to the front door, watching Cy lift himself and come on again. "Come here, you bastard," Cy said. "I'll get you."

Vito responded to the deep, shaking voice, a bad one now. "All right," Vito said. "Just cut it out. Cut it. That's enough."

Cy did not obey, but stepped closer towards Vito, who quickened his step, reached the door, opened it and ran out, letting the door slam at Cy.

The sound stopped Cy. He heard his breath, like a blower spinning up from his stomach, rough and thick. He coughed, and phlegm came into his mouth, and he swallowed it. He stepped to the door and placed a hand on the knob.

He leaned on the door; he felt weak; his body wanted to rest. There was no sound outside, none from behind him. His shirt was wet and twisted almost half round to his back. He waited at the door for a long time, then walked to the living room and sat in his chair and looked around, his eyes beginning to examine the room for what might be missing.

The room was so silent that he heard the sounds in the upstairs apartment: a hi-fi playing, steps going back and forth, like someone walking heels first on purpose. He did not know how much time passed before he received the thought to call Helen, no longer lost in himself, like a man in grief.

He leaned over slowly and removed his shoes and socks. Barefoot, he walked to the liquor bar and poured some gin in a large glass, then walked to the kitchen for the ice and Collins mix.

Returning, he shouted for Helen and sat down to wait. "You just better come in here," he added when he called a second time. While he waited he finished the drink.

He looked towards the bedroom door and then sat way back in his large chair, to get himself braced and calm.

At last, Helen came out. "You want a drink?" he said, but she turned her face away.

Cy stood up and walked to her and lifted her face so that she could see him. "I'm *talk*ing to you. I'm making you a Collins. Now you sit down."

While he was pouring the gin, she spoke. "Cy, what's the use of acting it didn't happen. I know what I did, Cy. You can't excuse it."

Cy took the glass of gin and started for the ice in the kitchen. Passing her, he took her hand and held it. "What's the matter? You afraid of me?"

It had been involuntary: she shrank from him, her shoulders in a spasm of hunching, her hands and arms close against her body.

He went inside and returned with her drink, then took his own and sat beside her. They drank silently; Helen did not wish to be touched, as though Cy were dirty.

2 8 3

"Look," he said. "Here's what I'll do. I'll leave Sol and Manny to do their proper share of the night work. And their Saturdays. I'll not go in on Saturdays; only for emergencies. After all, I'm the boss. I'll be home, then, more often."

His voice was thin; he held it back and tried to ride with reason, what was best, what he should say, his own peace treaty.

Helen smiled; she found herself grateful for this, but she was not sure of the meaning. His tone forgave: she waited.

"All right. We'll start a new page. Now let's go to bed." He finished his drink, stood up and removed his shirt. "Look at this thing, soaked through and through."

Helen watched him stretch and yawn, and she started to walk to the bedroom. "Wait a minute," she heard him say, and stopped. "No, no, it's all right. You go in. I'll meet you. I'm just going to check the doors."

Helen went to the bedroom silently. Cy locked the service door, then went to the front, opened the door and checked the knob from the outside, then shut the door and set the latch as well as the double top lock.

Coming back through the living room he heard the bell of the phone and stopped. When he related it to the phone, his mind feared it: it was invasion again, a screaming voice: the ship had sunk.

But it was Sol, asking him to come down tomorrow. "Sol, no, I just can't do it tomorrow." He heard the pause of his new partner, who must be thinking that the welching program had begun: they had joked about running out to play golf on each other. "No, no, Sol. I can't make it. I know this is customers. No, I can't come down tomorrow. It's like a holiday, anyway. I mean, people in the industry are taking off. What? I know it's customers. You said it. So let them stay another day; it can't break them."

Sol began with the usual crap: *what is this, Cy, what's going on here, Cy, what are you doing to me, Cy?*

"Sol. Listen. I'll pay for their room and entertainment. No, not *us*. *Me*, on my separate account. OK? Am I clear? And the decisions, whatever they are, you can make alone and I go along. Yes. You have my authority. Right now. I do, I do. I authorize you." Sol had changed tone, but he was still pushing the screw-your-buddy needle; now he became the poor, second-rate partner, mincing and inept. Mockie bastard. "No, Sol, it's not a question of my stopping in a few minutes just to check out what you decided. You go ahead." The thoughts were so boring to Cy, he heard his words as if said three times, coming back to him, rolling back over the other thoughts and words held back from Sol, swallowed by politeness. "This is something, Sol, from now on I have to do. Give my family time. No, no. Everything's all right here. Sure. Yes, yes, and stop. Sol, Sol. Just go down tomorrow. I'll see you Wednesday and we'll talk. The whole thing. And any extra time you put in, we'll make it up. We will. We'll sit down and split the thing equally. I guarantee you. You wouldn't be screwed. Yes. Yes. Goodnight. Good-bye."

When the phone was down, he moved his right hand to his neck and felt the wetness: the cool air of the machine had no effect upon him; the drops on his neck were large enough to flip off with his fingers; the water struck his shoulders and ran down his back; lines of sweat dripped along the sides of his face, from his head, through his hair already saturated. He rubbed at himself with one hand, slowly, until the sweat covered his hand; then he took out his clean handkerchief and wiped himself until the cloth was heavy and dark with gray-black streaks. He looked at the dirt for a moment — the soot had been hidden on him — then hid the handkerchief in his back pocket.

He stood up and looked down at the phone; his throat felt what he had kept back from Sol: blind bastards when Cy Steinman stays overtime. He's the boss; he should be there all the time. *Mockies.*

The anger seeped up, around, was in his head. *Helen. Helen.* That's it. He was not going to speak to her anymore. Let her get out. He would not sleep next to her. God dammit, he was not going in just like that, and be her baby. She'll talk fast. She'll talk the truth.

He walked to the bedroom silently, the indignation in his back, erect. Helen was lying on her side, facing away from him, her sheet covering only her legs. Cy stared at her; his face moved into a sneer: he became aware of it having formed on his face and rubbed his lips with the palm of his left hand, to set the anger in.

"Helen, look, I know you're not asleep." He watched her head move, but she did not speak. "I want some facts, and *now.* And fast. Fast." He had to stop to lick his lips. "The *truth.* If *you* can tell the truth. Now tell me: what the hell did you get yourself into? Did this kid trick you in some way? He is a kid; he looked eighteen. What were you doing with infants, if I may ask?"

Helen did not turn, but she spoke with her head on the pillow. "It was stupid. So it was stupid. It was all stupid. The whole thing was stupid. But I did it. I did it. That's what I'm saying. And I liked it, all of it, every time. And I'm no good. You know that. You know that."

"All right, all right. Now cut it out. *No good. No good.* That's not the point. Just tell me what was involved here. Did you go off your nut for a little? How many people know about it? Does the kid have anything on you? Talk about it, talk."

"There's nothing to tell." Her voice came off the density of the pillow and lost timbre. Cy had to strain to hear her. "*You* know what I did with him. You *know it*, exactly. You want me to do something — look, let me go and kill myself, instead of you beating me word by word." Helen lifted her head, turned, and looked up at him.

"Look, I don't even feel I can sleep in here anymore." He spoke very fast, and his head turned from side to side. "It feels dirty and filthy with the stink of that fucking thing you had here. You dirty, sneaky whore." Cy's breathing was fast, the echo of a wheeze coming through. "You probably gave him a key to get in anytime, too. So at least *tell me*, give me the *truth!*"

Helen picked up her pillow, stood up holding it and walked to the foot of her bed. "You're right, Cy. Look, I'll sleep in the living room. We'll talk about what you want to do, tomorrow."

"Oh, *stop* it. Cut it out. Sit *down*, here. *Sleep*, you sleep here. *I'll* go sleep in the living room. After all, it's your playground." He sat heavily on the bed and rubbed his forehead with his right palm. His tone of voice changed, plaintive, a boy's. "Oh, Helen, I don't know what to do. I'm so mad one minute, I'd like to kill you. Fucking around like that." The words made him lower his face into his hands. "How could you do it? Fooling me — with all that sensitive all alone bit. And I'm working my ass off downtown, and you're up here; you're not even thinking about me; you're *shacking*."

"No, Cy. No. It wasn't like that. It wasn't that."

"It's *not* like that." Cy's head fell into the pillow. "I don't know *how* it is. You don't *tell* me. You have this man in my bedroom; you do all of this to me when I can't *move*. What are you doing to me? Helen? I ask. What are you doing to me *this way?*"

Helen did not answer; her mind held some words she refused to say: she had been a good wife; she had waited for him and done plenty for him, waiting on his crude plodding. The thing had happened: a hole rent in her times, and loneliness had fluttered out like feathers from a suddenly torn pillow.

"Oh, stay here!" Cy said, and quickly stood up and walked to the bathroom to wash. He returned to find Helen still standing with her pillow, like a houseguest waiting to be assigned a bed.

*"You sleep here,"* he said.

Helen moved slowly along the bed and sat; Cy came to her, leaning down and caressing her cheek. She turned from him, fell upon the pillow, her tears on her face again, running uncontrolled.

"Come on, now," Cy said, and tried to lift her, but she squirmed out of his hold. "Come *on*, I said." He stepped back, erect again.

"All right, I'll tell you." Cy had offered forgiveness, expecting her to respond with herself to his touch, but her voice was angry. "The boy was Vito. Vic Phillips. The one you met last night. The boy who used to deliver. It happened the night we went to Leone's. He gave me a lift home, by accident—"

"All right, that's enough. Just forget it now." Cy leaned over her and lifted her shoulder and began to turn her towards him. "No, Cy."

He stood back again. "All right. So it was that kid. I didn't even recognize him: he looked like a kid right off the corners. All right. And you took me out there with my big mouth. I'm shaking his hand like he's my long lost brother. You must of had a good laugh, the both of you. Very nice stuff."

"No, Cy. And no. I only wanted to see him for myself. I did want you to meet him, but because he was nice."

Cy walked around the bed. "Because he was nice. Nice to me or to you." He leaned down again, and turned Helen's face up: when he saw the anger stuck there, he was surprised.

"We're both going to have to change, Helen." Cy said it unexpectedly, a reaction. "I mean, if we can work it out. If you'll tell me what this was to you. How deep. What could you *have* with a kid like that? There couldn't be anything but the bright lights in your eyes. You fell in a dream." Helen did not answer. "Helen? Can't you answer something? You're not saying. All right, then, do you want to split up? Is that it? Marry him?"

Helen turned and sat up. "I told you but you don't believe me. It was nothing. Nothing more than the thing I did. I did it and I liked it very much. It made me feel happy." She shook her head. "But it's bad, what I did to you. To you. You were always good, Cy."

Cy looked at her and then saw the dress on its hanger. "Did you want to go out tonight?"

"No, not now."

"That's good because my back is killing me. I waited down on that dock five hours before my old lady took off. Why does she *do* that all the time?"

Helen was quiet, but she nodded and looked at his face with concern.

"Why does she do that? Did that ever occur to you, Helen? All of a sudden, like she wants me to come down and hold her hand. Could she be going in her second childhood? Oh, the hell with her for a while. Two weeks, now, she doesn't exist."

Cy sat down on the bed and Helen lay back, staring at the ceiling. He leaned to kiss her, and she turned her face away. "Now, come on, Helen; *come on.*"

"I keep feeling, *how* could you want to touch me now. Tonight, especially."

"I told you, *forget* it. I'm trying to forget it. But you keep the thing going. All right, let's just stop then. OK? We'll stop trying. I don't care. I did my best. I worked on it."

He went to the dressing room and returned in his green silk pajamas and sat down and watched her. Helen was silent, her eyelids closed, in the same position, her face averted, unmoving.

He lay back on his pillow to sleep, but his thoughts rushed up like a wind inside him, pressing against his chest from within; his body shook as he glimpsed for a second, in his mind, an arm and a hand, large as a pole, coming down on Helen; there was no sound, no blood; only this vision, like a picture, breathing in and out, floated in his mind.

Then he felt he must cry, the crying that rose from the chest — *for the first time in twenty years!*

Then the feeling stopped, but in the minutes, his eyes had been touched with something stinging, his throat crusted with inner lumps, burning and dry.

*Why, Helen, why, Helen, why, Helen?* The words were going through his head. *Why, on this bed? Why, in this room? Why, on our beds? Why?*

Cy shifted his body, moving away from what was not there, like a walker avoiding puddles, his body jumping the discomfort in the sheets. The sheets shook; his insides shook; the winds in his body bruised his chest: it was too much, and he rose suddenly to a sitting position.

Helen heard the bedsprings and jumped up. "Cy. Cy? What is it? Are you all right?" Helen's voice came out of the darkness.

He sat up, but did not answer, waiting for her to speak again.

"Yes, I'm all right," he said after a long while. "You don't have to worry about me." He heard a sound of disgust as she went down again. "All right," he said. "And you go from this house tomorrow. You filthy bitch. You are getting out."

He lay back; his own words had made him cry a bit, as if he had said something else, had responded to a night voice of the past, down in the darkness of memory and night, where memory is always night; the punishment he gave was the pain he received.

*Oh you dirty pig.* Silent words appeared again inside his head after he had rested on his pillow a moment. The words were small and childish; they came up with feelings and fears: who was talking?

He was aware now that he had been grinding his teeth; once he had had a bite plate. He remembered the plastic and wires, the tinny taste of it blocking his mouth. How could you grind your teeth a long time and not know it, and then in a moment realize you had been doing it all the time, all your life.

His head pressed itself back into the pillow, to make a burrow.

*What do they want? Why do they do it? Why must they do things to you? They get you, they get you. They never let you go. They swallow you. They swallow you. Let go. Let go. Let go.*

# □□□ 25

C Y HAD NOT told anyone; he had gone through the days at the office with words piling up in his head, ready to scream them out. He would look at Sam or even Arnold Kent's little face, listening to them report something on the progress of the line, and his head would start screaming: *She left me. Do you know what Helen did? Got in bed with some damn singer. Do you know what that dirty whore did? Helen is gone. I kicked Helen out.*

At lunches he was silent, and while he listened to the talk, running along, made of malice and dirty jokes and business, his head would say it again to others around him. But they would see him only staring. His mouth pronounced his words silently, starting with her name: *Helen did this. Helen did that.*

On the way home in the evening limousine, he would glance at the people crowded against him in the rattling black Checker and feel that they knew but were turning away because of it. He wanted to ask aloud, *Well, what do you think about such a thing?*

In the apartment, he made sadness by cooking foods of the sick: cans of chicken soup, hard-boiled eggs which he

watched over in reveries; the saltines he ate dropped specks
into the boiling liquids and increased the dryness in his
throat. His mouth and throat were stiff: it was like dying.

*Well, there it is, pushed right in the face, the whole
thing. Just stand there and watch them laugh. Let her do
anything. Sure. And walk away and say, Good-bye, Cy,
take off for a while and when the bedroom's free again,
maybe I'll give you a ring. Oh no, oh no. Not like that. He
would ask her back here in a nice voice. Come on back, and
when she rang the bell and he saw the face at the door, a
big smile, that makes her take a step inside and then smash
the fucking door in her face. The ivory metal face of it
against her nose, her cheekbone, the sound of cracked bone,
her body falling back against the opposite wall outside, falling down on the rug, her skirts up, high heels caught on the
nylon hall rug, breaking her goddamn ankles.*

*Or let her in —* HELLO CY *—* HELLO HELEN *— Her face
looking up for a kiss hello and then a slap.* NO, DON'T, CY,
PLEASE *— Following her across the room and another slap,
sideways across the face, and following her to the wall
where she has to stop.* DON'T HIT ME, CY. DON'T HIT *—* ALL
RIGHT. NO HITS. ONLY THIS *— and his hand ripping her
dress right down the front —* NOW WALK!

He sat at the kitchen table and ate with his legs spread
apart, the way they used to sit on Saturdays in the old place
on Twenty-third Street, when customers came in all day to
buy from the rack, wholesale: you jumped up so often that
your legs were always ready: the elevator chains would be
your signal, a low sound like marbles dropped into a pillow,
and you were up, something inside you going constantly.

Cy saw himself: he had been seeing himself for all these
days: he did something and then he had a moment of sight,
watching himself do what he did. It was a going back, and

it shut out the screams he had prepared for Helen; it oblit-
erated her and made him bloated with himself in a way he
did not like.

He wanted the picture before his eyes, her last acts re-
viewed and seen. In three days he had no strength of fists to
beat them down in this condemning silence: he became
judge in the loneliness, but alone it was foolish — even a
destruction — to judge.

He would call and ask her back, now, but as soon as she
came, the hands of his mind would rise to hit her again.
That was his wish, to break her into pieces, yet there was no
condemnation in that. Judgment was different; judgment
was handing down a sentence, with lawyers' words, while
she stood all dressed up, seen by everyone, photographed by
the papers, cast into shame and at the same time taken away
from him. To break her in pieces was the help of his hands;
he would be justified, and she could then grow together
again.

The thoughts ran every day and night; by Friday night
the rooms were stale with silence, his head swollen as if
placed in the center of a thousand horns blowing. He sat at
the phone for an hour and finally called his mother to tell
her.

"Left you? I don't believe it," she said. "What happened?"

When he did not answer, she told him to come quickly to
her apartment.

"I couldn't talk anymore on the phone," he said when he
came in. "This is one thing you can't phone about."

"Well, sit down," she said. "Son, I'm sorry for you."

He told her about Vito, briefly, without the stories his
mind had added to it, with no mention of his visit to the
club.

His mother walked among her furniture. "I just want to ask you what you think you've got," she said.

"You mean what I think Helen is —"

"No. I mean what you think your marriage is. Or what it is to be married to her. Is it anything? What does she do for you?"

"Well, I love her." Cy stood up to say it.

"Relax. Sit down, Cy. Think about what I'm saying."

"All right. I'm completely relaxed. See?" He sat down and smiled for the first time in a week. "Now why don't you make me a relaxing Scotch on the rocks?"

"*Then* you'll be relaxed. Oh yes." She went to the kitchen, poured the drink and brought it to him.

Cy was waiting to speak: "Well, I don't know how to answer your question. What do you mean? Is it a happy marriage? Is that what you're asking? Does it run smooth? I've been a jerk a lot of times. And she whines like a cat. I know. It takes two to tango. I know all that. Do you think I just hate her now?"

"Yes, you hate her."

"No, I don't hate her."

Mrs. Steinman sat down slowly; Cy noticed she had brought herself a can of peanuts. He watched her eating them and felt hungry but would not ask. She cleared her mouth of the food. "Of course you hate her," she said. "You'll hate her for as long as you hate. But you're a *mensch*, Cy."

"Thanks, thanks. But not good enough, though. Have you got any cigarettes here, Mom?"

Mrs. Steinman stood up slowly and went to a shining armoire, took out an unopened package of Kents and a flowered ceramic ashtray. She placed them at the table next to Cy's chair. "You got a match?" he said.

"That bird is a lighter."

Cy picked up a ceramic bird set in a square wood base and pressed its head. A small flame shot up. He put it down again, opened the package of cigarettes and lighted one with the bird.

"How much of your life is Helen?" his mother said. "Do you understand that?"

"What *is this*? Are you starting to blame me now?"

"No, I'm not blaming you. I'm blaming her. She's a stupid girl. And now she's dishonest, too. But you're the one who's going to take her back — *if*."

"I told you I love her. She's my wife. What the hell are you asking? This woman is *my* wife."

"Do you know what belongs to us?" Mrs. Steinman sat down again and shut the can of peanuts. "Practically nothing belongs to us. You don't own Helen no matter what the hell she is."

"So that means she can go and get her kicks whenever some guy shows up who warms her up."

"Don't be stupid. You think a woman like that does this thing every day? You told me it was just a young fellow. A kid. Is that the truth?"

"Is that the truth? Do you think I made this all up?"

"Then tell me."

"Well, what do you think it means. A kid has a — a kid is a man who's a little younger. He does the same thing an older man does." Cy finished his drink. "I'll make a little one myself," he said, and walked to the kitchen, coming back with his glass full. "Don't tell me that a kid is nobody you take seriously."

"That's right. That's what I'm telling you. If you know what the hell you're doing in a marriage. Look at this kid's age and look at his background." She smiled. "He's even a *goy*. But really, he's a nothing."

"OK, *he* is nothing. But *he* got in bed with *she*." Cy smiled.

"Cy, you don't live in bed. Bed, bed, bed. Your mind keeps going into bed."

"Mom, you are nuts. Did you know that?"

His mother laughed. "Well, you're getting a little sense of humor back. Maybe you'll understand me now."

"OK, so tell me the whole story, without the beds." Cy was beginning to move about in his chair.

"Look. Does your wife want what this man wants? Don't make me laugh. They are different as night and day. And you must know this. They want different things. This is a kid who's going to knock over the world in five minutes. A singer. She doesn't live like that. She lives like you live. You think she doesn't know that? That you go out eight hours a day and stick to it. And you bring it *home*. And you'll be around, always."

Cy nodded and looked at her face. "Maybe she wants singers now."

"Go home and call her. Take her back. Try again. She'll take you."

"I am supposed to take her back again. Just let her walk right in."

"All right, you can talk that way. You can throw her out."

"All right, all right. And you tell me what's going to stop her from doing it again. I can't put a cop on her."

"You will stop her. *You*. By yourself."

"Well, I'm not taking anymore of that crap."

"Then she's not going to give you anymore."

"Ha, ha. Very good, Mom. Very good. *I'll* be the cop."

Mrs. Steinman did not answer. She looked at Cy, whose

297

face had become animated. "Do you think," she said slowly, "that it gets any better the second time around? That even *I* couldn't have found a second husband? Or you can find it better getting another one? Take a little heartache and learn yourself."

"You talk —" Cy stood up and came towards her. "You talk as if this whole damn thing does me some kind of favor. I'm supposed to be saying thank you."

"Don't say thank you for anything. You don't *get* anything to say thank you about. Nothing is given. I'm telling you, sweetheart, just learn something. It was a bad season."

Cy walked away, into the kitchen. "And don't ask the Scotch," his mother called in.

He came out again. "OK, Mom, I'm going home. I'm going to make up my mind."

"Make up your mind to keep the things you have. You know what you want."

"What do *you* want, Mom? Do you know?"

"Don't change the subject. Goodnight, my son." She came to him and embraced him. He walked to the door with her, kissed her suddenly on the cheek, and left.

□□□ 26

HELEN had spent another day in Rachel's rooms. Over two weeks without divisions in the days: light, darkness, and dinners, talking politely with Morty, who was loud and friendly, telling the latest jokes he'd heard, passing her the potatoes three times, squeezing her hand when she said a few words to Rachel's soupy face.

She had looked at the Concourse from the windows, morning and afternoon; the crowds jamming the trading-stamp store seemed to have all the happiness she had lost: they came out, steadily, each carrying packages — electric fry pans, plastic fire engines, wrought-iron stands, stack trays — threw the stuff in cars and drove away.

Her mind considered herself in terms of those strangers, who did not think about her, who did not care if she dropped from the third floor or stayed in the midst of the big chairs and couches for the rest of her life listening to Morty and Rachel, who nodded and understood and knew nothing.

Vito was in one part of her mind, a group of facts that rose when some sign called him up: he was in the young boys she saw standing near the Ascot Theatre; they were chained to their block, with minds in the places they had never seen; she knew that, yet they moved.

Vito was somewhere in a club, worried and important, having left the streets, never to be part of walls and rugs, never needing to look at others for his pleasures and peace.

For the rest of her life he would be someone waiting to be known, substantial only when she dared him in thought, in the air above her bed.

Until Cy came to erase it. Cy was the one who must master the wishes; if he decided that now they would continue, she would prepare to turn to him whenever he came in, forever. Shut in the apartment of others, she made these thoughts and took comfort from the feelings. The rooms were blank to her: they could be the platform on which to alter the events that had taken place and to raise Cy up again.

He had not called; perhaps he was seeing lawyers, and she would hear from them. But Manny had phoned, explaining that Cy had told him about it one night, and only him, and kept repeating *hang on, hang on*.

She did not abandon herself by forgetting her looks. She dressed neatly each day, had gone to movies, bought two books, intending to mail one to Cy, the life of Sammy Davis.

Mother Steinman had not called. She had been back for a few days and must know: Helen imagined her crossing Helen's name off the books; she had tried to say some nasty things about the old lady to Morty and Rachel, but could not.

In the third week she went to a musical with Rachel and Morty. Returning, they sat in the kitchen and had a cup of tea. The phone rang and Morty answered and handed her the phone with a smile.

"Helen, this is Cy." The voice was curt, but not angry. "Look, I'll be brief. I'm here at the apartment. It's *very* quiet. I want to see you. I want to talk to you. When can you come back?"

"I'll come tomorrow morning if you want."

"Then I'll take the day off." They waited. "I said I'll take off from work," Cy said.

"All right, Cy. I'll be over early. I'm so glad you called."

"Well, this place is nothing without you being here," he said, and hung up.

Next morning, when she arrived, he kissed her cheek discreetly, an uncle's kiss, and stepped back. Helen made herself walk in quickly. "I'd better get to work," she said. "I can see this place hasn't been touched."

"Sit down a minute." Cy's voice was behind her. "First, I want to tell you what I did."

"You don't have to." Helen sat on the couch.

Cy began to pace. "I came home every night. And every night I walked in, I was sure you were going to be here. I got so mad at you because you weren't here." He went to the bar.

"It's a little after nine in the morning," Helen said, and he stopped.

"This stuff has been my medicine." Cy put the bottle back and shut the bar door. "I got madder and madder. Then I started thinking. *I* expected *you* to be *on duty*. I learned that, Helen. I really learned that."

Helen stood up and came to him. Cy let himself be kissed, not taking her in his arms.

"You've got to believe that," he said.

"Of course I believe it." She took his hand and led him to the couch to sit. "And what about me?" Helen said. "What did you think of me?"

"You're my wife," he said, and began to cry, letting his head drop on a white pillow. But it was brief. "And then," he said, coming from the crouch of tears, "I remembered the bedroom, the night I came in." He stared at Helen. "And I even tried to erase it. I sat by myself and tried. But you killed trust. You know that."

"We both did," she said.

"We both did? Oh, come *on*. Just like my old lady. What did *I* do? Tell me that; what did *I* do that compares to you, *you, fucking,* fucking a man in *our* apartment."

"Please don't talk that way. I hate those ugly words."

"You've just got to face that, Helen. You *did* that. You did do *that*. And that's what I'm trying to get out of my system without busting your head in with a brick. Without beating you good. So *don't*, so please don't go saying we both did something, like the thing is balanced. Like I got to get *over* something —"

As Helen turned her face away, Cy stopped: she had removed her hands from him and placed them in her lap. Cy watched the hands withdraw from him. "Let's face the truth," he said. "You just look in my eyes. Are you going to see this guy? Do you have any ideas?"

Helen turned again to look at him. Her voice was going to respond slowly and heavily. "You did something, Cy. You fucked money," she said.

"Oh, that's it. That's my *problem*." He was nodding and remembered the comedian Woody Allen and nodded in imitation of his nightclub manner. "Yeah. All my money is bad. It gets you dirty. It buys bad rugs, bad clothes —"

Helen turned her face away: her own words had hurt her. "Let's just see if we can start out on a new foot."

"All right. Good. Let's start. Start with a trip." Cy was up. "Let's take a trip. OK? A little trip. Up to the mountains. Maybe the Concord. It's just before the holidays."

"What holidays?"

"Rosh Hashanah. Yom Kippur."

"Oh yes."

"We'll fly up. How about that. There's a new service in light planes. You know, I'm having those flying dreams again. Maybe that's it."

"Are they all right?"

"You mean the dreams? Sure. I'm always flying. So I thought about plane trips. Why not?"

"All right," Helen said. "But now let me get this place fixed up a little."

"Let's go for a walk first." Cy was moving in front of her. "Get into slacks. No, wait. I'll make a few calls to the place while you work. Then we'll go out for lunch around here."

In the bedroom she found his clothes all over and laughed while she picked up socks and undershirts and shorts: it was the pleasure of handling a creature who did not see himself in the things that covered him. It was a relief to live with such reminders when she had to stand at a mirror for an hour before going out of the house.

She changed the sheets and began to work more slowly: she was in it again, as though no break had occurred, the smells she knew, the crumpled sheets in the corner waiting for the laundryman to ring the bell. Her mind wandered to the freezer and suppers, to calling the rug man for fall shampooing, then having Rachel and Morty up as soon as possible.

When she was done, she showered: it was the one thing she could not do at Rachel and Morty's. Her own bathroom was the only place that permitted it; she had not known why.

She rubbed on bath-oil pads, then went to the bedroom, dressed slowly and combed her hair. "Hey, you look like a kid," Cy shouted at her when she came out with her hair tied back.

"I've got to get it done this week."

Cy took the phone off his lap and got his madras jacket and they went to Johnson Avenue.

There were no neighborhood men on the walks: it seemed unnatural to be walking with Cy on a weekday, as though a death had occurred.

The Chinese restaurant was empty; but as they sat waiting for their food, two women and a child came in and sat in a back booth. The child, about five, wandered back and forth down the aisle.

Cy had ordered some special dishes learned about on the San Francisco trip. "The man who took us out, one of the managers in the new chain — you wouldn't believe it. They said it was forty courses. A waitress for each guy. Oh, that was treatment."

Cy was smiling in a party discovery; his voice did not fit the time of day, the women shoppers passing, two shopkeepers talking outside. Helen listened to Cy and looked over his shoulder at the street in the sun and the people still slow from the last of the summer heat.

When they finished, Cy sat back and admired Helen. "Stuffed at noon," he said. "It's kind of nice."

"Let's walk a little." Helen led the way; they walked along Johnson Avenue, but the people and the stores held them up in watching: women chasing their children, crates

304

blocking traffic, crowds of schoolboys at the pizzeria, trucks unloading, cars trapped by double parkers, the drivers angry, honking their horns at the empty cars blocking them.

They left it quickly because Cy was sleepy. While he napped at home, Helen continued to work, getting the kitchen ready. The order she called for arrived at three: it was the Negro boy; she paid him with a blank face, and he gave back blankness.

Everyone was letting the past bury itself; she had only to keep the expression, masklike, of a person who was interested in other things: her face alone could dismiss the old meanings. It had worked on the Negro and was working in the apartment; Cy was talking in a different way, happy with present moments, making his own burial.

Supper was quiet and pleasant; they left the kitchen together to watch a CBS Special and then a variety show with top stars.

The eleven o'clock news was like a curtain coming down on the night. Next would be the dark, dry hours of the late movie, sitting up as eyes and back began to ache, talking a bit during the commercials, sometimes remembering the awful news and regretting the war, but then stopping as soon as the movie began again. Then on, into the silence beyond midnight, traffic noises getting softer, steps and sounds of neighbors gone, and still eating crackers and cheese and pears and drinking sugarless soda with its medicine aftertaste.

Finally, the end of the movie would be painful, bringing the truth of lateness, regret at the lateness, the loss of sleep, face sweaty, annoyed by the stink of the ashtrays. And the last, getting up in silence, too tired to embrace but awake enough to think that tomorrow was only five hours away.

"Cy, I think I'm going to bed right now," Helen said.

"I'll be right in." Cy sat up in his chair and faced her. "I like to see the first segment of the movie. Then it drags."

Helen went inside and dressed for bed. She sat at her vanity table and combed out her hair, looking into the familiar reflection, this backward look at the room that was always the start of sleep.

It was without a person now; she was grateful to Cy for letting her back into this. She would have it as long as she liked, if she kept the mirror free. Even if he were away, he must have his rooms kept empty: there was no other way.

She became annoyed. Alone, yes, without men. But she would act; she would do things. She would get going on some idea and she must be allowed to do it.

She brushed her hair for a long time and then rubbed herself with new hormogenic cream. The mirror image became her; she looked at it until it was a person in the room behind her. It was all pleasant, the reflection of soft lamps behind her, the wall color and the shine of the silk spreads. She turned to look at the real room, and it was hers again, unconnected to the outside, a place without pain.

Finally, she went to her bed and lay down on the sheets, slowly drawing them up about her body. She gently pressed the sheets upon her, as she used to do, once hoping that Cy would like the outline of her figure as he came in. It was a vision of something she had once seen, in a movie; but by now it was her own pleasure, the cool sheets against her body, pressed into the space between her legs, between her outstretched arms and body. It held her in coolness and seemed to stroke her.

As she was dozing, Cy entered and smiled at her. He undressed, went to the bathroom, returned. "You awake?" His voice was soft.

"Yes," she said. "Just dozing."

"Isn't it nice here?" Cy had had her own thought.

"Yes, I love this room. Remember you used to call it the suite at the Plaza."

Cy walked towards the window. "That's before I saw what some suites looked like." He stopped. "Do you want this thing going all night?"

"No; open the window a little. It's not hot tonight."

Cy turned off the air conditioner, adjusted the window, and came back. He sat down on his bed, removed his shoes and rubbed his feet. "Helen?"

"Yes?"

"It's never good to be alone." He paused. "I spent two weeks alone here. I stopped noticing the place. I didn't look at anything. Now it's all lighted up again."

"It's good with you, Cy." Helen felt her throat dry as she spoke it. She was making an emotion like nostalgia: they were two who had come back from a long distance, and they were remembering a long past.

Cy lay back for a moment before getting under his blanket. "You know what my mother said?"

Helen did not answer.

"She said try again." Cy's voice was louder. He had turned towards her. "She said to me, keep what you have; try again."

"You wouldn't have been alone for long." Helen had to say it.

Cy placed his hand on her arm. "That's a very different thing. What you mean. It really is. It isn't your wife."

She removed her arm from the cover and held his hand. Cy leaned over and kissed her. "Well, we're back again," he said. "As far as I'm concerned, it never happened. Nobody knew but Manny and my mother. I didn't even tell Sol. And Rachel and Morty I'll never forget. I'm going to make it up to them. So, we've been here all the time."

He lay back on his bed. "Helen?"

"Yes?"

"Will we be here all the time?"

"Yes, we will. Yes." And she knew it was true. She was this, she and Cy together; they made all the colors here, the lamps and the furniture, vases — all of it, exist. They would be here all the time.

She looked up at the ceiling: it was the only room that never had footsteps overhead, which meant that the people upstairs had rugs in that room. She did not know them, had only met the woman across the hall, Bea Bienen, who had been a teacher in Newark before getting married. Bea was a beautiful, black-haired girl, with the vivacity of an actress, and it seemed impossible that she would have taught in a school of poor black kids in that Jersey slum.

Her stories were amazing, but Bea reported them with laughter: she had loved her kids, loved teaching, and now she loved her house and her life, or so it seemed because she was always full of smiles and recipes, like someone who had settled a new country.

Everything around Helen must converge now; she would talk to everyone and bring them in. Her house would contain their remnants when Cy came home, and the nights would start with laughter like Bea's. And Helen herself would entertain whatever happiness came out of Bea and the others not yet known in the different apartments; and sitting with women she would wipe out her stains and the tiger feelings that had been uncovered. Women would do it, women together, planning like teams. Together they would circumscribe life, as walls do a room, and if there were repetition, it would be buttressed by sharing as much as possible the sadness that also happened. There were movies and card games and the charades Bea always talked about: Helen would learn and do it.

"Cy, did you meet Bea Bienen yet?"

"Who?"

"The girl across the hall."

"I saw you talking to her once," Cy said. "She's a beautiful thing."

"We're going to be good friends, I think."

"That's good," Cy said. "What's her husband do?"

"He's a lawyer. He does civil-rights cases."

"Hey. That's the Bienen was in the papers. He's a big shot."

"So are you," Helen said, and reached her arm across to him again. Cy took her hand and kissed it. "The sleeper awakes," he said. "I'm practically Mister Clothing right now," he said.

"Mister Clothing." Helen repeated it and smiled. "Cy, you're funny."

"Nuts like my mother?"

"Well, yes, maybe a little bit. But with bigger muscles."

"Well, thank god for that."

"Cy, who lives above us?"

"Upstairs? I don't know. I never met the people. Why?"

"No reason. I was curious. There's a card club in the building."

"If you get to know them, see if the husbands play poker, will you?"

"All right, I will."

"Helen?"

"Yes."

"I'm feeling happy again. You know. It's settling down."

"Yes. And it'll get better." She lifted her head to look at Cy. He was smiling, holding her hand; his face was smooth, his hair not messed and dried out from a night's tossing on the pillow.

She leaned across the bed and kissed his neck; he twisted round and laughed. She ran her tongue along his neck, and his laughter changed to a moan. He edged his way to her bed and pressed his body against hers. "Helen, I love you," he said.

He rested his head under her left arm, his face against her breasts' softness. All this *was* his. It was, no matter what was said or who took away: this person and these rooms were covered, protected, by his own walls: he had earned it and he loved it. He would go on earning it each day, more and more, better and better.

He was aware of only himself in the room, and Helen became a soft, sweet-scented pillow, the embodiment of gratification through his own reflection, a feeling from a mirror, a pool, that made him alone in the room. And there was nothing else: once you saw yourself expanded to the size of what you possessed — your home and your business — the promises had been fulfilled: you had all the comforts.